AFTER T[...]

Sabina Cane was worried about performing at Hamilton Regan Thorndon's nightclub. The sexy, stubborn businessman had quite a reputation. But singing was Sabina's life, and she was grateful for any work she could get. Yet after the music ended, would she be in danger of losing her heart?

DREAM'S END

How could shy Eleanor Perrie ever get her handsome boss to notice her? Her typing speed won Curry Matherson's appreciation, but her prim and proper looks never would. So Eleanor came up with the perfect plan to put an end to her dream—by making it come true!

Dear Reader:

Back by popular demand! Diana Palmer has long been a favorite of Silhouette readers, and it is with great pleasure that we bring back these impossible-to-find classics.

After the Music, Dream's End, Bound by a Promise, Passion Flower, To Have and to Hold and *The Cowboy and the Lady* are some of the first books Diana Palmer ever wrote, and we've been inundated by your many requests for these stories. All of us at Silhouette Books are thrilled to put together books four, five and six of Diana Palmer Duets—each volume holds two full novels.

Earlier this year we published the first three volumes of Diana Palmer Duets, containing *Sweet Enemy, Love on Trial, Storm Over the Lake, To Love and Cherish, If Winter Comes* and *Now and Forever*, to universal acclaim and sell-out crowds. Don't miss this chance of a lifetime to add to your collection.

The twelve novels contained in the six "Duets" show all the humor, intensity, emotion and special innocence that have made Diana Palmer such a beloved name at Silhouette Books. I'd like to say to Diana's present, past and future fans—sit back, relax and enjoy!

Best wishes,

Isabel Swift
Editorial Manager

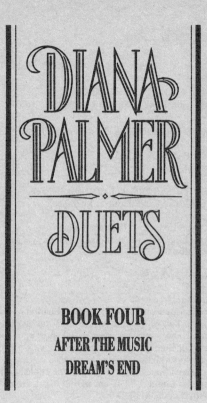

DIANA PALMER
DUETS

BOOK FOUR

AFTER THE MUSIC
DREAM'S END

Silhouette Books®

Published by Silhouette Books New York

America's Publisher of Contemporary Romance

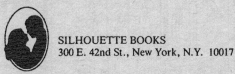

SILHOUETTE BOOKS
300 E. 42nd St., New York, N.Y. 10017

Silhouette Books edition published August 1990.

DIANA PALMER DUETS
© 1990 HARLEQUIN ENTERPRISES LIMITED

AFTER THE MUSIC © 1986 Diana Palmer
First published as a Silhouette Romance.

DREAM'S END © 1979 Diana Palmer
First published as a MacFadden Romance by Kim Publishing
Corporation.

ISBN: 0-373-48225-6

Contents

A Note from Diana Palmer

Dear Readers:

It seems like such a long time ago that I wrote the two books in this "Duet." The first, *After the Music*, was my sixth Silhouette Romance. It was published in 1986, but was written in 1985. In 1985, I received Waldenbooks Romance Bestseller Awards for both the Silhouette Desire line (*The Rawhide Man*) and the Silhouette Romance line (*Heart of Ice*), and I got my first *Affaire de Coeur* Silver Pen Award. I also found out that 20th Century Fox had received permission from Silhouette to use my book *The Tender Stranger* as a prop on a coffee table in their movie *Jumping Jack Flash* with Whoopi Goldberg. I got to see it, and even though it was only on screen for about two seconds, it was one of the high points of my life. I got a Reviewers' Choice Award from *Romantic Times* for *The Tender Stranger*, too. It was a banner year for me. And it was during this peak period that I wrote *After the Music*.

The idea for the story was one I'd had in the back of my mind for a long time, but I hadn't been able to market it successfully. When Silhouette acquired the proposal, I was over the moon. Then came the problem of producing the book! The idea involved having the heroine suffer a concussion toward the end of the story. But I have some wonderful resource people, and the two to whom I dedicated *After the Music* are my doctor and his wife—who also happens to be his nurse. When I was stuck for medical advice, I would take Hope to lunch. Not only is she a delightful lunch companion, she's smart! And what she doesn't know, her husband, Lamar, does. I couldn't have managed to do convincing hospital scenes without their help. They are very special people.

Sabina's love for opera comes from me. I support the Metropolitan Opera, and I have videotapes of Placido Domingo in *Carmen* and *Turandot* (my *very* favorite), and *La Traviata*. I grew up listening to light operettas—especially those made famous by Jeanette MacDonald and Nelson Eddy. My favorite movie when I was thirteen was *Indian Love Call*, which featured the famous duo. I graduated from operetta to opera, and now I never miss the televised ones on the educational channels.

One of the few disappointments of my life is that I have a poor voice for singing. My sister inherited our father's excellent ability in that direction, along with his facility for science and mechanical things. I can't complain, because I do love to write. But I always wanted to be able to sing the aria from *Madama Butterfly*. (I can at least play it on the piano after seven years of lessons—thanks to a wonderfully patient piano teacher).

Anyway, Sabina can sing it. I did enjoy having her background include that talent. I enjoyed Thorn just as much, because he was a hard-headed businessman who learned that there are things more important than making money. He wasn't hard on the eyes, either, and when I put that scene in his office on paper—the one where he climbs over the sofa to get to Sabina—I was laughing so hard that I almost fell out of the chair. Sometimes two characters play so beautifully against each other that a book practically writes itself. *After the Music* was one of those, a joy to work on from beginning to end.

Dream's End was originally published back in 1979,

and it was the eighth of the ten published with my first publisher. I was working at the *Tri-County Advertiser* during the time I wrote it, and that was one hard year to be a reporter. I also did occasional first-person opinion columns for *The Times* in Gainesville, Georgia, a daily newspaper on which I worked for a total of sixteen years as part of the district staff. I actually did a column on the dangers of overlapping fiction and reporting, in which an imaginary character became hopelessly involved in a county commission meeting. It read like fiction, but it was closer to the truth than I ever liked to admit! I spent all my lunch hours back then coming up with plot ideas and scenes, and I walked around in a perpetual daze. Looking back, I feel very fortunate that I didn't get fired from my day job as a result.

Dream's End was my first Cinderella story. I had in mind transforming an ordinary girl and making her into Miss Wonderful. In Eleanor Perrie, I had the perfect spinster, a girl raised in a strict home who was brought out—so to speak—by a friend. The hero is supposedly in love with another woman, a very sophisticated model, and about the time Eleanor discovers that *she* loves him, he announces his plans to marry the model.

It was fun to work with these characters. The spot where Eleanor and Curry have their picnic is based on a real place in South Georgia. When I was a little girl, my grandaddy and granny and I used to spend a lot of time fishing. Since Grandaddy farmed, he was pretty much his own boss, so we could go any time the mood took him if his work was caught up.

There was a mill pond near Cordele where we liked

to fish. We'd stop at a little country store down the road from it and buy Vienna sausages, soda crackers, RC Colas and Moon Pies. Then, between fish, we'd stuff ourselves. There's nothing like an RC Cola and a Moon Pie on a hot day, even if you don't catch any fish. More often than not, I didn't.

Dream's End is set in Texas, as a good many of my books are. I have a lot of friends out there, and I've spent some wonderful times seeing that enormous state and learning about it. I've stood in the Alamo and imagined the sound of guns, touched its walls and felt the coldness of fear along my spine as I tried to think what it was like for those brave men who died there.

I've seen the rolling countryside and the big cities, and I've loved every inch of it. Once, when my grandfather was a boy, he decided to go out to Texas and climbed on top of a yearling bull. His father pulled him off and sent him back home in short order, but I've often wondered what my life would have been like if Grandaddy had made it to Texas. He would have been a terrific cowboy. He was good with animals, and there was nothing he was afraid of. Zane Grey could have written some wonderful books about him.

In fact, I read almost every book Zane Grey ever *did* write. It was what got me fascinated with the American West from the time I was ten, and it's a fascination I've never lost. Writing has made it possible for me to afford trips to some of the places that intrigued me the most.

I've seen part of the Chisholm Trail, and I've stood where Doc Holliday stood in Tombstone during the gunfight at the O.K. Corral. I've been to ghost towns and abandoned mines in Arizona, seen the battlefield where thousands of Sioux and Cheyenne defeated Custer's 7th Cavalry in southern Montana. I've been over the Rocky Mountains where the mountain men and trappers ventured in the early days of the West.

All that traveling, all the wonderful people I've come to know, all that I've learned, I owe to those of you who read my books and share my dreams. Your loyalty is one thing I never take for granted. I think I owe you the best work I am capable of, the best writing I can do. It is a commitment and a responsibility that I try never to lose sight of.

I don't have much of an extended family anymore, just my husband and son, my sister and her family. But through the mails, I have become part of a much larger family: my very special family of readers. Many of you have corresponded with me from the very beginning, when I wrote the romances that are being reprinted by Silhouette Books. Georgia Walden and Mary Murphy in Augusta, Georgia, were the first people who ever wrote to me. We have visited over the years and still keep in touch, and I consider them close friends. I think I have someone in every state, and two adopted mothers, Alice in Chicago and Dorothy in California. I even have friends in foreign lands: a Romany gypsy in England, a college student in Bangalore, a housewife in India, a housekeeper and a business executive's wife in Australia, friends in Canada and Jamaica and the Philippines. There are Ophelia in Georgia, and Flo and Alice in Canada, and Rozanne in Oregon, and Doris and Kay in Texas, and Carolyn and Barbara in Iowa— and so many, many others who have made my life special and rich and blessed.

To all of you, thank you, with love. Diana Palmer is

AFTER
THE MUSIC

To Hope and Lamar

1

*

It was sad to see a tour end, Sabina Cane thought as she watched the electricians strike the lights at the auditorium where she and the band had performed the night before. It had been a sellout performance here in Savannah, and thank God for road tours. Times had been hard lately, and as it was, they'd make only a small profit after all the hands were paid. Sabina often wondered if there would ever come a time when she'd have financial security. Then she threw back her head and laughed at her own silly fears. She was doing what she loved best, after all. Without singing, she'd have no life at all, so she ought to be grateful that she had work. Besides, she and The Bricks and Sand Band were already booked for two weeks back home in New Orleans at one of the best clubs in town. And this month on the road had netted them some invaluable publicity.

She stared down the deserted, littered aisles, and spared a sympathetic smile for the tired men taking down equipment at this hour of the night. They had to be in New Orleans tomorrow for rehearsals, so there was no time to waste.

Sabina stretched lazily. Her slender body in its satin shorts and sequined camisole top and thigh-high cuffed pirate's boots was deliciously outlined by the fabric that was her trademark. The Satin Girl had wavy dark hair, which she wore down to her waist, and eyes almost like silver. Her complexion had been likened to pure pearl, and she had eyelashes no photographer believed were actually real.

Albert Thorndon grinned at her from the front of the auditorium, where he was passing the time with her road manager, Dennis Hart, who was also doubling as their booking agent. Dennis had done well so far for a young publicist seeking new directions. She smiled at both of them, waving at Al.

He was one of her best friends. She'd met him through her childhood pal, Jessica, who was hopelessly in love with Al. He was Jess's boss at Thorn Oil. Al didn't know about that infatuation, and Sabina had never betrayed Jess by telling him. The three of them went around together infrequently, and maybe at the very beginning Al had been mildly attracted to her. But Sabina wanted nothing from a man in any emotional or physical sense, and she let him know it right off the bat. After that, he'd accepted her as a friend. It was Al who'd managed to get them the club engagement in New Orleans, and he'd flown here all the way from Louisiana to tell her so. Thorn Oil had many subsidiaries. One of them was that nightclub in New Orleans. She wondered if his older brother knew what Al had done.

She'd heard plenty about Hamilton Regan Thorndon the Third, and most of it was unfavorable. The elder brother was the head honcho of Thorn Oil, which was headquartered in New Orleans, and he had a reputation for more than a shrewd business head. Rumor had it that he went through women relentlessly, leaving a trail of broken hearts behind him. He was the kind of man Sabina hated on sight, and she was glad Al had never tried to introduce her to his family. There wasn't much family, apparently. Only the two brothers and their widowed mother, who was on the stage somehow or other and spent most of her time in Europe. Al didn't talk about his family much.

At times, it all seemed odd to her. Al was always avoiding his family. He never even invited Jessica to those big company barbecues out at the family ranch in Beaumont, Texas, and Jess had been his secretary for two years. Sabina found his behavior fascinating, but she never questioned him about it. She'd thought at first that her background might have been the reason that he didn't introduce her, and she'd felt murderous. But when she realized that he'd left Jessica off the guest list, too, she calmed down. Anyway, Al didn't know about her past. Only Jess did, and Jess was a clam.

Al murmured something else to Dennis, and with a wave of his hand, went to join Sabina. His green eyes frankly approved of the baby-blue and silver-satin shorts that displayed her long, tanned legs to advantage. She laughed at the stage leer, knowing it was only an old joke between them.

"Well, aren't you the picture, Satin Girl?" he said with a laugh. He had dark hair and was just her height.

"I don't know. Am I?" She struck a pose.

"My kingdom for a camera," he sighed. "Where do you get those sexy costumes, anyway?"

"I make them," she confided, and laughed at his astonished reassessment of her garments. "Well, I did take a sewing course, and it relaxes me when I'm not singing."

"Little Miss Domestic," he teased.

"Not me, mister," she drawled. "I know all I care to about housework."

"In that tiny apartment," he sighed. "Don't make me laugh. You could mop the floor with a paper towel."

"It's home," she said defensively.

"It could be better stocked if you wouldn't give away everything you earn," he said, glaring at her. "Secondhand furniture, secondhand TV, secondhand everything, just because you're the softest touch going. No wonder you never have any money!"

"A lot of my neighbors are worse off than I am," she reminded him. "If you don't believe in poverty, let me introduce you around my neighborhood. You'll get an education in the desperation of inescapable struggle."

"I know, you don't have to rub it in." He stuck his hands in his pockets. "I just wish you'd save a bit."

"I save some." She shrugged.

"End of conversation," he murmured dryly. "I know when I'm beaten. Are you coming to my party tomorrow night?"

"What party?"

"The one I'm giving at my apartment."

She'd never known Al to give a party. She stared at him suspiciously. "Who's going to be there?"

"A lot of people you don't know, including Thorn."

Just the sound of his nickname threw her. "Hamilton Regan Thorndon the Third in the flesh?" she taunted.

"If you call him that, do it from the other side of a door, will you?" he cautioned, smiling. "He hates it. I've called him Thorn since we were kids."

"I suppose he's a stuffy old businessman with a thick paunch and a bald head?"

"He's thirty-four," he told her. His eyes were calculating. "Why do you react that way every time I mention him? You clam up."

She stared down at her black boots. "He uses women."

"Well, of course he does," he burst out. "For God's sake, they use him, too! He's rich and he doesn't mind spending money on them. He's a bachelor."

Her mind drifted to the past. Rich men with money. Bait. Using it like bait. Catching desperate women. She winced at the memory. "Mama," she whispered and tears welled up. She turned away, shaking with subdued rage.

"Odd that he isn't married."

Al was watching her with open curiosity. "My God, no one could live with Thorn." He laughed bitterly. "Why do you think our mother stays in Europe, and I have an apartment in the city?"

"You said he loves women," she reminded him.

"Nobody is allowed that close," he said flatly. "Thorn was betrayed once, and he's never cared about a woman since, except in the obvious ways. Thorn is like his nickname. He's prickly and passionate and rock stubborn. His executives bring jugs of Maalox to board meetings."

"I'd bring a battle-ax," she commented dryly. "Or maybe a bazooka. I don't like arrogant ladies' men."

"Yes, I know. You two would hit it off like thunder," he returned, "because Thorn doesn't like aggressive women. He prefers the curling kitten type."

She'd have bet he'd been hoping all his life for someone to match him. She was almost sorry because the pattern of her own life had made it impossible for her to be interested. It would have been fascinating to take him on. But she was as cold as the leather of the boots she wore onstage. Ironic. She was a rock star with a sensuous reputation, and her experience of men had been limited to a chaste kiss here and there. She found men unsatisfying and unreliable. Her heart was whole. She'd never given it. She never would.

She got up from her perch and flexed her shoulders wearily. It had been a long night.

"I could use a few hours' sleep," she said on a sigh. "Thanks for coming all this way to give us the news."

"My pleasure," he said. "The vocalist who had been hired by the club manager was involved in a car crash. She'll be okay, but she won't perform for a while. They were relieved that you and the band didn't mind rushing home to fill the spot."

Sabina smiled. "We're always rushing somewhere. We're grateful to get the work."

"About tomorrow night." He seemed oddly hesitant.

"The party?" She studied him and sensed something. "You're up to something. What is it?"

He shook his head ruefully. "You read me too well. There's this benefit."

"Aha!"

"I'll tell you more about it tomorrow night when I pick you up. I need some help. It's for underprivileged kids," he added.

"Then count me in, whatever it is." She stifled a yawn. "Who's the hostess for you?"

"Jessica." He looked sad and lost. His eyes met hers and fell. "I wish . . . nothing."

"You've never invited Jess to a party before," she remarked gently.

"Thorn would eat her alive if he thought I was interested in her," he said, grinding his teeth. "I told him I couldn't get anyone else to hostess . . . Oh, hell, I've got to run. My pilot's waiting at the airport. I didn't have anything better to do, so I thought I'd catch your last performance and tell you about the club date. Pick you up tomorrow night at six, okay?"

"Okay," she said, reluctant to let the matter drop. What a horror his brother sounded! "See you. And thanks for the club date, pal."

"My pleasure. Night." He turned and walked away, and her eyes followed him with open speculation. Could he be getting interested in Jessica? What a wonderful thing that would be. Her two best friends. She smiled to herself.

* * *

It was late afternoon when Sabina finally got to her own apartment. She walked up the steps, gazing fondly down at the block of row houses. She'd lived here all her adult life, ever since she'd left the orphanage at the age of eighteen. It wasn't a socially acceptable neighborhood. It was a poor one. But she had good neighbors and good friends here, and she loved the children who played on the cracked sidewalk. It was close to the bay, so she could hear the ships as they came into port, and she could smell the sea breezes. From her room on the fourth floor, she sometimes watched them as they passed, the heaving old freighters moving with an odd grace. But the very best thing about her apartment was the rent. She could afford it.

"Back home, I see, Miss Cane," Mr. Rafferty said at the foot of the staircase. He was about seventy and bald and always wore an undershirt and trousers around the building. He lived on his Social Security checks and had no family—unless you counted the other tenants.

"Yes, sir." Sabina grinned. "Got something for you," she murmured. She dug into her bag and produced a small sack of pralines she'd bought on the way home. "For your sweet tooth," she said, handing them over.

"Pralines." Mr. Rafferty sighed. He took a bite, savoring the taste. "My favorite! Miss Cane, you're always bringing me things." He shook his head, staring with sad eyes. "And I have nothing to give you."

"You're my friend," she said. "And besides, I've already got everything I need."

"You give it all away," he uttered darkly. "How will you heat your place with winter coming on?"

"I'll burn the furniture," she said in a stage whisper, and was rewarded with a faint smile from the pugnacious, proud old man who never smiled for any of the other tenants. He was disliked by everyone, except Sabina, who saw through the gruff exterior to the frightened, lonely man underneath. "See you!" Laughing, she bounded upstairs in her jeans and tank top, and Mr. Rafferty clutched his precious pralines and ambled back into his room.

Billy and Bess, the blond twins who lived next door, laughed when they saw her coming. "Miss Dean said you'd be back today!" they chattered, naming the landlady. "Did you have a big crowd?"

"Just right," she told them, extracting two of the huge lollipops she'd bought along with the pralines. "Here. Don't eat them before your dinner or your mama'll skin me!"

"Thanks!" they said in unison, eyeing the candy with adoration.

"Now I really have to get some sleep," she told them. "We've got a gig downtown!"

"Really?" Billy asked, wide-eyed. He and his sister were ten, and Sabina's profession awed them. Imagine, a rock star in their own building! The other kids down the block were green with envy.

"Really. So keep the noise down, huh?" she added in a conspiratorial whisper.

"You bet! We'll be your lookouts," Bess seconded.

She blew them a kiss and went inside. The twins' only parent was an alcoholic mother who loved them, but was hardly reliable. Sabina tried to look out for them at night, taking them into her apartment to sleep if Matilda stayed out, as she often did. Social workers came and went, but they couldn't produce any antidote for the hopeless poverty Matilda lived in, and threats to take the children away only produced tears and promises of immediate sobriety. Unfortunately, Matilda's promise lasted about an hour or two, or until the social worker left, whichever came first.

Sabina knew that kind of hopelessness firsthand. Until her mother died and she was put in the orphanage, she'd often gone hungry and cold herself. Losing her mother in the brutal way she did hadn't helped. But the struggle had given her a fixation about rich men and hard living. She hated both. With the voice that God had given her, she was determined to claw her way out of poverty and make something of her life. She was doing it, too. If only it had been in time to save her mother...

She lay down on the bed with a sigh and closed her eyes. She was so tired. She put everything she had, everything she was, into her performances. When they were over, she collapsed.

Dead tired. Sometimes she felt alive only in front of an audience, feeding on their adrenaline, the loud clapping and the cheers as she belted out the songs in her clear, haunting voice. Her own feet would echo the rhythms, and her body would sway. Her long, dark hair would fly and her silver-blue eyes would snap and sparkle with the electricity of her performances. She withheld nothing, but it was telling on her. All the long nights were wearing her down, and she was losing weight. But she had to keep going. She couldn't afford to slow down now, when she and the band were so close to the golden ring. They were drawing bigger crowds all the time wherever they appeared, and getting great coverage in the local press. Someday they'd get a recording contract, and then, look out!

Smiling as she daydreamed about that, she closed her eyes and felt the lumpy mattress under her with a wistful sigh. Just a few minutes rest would do it. Just a few minutes...

The loud pounding on the door woke her up. Drowsily, she got to her feet and opened it, to find Al on the other side.

"I fell asleep," Sabina explained. "What time is it?"

"Six o'clock. Hurry and throw something on. You'll feel better when you've eaten."

"What are you feeding me?" she asked on a yawn, preceding him into the apartment.

"Chicken Kiev," he told her. "Pommes de terre, and broccoli in hollandaise sauce—with cherries jubilee for dessert."

"You must have kept Susi in the kitchen all day!" she exclaimed with a laugh, picturing Al's cook, a stooped little Cajun woman cursing a blue streak as she prepared that luscious repast.

"I did," he said, green eyes gleaming. "I had to promise her a bonus, too."

"Well, she certainly deserves it. Make yourself comfortable. I'll be out in a jiffy." She took a quick shower and pulled on an elegant electric-blue satin dress with spaghetti straps, a square neckline, and a drop waist with a semifull skirt. It suited her slenderness and gave her gray eyes a blue look. Normally she'd never have been able to afford it on her budget, but she'd found it at an elegant used dress shop and paid only a fraction

of its original price. Bargain hunting was one of her special-
ties. It had to be, on her erratic salary. She wore black sling
pumps with it, and carried a dainty little black evening bag, and
put on the long cashmere coat, because nights were getting cold
in late autumn. She left her hair long instead of putting it into
a high French twist, as she usually did in the evening. When she
went back out into the living room, Al got to his feet and
sighed.

"You dish," he murmured. "What an eye-catcher!"

"Why does that make you look so smug?" she asked suspiciously.

"I told you I had a project in mind," he said after a minute.
"You remember hearing me talk about the children's hospital
I'm trying to get funds to build?"

"Yes," she said, waiting.

"I'm trying to put together a benefit for it. On local television. If I had a couple of sponsors, and you for a drawing card,
I could get some local talent and present it to the local stations." He grinned. "I guarantee we'd raise more than
enough."

"You know I'd do it for you, without pay," she said. "But
we're not big enough..."

"Yes, you are," he said stubbornly. "A television appearance here would give you some great publicity. Look, I'm not
asking you to do it for that reason and you know it, so don't
ruffle up at me. The kids will benefit most, and I've got some
other talent lined up as well," he told her. "But I can't sell the
idea to the television stations until I've got the sponsors. I want
to wheedle Thorn into being one of them."

"Will he?"

"If he's persuaded," he said, with a sly glance at her.

"Now, wait a minute," she said curtly. "I am not playing up
to your poisonous brother, for any reason."

"You don't have to play up to him. Just be friendly. Be
yourself."

She frowned. "You aren't going to paint me into a corner,
are you?"

"Scout's honor," he promised with a flash of white teeth.
"Trust me."

"I don't trust anybody, even you," she said with a smile.

"I'm working on that. Let's go."

He led her down the long flight of stairs.

"Couldn't you ask him yourself?" she murmured. "After all, blood is thicker..."

"Thorn's kind of miffed with me."

"Why?"

Al stuck his hands in his pockets with a sigh and glanced at her ruefully. "He brought a girl home for me last night."

Her eyes widened. "He what?"

"Brought a girl home for me. A very nice girl, with excellent connections, whose father owns an oil refinery. He was giving a dinner party, you see."

"My God!" she burst out.

"I called my mother after it was over, and she called up and chewed on his ear for a while. That made him mad. He doesn't like her very much most of the time, and he needs that refinery damned bad." He shrugged. "If I could get him a refinery, he'd sure rush over to sponsor my benefit."

"You could buy him one," she suggested.

"With what? I'm broke. Not totally, but I don't have the kind of capital I'd need for business on that scale. I'm a partner on paper only, until I come into my share of Dad's estate next year."

"I'm beginning to get a very interesting picture of Hamilton Regan Thorndon the Third," she said stiffly. "A matchmaker, is he?"

"That's about the size of it," Al confessed. He gestured toward his car when they reached the street. "I'm parked over there."

She followed him, scowling. "Does he do this to you often?"

"Only when he needs something he can't buy." He sighed. "You'd never guess how many businessmen have eligible daughters they want to marry off. Especially businessmen with refineries and blocks of oil stock and..."

"But that's inhuman!"

"So is Thorn, from time to time." He unlocked the car and helped her inside. "Haven't you wondered why I usually keep you and Jessica away from company parties?"

"I'm beginning to realize," she said to herself. She waited until he got inside the green Mercedes-Benz and started the engine before she added, "He doesn't want you associating with the peons, I gather?"

He stiffened, started to deny it, and then huffed miserably. "He's not marriage-minded himself. Thorn Oil is worth millions, with all its subsidiaries. He wants an heir for it. But with just the right girl, you see. Jessica has been married before, and her family isn't socially prominent," he said, biting it out. "Thorn would savage her."

It all became crystal clear. Everything . . . how he felt about Jessica, why he'd been so secretive. "Oh, Al," she breathed piteously. "Oh, Al, how horrible for you!"

"Next year I can fight him," he said. "When I've got money of my own. But for now I have to lie low and bide my time."

"I'd punch him out," she growled softly, gray eyes throwing off silver sparks, her long hair swirling like silk as her head jerked.

He glanced at her as he drove toward his apartment down the brightly lit streets. "Yes, I believe you would. You're like him. Fire and high temper and impulsive actions." He smiled. "You'd be a match, even for my brother."

"With all due respect, I don't want your brother."

"Yes, I know. But please don't take a swing at him tonight. I need you."

"Now, wait a minute . . ."

"Just to help present my case, nothing else," he promised. His smile faded as he studied her. "I wouldn't strand you with him. Thorn isn't much good with innocents. You'll know what I mean when you see the woman he's got with him tonight. She's as much a barracuda as he is. I only want you to help me convince him to sponsor the benefit. I'll get an accompanist and you can do the aria from Madama Butterfly for him."

"He likes opera?" she asked.

"He loves it."

She eyed him closely. "How does he feel about rock singers?"

He shifted restlessly, and looked worried. "Well . . ."

"How?"

His jaw clenched. "Actually, he's never said. Don't worry, we'll find out together."

She had grave misgivings, but she didn't say anything. After all, his older brother would probably be nothing like she imagined. He might like women, but she pictured him as a retiring sort of man like the pictures of businessmen she'd seen in magazines. She knew all too well that a rich man didn't have to be good-looking to get women.

Al's house overlooked the bay, and Sabina dearly loved it. It was white and stately, and had once belonged to his grandmother. She could picture the huge living room being the scene of elegant balls in the early days of New Orleans. There were shrubs all around it, assorted camellias and gardenia and jasmine. Now, of course, everything was dormant, but Sabina could imagine the grounds bursting with color, as they would in the spring.

Jessica came darting out of the big living room, where several people were socializing over drinks, and her face was as red as her hair. She was small and sweet, and Sabina loved her. She and Jess went back a long way. They'd shared some good times when Sabina was at the orphanage just around the corner from where Jessica lived. They'd met by accident, but a firm friendship had developed, and lasted all these years.

"Hi, Sabina!" Jessica said quickly, then turned immediately to Al. "We're in trouble. You invited Beck Henton."

"Yes. So?" Al asked blankly.

"Well, he and Thorn are competing for that oil refinery in Houston. Had you forgotten?"

Al slapped his forehead. "Damn!"

"Anyway, they just went out the back door together, and Thorn was squinting one eye. You know what that means."

"Damn!" Al repeated. "I was going to ask Beck to help sponsor my benefit," he growled. "Well, that's blown it. I'd better go and try to save him."

Sabina stared after him with wide, curious eyes. She was getting a strange picture of the sedate older brother.

"I'd better get Beck's chauffeur," Jessica said miserably. "He'll be needed."

"Before you go, is there any ginger ale in there?" she asked, nodding toward the bar in the living room.

"Not a drop. But I left you a bottle in the kitchen. I'll see you in a minute."

"Thanks!" Sabina darted quickly into the kitchen and filled a glass with ice. She was just reaching for the bottle of ginger ale when the back door suddenly flung open and, just as quickly, slammed again.

She turned, and froze in place when she saw him. He was tall and slender, with the kind of body that reminded Sabina of the men who appear in television commercials. He was powerful for all that slenderness, and the darkness of his tuxedo emphasized his jet black hair and the deep tan of his face and hands. His eyes were surrounded by thick, black lashes, and they glittered at her.

"Hand me a cup of that," he said in a crisp voice, holding out a lean, long-fingered hand. There was no jewelry on it, but she got a glimpse of crisp black hair on his wrist surrounding a Rolex watch.

She handed him the ice automatically, noting a faint scar on his cheek, near his eye. His nose was arrow-straight and gave him a look of arrogance. He had a jutting jaw that hinted of stubbornness, and his mouth was perfect, the most masculine mouth she'd ever seen. He was fascinating, and she couldn't take her eyes off him.

"What's so fascinating, honey?" he drawled. "Haven't you ever seen a man with a black eye before?"

This, she thought, must be the Beck Henton they'd discussed, because he certainly didn't fit the long, pretentious name Al's brother had.

"Not many walking around in tuxedos." She grinned. He did fascinate her, not only with the way he looked, but with that air of authority that embodied him.

She seemed to fascinate him, too, because a smile played at the corners of his mouth as he wrapped the ice in a tea towel and held it just under his bruised eye. He moved closer, and she saw that the glittering eyes under the jutting brow were a pale, icy-blue. The color was shocking in so dark a face.

He let his gaze fall to her smooth, faintly tanned shoulders and down the bodice of the trendy dress to her long, slender legs encased in blue-patterned stockings. They moved back up slowly, past her long neck and over the delicate planes of her face to her soft mouth, her high cheekbones, her dark, wavy hair and to the incredibly long lashes over her silver eyes.

"Why are you hiding in here?" he asked, breaking the silence.

"I came for some ginger ale," she confessed, showing the bottle. "I don't drink, you see. Jessica hides some soft drinks for me, so I don't have to look repressed in front of Al's guests."

He cocked his head. "You don't look repressed." That faint smile was still playing on his firm mouth. "Al's secretary must be a friend of yours?"

"A very good one."

"Jessica's all right. Al said he couldn't get anyone else to hostess for him, and she's doing a pretty good job."

Faint praise, she thought, and a bit condescending, but he had a right to his opinion. "You're going to have a gorgeous shiner, there," she remarked.

"You ought to see the other guy," he mused.

She sighed. "Poor Hamilton Regan Thorndon the Third. I hope you didn't hit him too hard."

His dark eyebrows arched, and his eyes widened. "Poor Hamilton...?"

"Al said the two of you were competing for an oil refinery," she volunteered, grinning impishly. "Why don't you just leave the oil in the ground and pump out what you need a little at a time?"

He chuckled softly. "You're impertinent, miss."

"Why thank you, Mr. Henton. You are Beck Henton, aren't you?" she persisted. "You certainly couldn't be Al's brother. You don't look like a man with a mile long name."

"I don't? And what do you imagine Al's brother looks like?"

"Dark and chubby and slightly graying," she said, fascinated by his faint smile.

"My God, I never knew Al to lie."

"But he didn't. I mean, he didn't ever describe his brother."
She poured ginger ale into her glass, lifted it up and peeked at
him over its rim. "You really shouldn't have hit Al's brother.
Now he'll leave and I won't get a shot at him."

One eye narrowed. "Why did you want to?"

"Well, he's got an oil company," she said. "And there's a
project . . ."

Before she could tell him why, his expression grew stern and
he laughed unpleasantly. "There's always a project." He moved
closer. "Why don't you have a shot at me, honey? I've got an
oil company myself."

"Aren't you . . . with someone?" she asked nervously. He was
so close that she could feel the vibrant energy of him, smell his
expensive cologne. He towered over her.

"I'm always with someone," he murmured, letting his fingers toy with strands of her soft hair. "Not that it matters. They
all look alike, eventually."

"Mr. Henton . . ." she began, trying to move away.

He backed her against the counter and pinned her there with
the formidable, controlled weight of his body. He was almost
touching her, but not quite. Her hands shook as he took the
glass from her and set it aside on the counter.

"Shhh," he said softly, touching her mouth with one long
finger. He wasn't smiling now. His eyes were darkening, in-
tense. He tossed the towel and ice aside, and framed her oval
face in his big, warm hands. They felt callused, as if he used
them in hard work, and she felt threatened.

"You mustn't . . ."

"We're cutting a corner or two, that's all," he whispered,
bending. "You're very lovely."

She should move, she should push away! But her hands flattened helplessly on his shirtfront, and she felt hard muscle and
warmth against her cold fingers. His breath teased her lips as
he poised his mouth over hers.

"No," she protested weakly and tried to move away.

His hips pressed her into the counter, and the twisting motion of her body provoked a shocking reaction. He drew in a
sharp breath, and his fingers tightened on her face. "My God,

it's been years since that's happened so quickly with a woman,'' he said curtly and then his mouth was on hers.

She stiffened, feeling the shock from her head to her toes, which tried to curl up in her high heels as his lips relented. He seemed to feel her uneasiness, her reticence. He drew away and searched her face with odd, puzzled eyes. Then, slowly he lowered his head again and traced her bottom lip with his teeth, slowly, gently in a masterful exploration that was years beyond her experience of men. Her fingers clung to the lapels of his jacket and her breath came quickly. She could taste him, the smoky and minty warmth of his mouth doing wild things to her pulse.

"Yes, like that," he whispered into her slowly parting lips. "A little more, honey...yes. Kiss me back this time. Kiss me..."

He incited her in wild, reckless ways. It was like some wild fantasy, that she could be standing in an intimate embrace, kissing a man whom she'd only just met in a deserted kitchen. He was no ordinary man, either; he was an expert at this; he knew ways of using his mouth that she'd never even imagined.

She gasped as his tongue probed and his mouth demanded. All at once the hunger broke through her natural reserve and she felt warmth spread through her body. A tiny, surprised moan broke from her lips as she went up on tiptoe and gave him her mouth hungrily. Her hands reached up to the thick, cool waves of his hair and she held his head to hers.

"God!" he groaned. His arms lifted her and the room seemed to whirl away. It was the wildest, deepest, hungriest kiss she'd ever shared with a man, and it didn't seem as if he had any intention of stopping. She should be fighting him. Why couldn't she fight?

A long minute later, he set her back on her feet and looked down into her wide gray eyes with curiosity and caution. One of his blue eyes narrowed, and a warning bell rang somewhere in her mind, but her body was throbbing wildly and she hardly connected the telltale sign.

"You're gifted, lady," he breathed, studying her. "Not very experienced yet, but I can take care of that. Come home with me."

Her face burned and her lips trembled. "I can't," she whispered shakily.

"Why not?" His eyes blazed down at her body.

"I . . . what about Al?" she began.

He made a rough sound under his breath. "What about him, for God's sake? Have you got some wild crush on him? You won't get to first base, I promise you. Al's bringing that damned rock singer he's courting. I came because of her, but I can deal with her later." He touched her cheek gently and seemed oddly hesitant, mistaking her frozen posture for fear instead of the shock it really was. "I won't hurt you," he said mildly. "I won't rush you, either. We can discuss . . . projects."

The words began to take effect on her numb brain, and she stared up at him with dawning comprehension.

"Rock singer?"

He looked utterly dangerous, the tender lover suddenly growing cold and businesslike and threatening. "Al's got himself a new girl. But not for long," he added on a short laugh. "That's got nothing to do with you and me. You said you need money; let's go talk about it."

"You're . . . Hamilton Regan Thorndon the Third," she said.

He cocked an eyebrow. "Smart lady. Does it make a difference? I told you I had an oil company. Come on, honey, let's get away from this crowd." He touched her shoulder, lazily, caressingly. "You won't go away empty-handed, I promise."

She felt sick all over—sick that she'd let him kiss her, that she'd responded. She felt as her mother must have years ago, but with one major difference: she wasn't desperate. She'd never be desperate enough, and her kindling eyes told him so. She began to tremble with the force of her anger, her disgust.

"Hey, what is it?" he asked suddenly, frowning.

"You have such a line, Mr. Thorndon the Third," she said with a voice as cold as ice. Her fists were clenched at her sides as she backed sharply away from him. "'You won't go away empty-handed,'" she mimicked.

"How suddenly principled you are, lady," he said bitterly. "You're the one who started talking terms right off the bat. Okay, I'm willing. How much?"

Oh, Lord, what a mess she'd made of things. Why hadn't she said something about the project? Now he thought she was a prostitute! But what a monumental ego he had, she thought, glaring up at him. "You couldn't afford me," she told him.

His eyes ran over her body again and this time there was no appreciation in his stare. "You overestimate yourself. I'd say twenty dollars would do it."

She slapped him. It was completely unpremeditated, without thought, but she wasn't taking any more insults from this creature, even if he was Al's brother.

He didn't even flinch. His cheek turned red, but he simply stared at her with those icy eyes.

"You'll pay for that," he said quietly.

"Make me," she challenged, backing away. "Come on, oil baron, hit me back." She was beautiful in her fury, silver eyes flashing, black hair flying, body taut and poised and elegant. "I'm not afraid of you."

His face gave nothing away; his gaze was unblinking and hard. "Who are you?" he asked sternly.

"I'm the tooth fairy," she said with a mocking smile. "Too bad you didn't lose any to Mr. Henton; I've got a pocket full of quarters."

She turned, forgetting her ginger ale, and strode out the door and through the house. She was livid by the time she reached the crowded living room.

Al spotted her, moving forward with a glass in his hand. He looked worried and nervous, but when he saw Sabina's face he looked shocked.

"What happened?"

"Never mind." She would hate to tell him. "Where's Mr. Henton?"

"Gone home in a snit, with a broken nose," he grumbled. "So much for that potential sponsor." He sighed. "Well, we'll just have to work on Thorn."

"Al, about working on your brother..."

A door slammed, and even amid the noise of the guests, she knew who it was and why. She stiffened as Al looked over her shoulder and grinned.

"Well, Beck sure left you a present, didn't he?" Al chuckled. "Why didn't you duck?"

"I did," came a familiar, cold drawl from behind her. "Are you going to introduce me?" he asked, pretending ignorance.

"Sure." Al placed a casual arm across Sabina's shoulder and turned her to face the man with the black eye. Al sounded casual, but his arm was tense and trembling a little. "This is Sabina Cane."

The tall man looked suddenly murderous. "The rock singer?"

"Yes," Al said defensively.

The man who'd kissed her so passionately not five minutes before glared at Sabina as if he'd like to cut her throat.

"I should have known," he said with a harsh laugh, ramming one lean hand into his pants pocket. "You look the part."

She curtsied sweetly. "Thank you, Mr. Thorndon the Third."

Al glanced from one to the other with open curiosity. "Thorn, there's something I want to talk to you about," he said.

"Forget it," Thorn told him. He gave Sabina a long, insulting appraisal. "Your taste in women stinks." He turned and walked straight toward an elegant blonde in a gold lamé bodysuit. The woman slipped into his arms, clinging to him like glue.

Sabina glared at him with eyes that burned when she saw him bend to kiss the blonde warmly on the mouth. She averted her gaze. "Al, I can't stay here. I can't possibly."

"Sabina, I'm sorry . . ."

She spotted Jessica and motioned to her. "Can you run me home?"

"Sure, what's wrong?"

"I just have a bad headache, Al." Sabina lied smoothly. She couldn't go into it now. "I'm sorry, I thought it would get better."

"If it's because of Thorn," he began, glaring at his brother, "I apologize for his bad manners."

"I'd like to tell him what to do with them, too," she told Al. "But my head's splitting. Jessica?"

"I'm ready. Come on. See you later, boss," she told Al with a shy smile.

"I'll talk to Thorn," Al said brusquely.

"Don't waste your breath on him," Sabina added. "Good night."

She walked out the door with a breathless Jessica right behind, grateful for the nippy autumn air and the dark.

"What happened in the kitchen?" Jessica demanded as they were driving back toward Sabina's apartment.

"I antagonized him," Sabina said stiffly. "Al will never forgive me, but I couldn't stand that man another minute!"

"Al says that Thorn is used to expecting the worst and he usually finds it. He's a sad kind of man, really. He doesn't let anybody get close; he spends most of his time all alone."

"Alone?" Sabina said gruffly. "That's not what I saw..."

"Window dressing," Jessica replied as she sped down the street where her friend lived. "His women come and go. Mostly they go."

"How do you know so much about him?" Sabina asked.

"He comes in and out of our office. His own offices are in the new building, the addition. But he and Al have business dealings they have to discuss now and then. He's always polite. Once, he even brought me coffee when I was hurrying to get some correspondence out for him and Al," she added with a smile.

He could afford to be polite to Al's secretary, Sabina thought angrily. But if Al got serious about Jessica, he knew Thorn would wage a desperate battle. He had said as much with that offhand remark at the party. And Al did feel something for Jess, Sabina was sure of it. She wanted so much to tell Jessica what she suspected.

"Thorn probably bribes people when he can't get them any other way," Sabina grumbled.

Jessica pulled into a parking space outside the apartment building and glanced at her friend. "I'll bet he's never needed a bribe," she sighed. "But Al's terrified of him, you know? So am I, really. If I ever looked twice at Al, I'll bet Thorn would have me transferred to Saudi Arabia or somewhere."

Yes, Sabina thought miserably, being nice to Al's secretary was one thing. But Hamilton Regan Thorndon the Third would cut Jess up like sausage for merely smiling at his brother.

"Just remember one thing. Al isn't blind about you," Sabina said softly. "And if he cared enough, he'd even take on big brother."

"He'd only notice me if I died and there was nobody to make coffee," Jess groaned.

"Ha! Well, I guess I'll go up and eat some toast. Damn Hamilton Regan Thorndon the Third, anyway," she muttered. "He's cost me my supper. Imagine having to work for him!"

"His secretaries kind of come and go, like his women," Jessica confided. "He's hard on women. They say he hates them."

Sabina felt herself shudder. "Yes, I felt that. He's very cold."

"Not in bed, I'll bet," Jessica said under her breath.

Sabina's face flushed, and she got out before Jess could see it. "Thanks for the ride! Want to have lunch one day?"

"I'll call you. Are you sure you're okay?" Jess added with a worried frown.

Sabina shrugged and smiled. "Just a little battlescarred."

"What did you say to him?"

"I hit him," she said, noticing the wary look on Jess's face. "Then I dared the oil baron to hit me back."

Jess looked uneasy. "That wasn't wise. He has the memory of an elephant."

"He tried to buy me for the night," Sabina said curtly.

Jess made a soft sound. "Oh, my. No wonder you hit him! Good for you! Will you tell Al?"

She debated about that. "I'd rather not. Al doesn't know about my background. Just tell Al I'm not sorry I did it, but I'm sorry I embarrassed him."

"Al doesn't embarrass easily." Jessica toyed with the steering wheel. "I was pretty shocked when he asked me to hostess for him." She glanced up. "He's never invited me to his apartment before."

"He's started to notice you," Sabina said cautiously.

"Well, at least Thorn didn't toss me out tonight," Jess replied sadly. "He strikes me as a little snobbish where his family is concerned."

Sabina's temper flared again, "What he needs is someone who can put him in his place. And if he isn't careful, I may blacken his other eye for him!"

Jess laughed. "I can see it now—a TKO in the fifth round..."

"Good night," Sabina said, closing the car door behind her. She waved at Jess and went upstairs. Of all the unexpected endings to what had begun as a lovely evening. Closing the door of her apartment, she decided to skip dinner. She'd lost her appetite anyway. Sleep would be a welcome relief. But instead of losing herself to dreams, her mind replayed an image of Thorn and the way he'd kissed her. He'd touched her deeply, in ways she'd never expected to be touched.

How could she blame him for thinking she was easy, after the way she'd reacted to his unexpected ardor? He couldn't have known about her childhood, about her mother. She turned her hot face into the pillow. Now she'd made an enemy of him, and what was Al going to think? If only she'd stayed out of the kitchen, none of it would have happened.

She had a feeling she was going to be under siege shortly. The oil baron wasn't going to stand for having her in Al's life after this. She'd have bet money that he was already brooding about ways to get her away from Al, because she knew he had the impression that she and Al were more than friends. And part of her was even looking forward to the confrontation. She liked a sporting enemy.

2
*

Sabina got up the next morning with a feeling of dread. Immediately, her mind raced back to the night before, and her heart burned at the memory of a hard mouth invading hers.

It had been the first time she'd ever felt like that. How ironic that it should be with a man who was quickly becoming her worst enemy. She had no inclination whatsoever for the lighthearted alliances other women formed. She knew too much about their consequences.

How odd, that Hamilton Thorndon the Third should think that she was easy. She almost laughed. If there was one woman in the world his money couldn't get, it was Sabina.

With drooping eyelids she dragged herself into the exclusive Bourbon Street nightclub where she and the band were working. She'd never felt less like working, but the rehearsals went on regardless.

It was late afternoon, barely an hour from curtain time, and she was just finishing a tune about lost love, when Al came walking in. He looked as miserable as she felt, and his face looked sullen.

"Can you spare a minute?" Al asked.

"Sure," she said, jumping down from the stage in her satin shorts and top, and black leather boots. "Be right back!" she called to the boys.

Ricky Turner, the tall, thin band leader and pianist, waved back. "Ten minutes, no more. We've still got two numbers to go over."

"Okay," she agreed. "He worries," she told Al as they sat down at a nearby table while around them busboys put out napkins and silver and glassware. "He's terrified that the stage will fall through, or the lights will come down on our heads, or that I'll trip over a cord and bash in the drums." She laughed softly. "Concerts are hard on Ricky's nerves. He's just started to relax since we've been doing this gig."

"What happened last night?" Al asked bluntly.

She flushed and averted her eyes. "Ask your brother."

"I did. And he said the same thing. Look, if he hurt you..."

"I think I hurt him more," she said angrily. "I hit him just as hard as I could."

His eyes widened. "Thorn? You hit Thorn?"

"Just as hard as..."

"I get the message. No wonder he was so icy." He studied her. "He wants to see you."

Her mouth dropped. "Oh he does, does he? Did he say when?"

"In fifteen minutes. Now, before you go up in flames and say no, listen to me. I called my mother and told her I wanted to bring you to the ranch for a few days over Easter. She called Thorn and talked to him. Apparently he's ready to back down a little. I think all he wants is to issue you a personal invitation. But if you don't go to see him, everything's off. Including," he added gruffly, "my children's hospital benefit. I can't get another backer. Without Thorn, we'll just have to do a one-night live concert at some theater. We won't raise nearly enough money that soon. I haven't told him much about the benefit. He won't even listen to me right now."

"And you think he'll listen to *me*?" she said crisply. "And I don't think I want to spend Easter with your family."

"Sure you do. It'll be great fun. You'll like my mother."

"I'm sure I will, but I don't like your brother!"

He sighed. "The new hospital wing would cater to families who can't afford proper medical care," he said, eyeing her. "Especially children with fatal illnesses, like cancer. It would boast a research center as well."

Her eyes glittered at him. "Al..."

"Of course, it will eventually get built. In a few years. Meanwhile a lot of children will have to go to other cities, some won't be able to get treatment..."

"I'll do it, you animal," she said irritably. "You know I can't turn my back on any kind of benefit. But if your horrible brother tries to cut me up again, I'll paste him one!"

"That's the girl." He grinned. "Get over to his office and give it to him!"

She left him to explain her departure to the band. She was just going out the door, still in costume, when she heard Ricky wail. Sabina quickened her pace and tried not to grin.

Minutes later, she paused at the door of the plush New Orleans office that housed Thorn Oil's executive officer. Taking a deep breath, she forced her racing heart to slow down. She told herself not to let her apprehension show or give the enemy any weakness to attack. Anyway, there was no reason to believe that old poisonous Hamilton Regan Thorndon the Third might want anything worse than a pleasant chat.

She laughed to herself. Sure. He just loved having the youngest son of the family mixed up with a rising young rock star and wanted to tell her so.

With a resigned sigh, she opened the door and walked into a lavish but sleek office, where a lovely blond receptionist was typing at a computer keyboard.

"Yes, may I help you?" she asked politely, smiling at Sabina.

"I'm here to see Hamilton Thorndon the Third," Sabina said, returning the smile. "I believe he's expecting me?"

The blonde looked wary as her eyes examined the slender figure in thigh-high black leather cuffed boots, tight pink satin shorts with a low-cut white satin camisole and silver beaded vest under a thin jacket. Sabina almost chuckled. The outfit was so outrageous. But she had a performance in less than an hour and no time to change clothes, so the big man would just have to see her in her working garb. Her expression darkened with worry. She had grave misgivings about this. Especially after last night. But this business was best taken care of now. Thorn was the kind of man, from all description, who wouldn't mind walking up on the stage right in the middle of her nightclub performance to question her.

"Uh, I'll announce you," the blonde stammered, then buzzed the intercom. "Mr. Thorndon, there's a..." She put her hand over the receiver. "Your name, please?"

"Tell him it's Sabina," she replied in the clear voice that was her trademark.

" . . . Miss Sabina here. She says you're expecting her. Yes, sir." The receptionist hung up. "Mr. Thorndon will see you. Go right in."

Sabina was waved to a door beside the desk. Smiling coyly at the blonde, she opened the door and poked her head in.

Immediately she regretted the lack of time to change into something more suitable. She'd have to bluff her way through. As usual.

"Here I am, your worship," she told the man behind the desk as she closed the door breezily behind her. "Fire away, but make it fast. I've got a performance in less than forty-five minutes."

He rose from the desk like a shark slicing through water, all sleek, smooth pursuit. The tan suit he was wearing did nothing to disguise the huge muscles of his arms, chest and legs. As he moved around the desk toward her, she felt his eyes sweep over her, as if she were being brushed all over with a flammable liquid.

His disposition was as cold as she remembered it. Sabina tried to block the previous night out of her mind while his blue, unblinking eyes were riveted on her.

A finger hit the intercom button. "No calls, honey."

"Yes, sir," came the edgy reply. Then there was silence while the oil magnate did what he was best at—intimidation.

He folded his arms across his chest and his blackened eye narrowed as he studied her graceful figure. "You do advertise it, don't you?" he murmured with a faint smile.

"This is my stage costume. Al said you wanted to see me immediately, and I just dropped everything and rushed right over. Satin is my trademark," she reminded him.

"So I've heard. How much do you want? What'll it cost for you to promise to leave Al alone?"

"Characteristically blunt," she remarked, eyeing him. "Have you ever found anything your money couldn't buy? Besides that oil refinery, I mean. Obviously, it's much more important than a little thing like Al's happiness."

An eyebrow jerked and the blackened eye squinted. She remembered that telltale signal, but she ignored it. "I hear through the grapevine that Al flew to Savannah to tell you about that singing engagement in my nightclub."

"Your nightclub?" she asked. "I understood that it was jointly owned by the two of you, and your mother."

At the mention of his mother, his body went rigid. "Al caused one hell of an argument last night. I do not want you at my ranch over the holidays. That's the one place I don't have to suffer women."

Her chin lifted. "I like Al," she told him. "And if he wants me to join him for Easter, I'll be delighted to accept." As she said that, she wondered vaguely why Al had invited her when Jessica had his whole heart. Was he trying to put up a smoke screen?

"Listen to me, you half-baked adventuress," he said suddenly. "I'm not having my brother taken over by a wild-eyed rock singer with eyes for his bankbook!" Moving toward her, he reached into his vest pocket, caught her roughly by the arm, and stuffed a piece of paper into the valley between her high breasts. "You take that and get the hell out of my brother's sight. I make a bad enemy. Remember it!"

He escorted her to the door and shoved her out of his office. "I'll make your apologies to my mother," he added sarcastically. The door slammed shut behind her.

The blonde stared at Sabina who stood there trembling, her face red and hot with hurt and humiliation, her eyes brimming with tears of fury. Just like old times, she thought wildly, just like my mother. She reached blindly for the check—she knew it was a check. Her trembling fingers unfolded it. It was made out to her, $20,000 worth. She stared at it for a long minute, until her face went purple.

Without a single regard for good sense, she whirled, opened the door to Thorn's office and stormed back in. She slammed the door behind her, watching his pale blue eyes widen with shock as his head jerked up.

She had a feeling that no one had ever dared cross him before. If she hadn't been so furious, she might have backed down, but it was too late for that now. Crossing the room with exquisite poise, she crumpled the check without looking at it, and threw it at him.

"You listen to me, you blue-eyed barracuda," she said, her eyes flashing venomously over the desk at him. "Al's invited me to the ranch, and I'm coming. You can take your bribe and stuff it up your arrogant nose!"

With a fierce look, he stood up and moved around the desk like a freight train barreling down a mountain.

She actually backed away, positioning herself behind the big leather sofa, her eyes widening with mingled fury and fear as he kept coming.

"Don't you do it, Hamilton Regan Thorndon the Third," she challenged, glaring at him. "You lay one hand on me, and I'll have you in court so fast your head will swim!"

"It will be worth it," he said, walking up onto the sofa, boots and all.

"You take your hands…!" she cried as he bounded over the leather back and jerked her into his arms. She never finished the sentence. He had her mouth under his, and he was hurting her.

She fought him, twisting, hitting him with her clenched hands. He backed her into the wall and held her there with the controlled weight of his body. After a moment or two, the bruising mouth relented a little and stopped demanding. It grew unexpectedly gentle, and as his hips pressed deeply against hers, she felt the sudden impact of his masculinity and caught her breath. He lifted his devouring mouth a breath away, and his hands slid down her waist to her hips, holding her as his eyes met hers. His chest rose and fell roughly, brushing her sensitive breasts.

"You're hurting me," she said unsteadily.

"And frightening you?" he asked quietly as he saw the apprehension in her eyes.

"Yes," she confessed.

He let her move away a little, so that the shocking evidence of his arousal was less noticeable. Her heart stopped pounding so feverishly. "Do you make…a habit of chasing women…over sofas in your office?" she asked breathlessly, trying to keep her sense of humor.

He didn't smile, but the corner of his mouth twitched. "No. Most of them have the good sense not to challenge me." He let her go with a rueful laugh. "On the other hand, I've never had a woman arouse me the way you do."

She averted her face to the window, trying to fight down the blush that was forming there.

"So I can't buy you off, is that what you're telling me?" he asked, moving away to his desk to light a cigarette.

"Chapter and verse," she proclaimed.

"There are other ways," he said, smoking quietly as he watched her smooth the hair his hands had angrily disheveled.

"Like seducing me?" she challenged, facing him. "No way. I'll never let you that close a second time."

"A third time," he corrected, and a faint gleam touched his eyes. "If you come out to the ranch, you could find yourself in a difficult position. Ask Al how I react to a challenge."

She didn't need to. She already knew. "You just want to choose Al's wife, is that it? You want him to marry a woman who would work to your advantage, of course, not his."

That eye narrowed again. "Think what you like about my motives. But you'll have to go through me to get to Al. Give it up before anyone gets hurt."

"Threats?" she chided.

"Promises." He took a draw from the cigarette and something alien flared in his blue eyes. "I'm a reasonable man. You can still have the check if you want it. No strings. How's that for generosity?"

She stared at him, calculating. "Suppose I show up at the ranch for Easter?"

He took another draw from the cigarette. "Try it."

She pursed her lips. That check would go a long way toward Al's goal for the children's hospital wing. And it would needle the hell out of this overprotective oil magnate. She held out her hand.

He looked faintly disappointed, even as he reached for the check, yet he tossed it to her with careless accuracy. "Smart girl."

"You don't realize how smart. Yet," she added. She blew him a kiss and walked out. "Have a nice day," she called to the blonde secretary as she breezed out of the office.

An hour later, Sabina went onto the stage at the exclusive Bourbon Street nightclub feeling wildly reckless. Consequently, she gave the best performance of her short career. The band beat out the thick rhythm, and Sabina, in her satin and sequins, sang in her piercingly clear voice, every word discernible, her body throbbing with the drums. She could feel the music, actually feel it, and the overflowing audience seemed to feel it with her, clapping and keeping time with her, smiling appreciatively as she took them with her to the heady finale. She moved across the stage, bathed in colored lights, and held her audience spellbound as the last notes died. In the audience, Al watched her with a worried frown.

After the final set, she walked off the stage and sat down with him. Anger still glittering in her eyes.

"What's wrong?" he asked quietly.

"Read me pretty well, don't you, my friend?" she asked. She ordered a cup of coffee from the waiter and smiled at Al. "Your brother and I went two more rounds."

"Again? For God's sake! I should have known better," he growled, running a hand through his hair. "I never learn, never!"

She pulled the check out of her pocketbook and showed it to him. "This is how much he thinks you're worth to me. I'd be insulted if I were you. You're worth a hundred thousand, at least!"

Al's face went blood red and he started shaking. "I'll break his head," he hissed.

"I'll get you a hammer."

"You didn't turn around and throw it at him?" he asked, watching her fiddle with it.

She burst out laughing. "Of course I did." She grinned, neglecting to mention what had happened next. "Then he dared me to come to the ranch, and I told him hell itself wouldn't keep me away. How's that for friendship?"

He let out a breath. "My gosh! You got away with it?" He laughed. "Sabina, you're the greatest!" he said enthusiastically. "Are you coming with me, really?"

"Sure."

He seemed to grow an inch. "Fantastic." He eyed her. "Now, if I can just sell you on the rest of the plan. By the way, what are you going to do with that check?"

She unfolded the $20,000 check. "I'm giving this to you for your new project. In your awful brother's name, of course." She smiled at Al's expression as she endorsed it and handed it to him.

He took it, but his eyebrows arched. "But he'll think you took the bribe!"

"Let him," she said, leaning back.

He started to laugh. "He'll be out for blood. You haven't ever seen Thorn in action."

Want to bet? she thought amusedly. "I've lived dangerously all my life."

He reached across and caught her hand in his thin one. "Prodding Thorn isn't any way to get even. He could hurt you."

"Because he's rich?" she asked with a laugh.

"No. Because he's Thorn. Money doesn't make any difference whatsoever."

"I hate being made a fool of," she muttered. "I hate being humiliated. He's not getting away with that. I'd dearly love to pay him off."

His eyes wandered over her face. "Do you really want to get even with him and help me out at the same time?"

"Of course!" she said without hesitation.

"Then let me buy you an engagement ring."

Sabina all but fainted. The look on her face spoke volumes, and Al couldn't help laughing.

"No, you've got it all wrong. I'm very fond of you. I'm sure you're fond of me. But I don't have marriage in mind."

"A bogus engagement, then?"

"Exactly." He chuckled softly. "I'm so damned tired of having Thorn scare away girlfriends because he doesn't think I can manage my own love life. I'd purely enjoy setting him down hard for once. He's only ten years my senior, but he acts as if he were my father."

"How old did you say he was?" she asked curiously.

"Thirty-four."

"Are you really only twenty-four?" she asked, grinning. "I thought you were at least sixty."

"Shame on you. Attacking a man who's trying to assist you in a monumental vendetta!"

"What would I have to do?" she asked, pursing her lips.

"Be seen everywhere with me. Especially," he added with a hot grin, "at the ranch. That would kill him."

"What about your mother? I'd hate to play such a trick on her."

"Oh, she'd be no problem. She spends most of her time in Europe, especially since our father died ten years ago. Odd thing, Thorn was effortlessly running Thorn Oil at my age. And here am I fighting tooth and nail to keep from being taken over."

"You're not like him," she said quietly. "And I mean it as a compliment."

He cocked his head and smiled slightly. "Do you? Most women find him fascinating and wildly sexy."

"I don't like domineering men," she said flatly. "I can run my own life without being told what to do. I rebelled at an early age."

"I wish I had. I was too busy learning the oil business at Thorn's knee to fight being overrun." He smiled sheepishly. "Now that I want to cut the strings, I'm finding that they're pretty tough. I don't come into the trust until I'm twenty-five. That gives brother Thorn another year of absolute domination."

"And then?"

"Then I'll have a sizable share of stock and enough money to start my own damned oil company, if I feel like it." He brought her hand to his lips and kissed it gently. "Help me declare independence. Wear my ring for a few weeks and watch Thorn paw the ground."

"As long as he doesn't try to paw me," she said with a hearty laugh. "I'd rather take poison."

He studied her flushed face quietly. "He really got under your skin, didn't he?"

She shrugged. "It was bad enough at that party. But today was the biggest slap in the face I've had since I was a kid." She looked up. "I'll wear the ring for you. But make it something inexpensive, okay? And something you can return!"

"Will do!" He chuckled.

The ring he brought her the following day was an emerald, not too flashy but surrounded with diamonds in a platinum setting. She gasped.

"Remember that I'm not a poor man," he said before she could protest. "To me, this is an inexpensive ring."

She slid it onto her finger, shaking her head. "When I think of all the heating bills it would pay for my neighbors..."

"No," he said. "Absolutely not. You can't hock the ring."

She laughed delightedly, her eyes sparkling. "I wouldn't, you know. But I feel kind of guilty wearing it all the same."

"It suits you. Emeralds make your skin look creamy." He hesitated a moment. "Thorn called me."

She felt her face draw into a scowl as her mood darkened. "Did he?"

He leaned back in his chair with a drink in hand. "I told him I'd just bought you a ring."

"What did he say?"

"I don't know. I hung up in the middle of it." He chuckled. "He was fit to be tied!"

"When do we leave for the ranch?" she asked apprehensively.

"Day after tomorrow."

"So soon?" she murmured, her eyes and voice plaintive.

"I'll protect you, don't worry," he promised. "We'll only be there a few days. Besides, Thorn doesn't spend a lot of time at the ranch, even on holidays. Especially now."

"Because of me?" She felt unwanted and nervous as she studied the ring. "Maybe this isn't such a good idea, Al."

"You can't back out now," he said merrily. "I'll sue you for breach of contract."

Sabina burst out laughing. "Oh, you," she muttered. Her breasts rose and fell with a heavy sigh. "Al, I'm afraid of him," she admitted softly.

"Yes, I know." His eyes were calculating. It was the first time he'd ever seen her afraid of any man, and he wondered why. "Sabina, he won't hurt you. Not physically."

Her lower lip trembled. Hating that tiny betrayal and fearing that Al would notice, she got up from the table. "I'll be packed and ready to go," she promised. "Now I'd better get some sleep. Walk me home?"

"I'll drive you," he said. "Don't worry. It will be all right."

She hoped he was on target with that prediction. She truly was afraid of Hamilton Regan Thorndon the Third, and he hated her. This was an insane thing to do; she needed her head examined. Of course, maybe he wouldn't be at the ranch. She comforted herself with that hope. Then she realized something else.

"Jessica!" she burst out as he pulled up in front of her apartment house.

He stared curiously. "What?"

She swallowed. "Uh, I was just wondering what people will think."

"That's not what you said. Sabina, please. What's going on?"

The painfully hopeful expression on his face made her come out with it. Jess would kill her, but maybe it would be worth it. "She'll kill me for telling you. But..." she sighed, eyeing him. "Well, you see, Jess is in love with you."

He seemed struck dumb. At a loss for words, he stared at the dashboard as if he'd never seen it. His fingers toyed with the key in the ignition. "She is?"

Sabina didn't reply. She just sat and watched him. He took a deep breath and began to smile.

"Are you sure?" he asked, glancing at her.

She nodded, smiling back.

"Damn!" He took another deep breath. "Jess..." Then the sudden exaltation faded and his face fell. "What difference does it make now? Thorn won't let me have her. She doesn't have an oil refinery."

"I'm going to be the decoy, remember?" She grinned at him, flashing the emerald. "Go tell Jess you just got engaged to me. She's home alone tonight. I was going to have a late cup of coffee with her after the show. You can go instead of me."

He frowned and then smiled. "Well—"

"Go on, for Pete's sake! Thorn won't know unless you tell him!"

He shrugged. "Well—"

"Faint heart never won, etc., etc.," she quoted.

"You're right." He glanced at her. "You aren't afraid to go through with this?"

Sabina shook her head. Inside she was trembling, but no one would ever know it. Jess was her best friend. Al was as much to her. She could do this one thing for them. Besides, she thought angrily, it would do the oil baron good to be set on his heels for once. And she was just the girl to do it.

"Okay. Here goes nothing. See you tomorrow."

She got out of the car. "Don't blow it, Romeo," she teased.

He made a face at her and pulled back out into traffic, preoccupied and thoughtful. She thought about calling Jess to warn her. But then she reasoned that Jess was a divorcée with a sharp mind, and didn't. Jessica could take care of herself. Or, at least, that's what she thought until the next morning.

Just as she was having her first cup of coffee, there was a hard knock on her door.

She got up and opened it, shocked to find Jessica standing there, her eyes red-rimmed, her red hair disheveled.

"Jess!" she burst out. "What's wrong?"

"Everything," came the wailing reply. "Can I have some coffee, please?"

"Of course." Sabina pulled her robe closer and got a second cup from the cupboard. When she came back into the room, Jessica was sitting at the small table with her head in her hands. "What happened?"

"Doesn't it show?"

Sabina took a long, hard look at her best friend, shocked by her unruly appearance, the dark shadows under her eyes.

"Al and you . . . ?" Sabina said.

"Bingo!" Jessica poured herself a cup of coffee and sipped it nervously. She looked up with a pained expression. "What did you say to Al last night?"

Sabina blinked. "Nothing." She lied.

"You must have said something, you must have," Jessica moaned. She put the coffee cup down. "He came to the apartment. He was passing, he said, and thought I might have a spare cup of coffee. You know how I feel, how I've felt for months. Well, he said you and he had just got engaged, and I went crazy. I threw a lamp at him and swore." She smiled sheepishly. "Well, one thing led to another, and he kissed me. Then he told me the engagement was just to throw Thorn off the track. And he kissed me again." She drew in a short breath. "Oh, my, oh, my, I guess it blew my mind, because when he started toward the bedroom, I followed. It was the shortest night of my whole life. Now I can't go home because he's still there, and I'm afraid to go to the office. I'm afraid he'll think I'm cheap, and I'm so much more in love with him this morning than I ever imagined I could be!"

Sabina's face lit up as she laughed and hugged her friend. "He cares!" she said. "He does; he has to. You know Al, for God's sake! He'd never take you to bed on an impulse; he's too deep."

"But he'll think I'm easy!" Jessica wailed.

"Wanna bet?" Sabina went to the phone, throwing herself down into the armchair beside it. She dialed Jess's number.

"No, you can't!" Jessica screamed, diving for the phone.

Sabina struggled with her, grinning. "No, you don't. Be quiet!"

It rang and rang until Al answered it drowsily. "Hello?"

"Hi, Al," Sabina said.

"Hi." He moaned, then all of a sudden, there was an exclamation. "Jess!" he burst out. "Sabina, is Jess with you? Oh, God, what she must have thought.... Is she there?"

"Yes," Sabina said, watching Jess hide her face in her hands. "She is. And feeling pretty low."

"Oh, God, the fat's in the fire now," Al groaned. "Thorn will send her to Siberia the second he knows... Let me talk to her, please!"

"He wants to talk to you," Sabina said, handing the phone to her nervous friend. "Go on. He sounds frantic."

Jessica took it. "Hello," she said unsteadily, brushing back her hair. "Yes. Oh, yes." She began to calm down. She smiled. "Yes." Jess sat down in the chair and Sabina left the room.

Sabina sipped her coffee in the tiny kitchen. Minutes later, Jessica came through the door, looking subdued and happy and sad, all at once.

"I'm going home to talk to him," she said. "But it seems pretty hopeless. Thorn wants him to marry the oil refinery, you see." She shrugged. "I guess a divorced nobody of a secretary wouldn't be good enough." She looked up. "Listen, you weren't sweet on Al, were you?"

"Al and I are just buddies. In the beginning he worked up this false engagement to get big brother off his back. But now it may serve a different purpose. As for being sweet on anyone... You know what it was like for me when I was growing up. You know I don't want involvement, and you know why."

"Yes," Jess sighed sadly. "I understand. It's just that I wish you could be as happy as I am, my friend." She picked up her purse. "I'd better go. Al said he wasn't going to work until we talked. I think he and Thorn got into a spat yesterday over the refinery heiress again."

"Big brother just radiates love, doesn't he?" Sabina said coldly.

"He's trouble. Watch out."

"You're the one who'd better take that advice," Sabina murmured. "I'm just the red herring. You're the fox." She grinned.

"Some fox." Jessica laughed. "Don't take any chances. You're the best friend I ever had."

"Same here." Sabina flashed the engagement ring. "I'll keep this warm for you," she added wickedly.

Jess only laughed. "It wasn't funny when he first told me. But now, I think it's just great!"

"I wish I could have seen your face."

"It was a fascinating shade of purple," Jessica grinned as she headed for the door. "Thanks for the coffee!"

"Any time," Sabina murmured dryly. "See you later."

Jessica barely nodded, and then she was gone.

But if Sabina thought that was going to be the end of it, she had a surprise waiting the next evening after her performance. Al and Jess were waiting for her, all eyes and expectations after she'd changed into her street clothes and grabbed her long secondhand cashmere coat and joined them at their table.

"Hi." Jess grinned.

"Yes, hi," Al seconded.

She studied them with pursed lips. "You look like crocodiles with your eyes on a fat chicken. What have you cooked up that's going to get me in trouble?"

"You volunteered," Al reminded her with a laugh.

She glared at the engagement ring on her finger. "Yes, but I'm only keeping it warm for Jess."

"Jess and I are going to get married next week," Al said.

Sabina perked up at that. She beamed, then almost cried at the look of happiness on their faces. "Marvelous!"

"Once we've actually done it, there's not a thing big brother can do to me," Al said. "Besides that, there's this tricky little loophole in the trust—if I get married, I inherit the trust immediately." He looked gloriously happy. "Thorn will never be able to tell me what to do again. And Jess and I can stop worrying about Thorn's matchmaking attempts."

"So I'm to divert him, is that it?" she asked.

Al nodded. "We'll be in Beaumont at the ranch for several days, but with Mother and me to run interference for you, it will be okay. He's in and out of the ranch because of his responsibilities and while he's working I'll sneak out with Jess to make the arrangements."

Sabina was thoughtful. Of course she wanted to help, but crossing Thorn this way could backfire. She hadn't forgotten the way she'd felt in his arms, and she didn't like being vulnerable. He probably knew how he affected her. She wouldn't put anything past him, especially if he thought the engagement was for real. He'd stoop pretty low to save his brother, and she was uneasy about the tactics he might use.

"We leave tomorrow morning, you know," Al reminded her.

"Yes, but what about the performances . . . ?"

"We've got a vocalist to fill in for you," Al responded quickly. "I'm sorry, I know you don't like that, but Thorn did mention that if you were going to be at the ranch, it wasn't practical for you to commute back and forth for the week."

She felt a burning sensation. "Will I have a job to go back to?" she asked.

"Of course," Al said. But he didn't look that confident. He swore softly. "Damn, Sabina, I'm sorry. I'm not up to Thorn's weight. My God, who is?"

"I'll discuss it with him while we're at the ranch," Sabina said. She even managed to laugh. She couldn't blame Al for being himself. Her protective instincts were what had drawn her to him in the first place. He was like a baby brother. And she loved Jessica too much to pull out now. She could handle the oil baron. She'd just be a decoy, after all. "I'd better go pack!" she said with a smile. "Now, Jess, don't worry about a thing. I'll make sure big brother doesn't take a single bite out of your intended."

Jess got up and hugged her warmly. "I love you," she said fervently. "Please be careful." She looked at Sabina, and her eyes said it all. "You're much more vulnerable than anyone realizes."

Sabina straightened. "Don't worry, I believe in self-preservation. See you in the morning, Al!" she called.

"You're a pal," he told her, and he meant it.

"I'm a nut case," she muttered to herself as she left. She had a feeling this was going to be the worst mistake of her life—like prodding a cobra with a straw.

3

*

The Thorndon ranch was just outside Beaumont, Texas, surrounded by white fences and huge oak and pecan trees. The house was a two-story Victorian model, gleaming white, with intricate gingerbread woodwork and a huge front porch and a lawn that was glorious in spring. The trees were bare now, because it was late autumn, but Sabina could picture it in warm weather with flowers all around. She'd seen a house like that in a storybook at the orphanage when she was a little girl, and she used to dream of living in one. Her eyes were wide and sad as she studied the sleek lines of the Rolls-Royce parked in the driveway. The oil baron's car, no doubt, she thought bitterly. He had so much, and she'd had so little all her life. Her mother's lover must have been just such a man....

"This is home," Al told her, stopping his Mercedes-Benz just as a solitary rider came into view against the backdrop of the trees. Wearing a tan sheepskin coat and a creamy white-brimmed hat, the rider sat astride the most magnificent black stallion Sabina had ever seen.

The rider was coming toward them at a gallop, through a herd of white-faced, red-coated Herefords, so close to his horse that they seemed to be irrevocably joined. Sabina watched him, fascinated, and wondered if he was one of the cowhands who worked for the Thorndons. That lean, easy grace spoke of hours in the saddle.

"He rides beautifully, doesn't he?" Al murmured. "I remember watching him when we were boys and wishing I could do it half as well. He used to ride in rodeo competition, but then Dad died and he had to take over the oil company. I don't think he's really been happy since."

Sabina frowned slightly as the meaning of the words penetrated. The solitary rider had closed the gate he'd just ridden through and remounted, coming near enough that his face was recognizable. He cocked his hat over one eye and gave Sabina a slow, insolent smile. The black eye had lost some of its vividness. Now just a faint discoloration attested to its existence.

"Hello, rock singer," Hamilton Regan Thorndon the Third said mildly. "Fancy you on a ranch, cream puff."

She looked at him expressionlessly, as if he were a faintly interesting exhibit in a museum. "Yes, I know, I'll just be bored silly. But I'll muddle through somehow, oil baron," she said with a sweet smile.

He didn't like that cool appraisal or the taunting words, and his eyes narrowed as he lit a cigarette.

"How's it going?" Al asked casually.

"Feed's low," Thorn said. "We'll have to supplement the stock through the winter. I've sold off the culls already."

"That's the cattle business for you," the younger man agreed. "Is Mother here yet?"

Thorn's face grew colder. "She isn't coming."

Al stared at him. "Not coming?"

"The new boyfriend doesn't want to come all this way for a holiday," the older man said with a mirthless laugh. He drew on the cigarette. "And Mother doesn't want to leave him. Early days, you know."

"I'm sorry," Al said. "I'd hoped... It's been over a year since she's set foot on the ranch."

"She doesn't like the smell of cattle." Thorn's eyes went to Sabina, chilling blue eyes. "You won't be able to wear satin shorts around here, honey," he added.

"Okay." She shrugged. "I'll just go naked. Al won't mind," she said with a grin.

Thorn threw his cigarette to the ground. "You'll have separate rooms here," he told them. "And no midnight wandering, or so help me God, I'll throw both of you out the door!"

He turned his horse without another word, leaving Sabina spellbound.

"Whew!" Al sighed, easing the car up the driveway. "Mother really must have upset him this time."

"Does Thorn resemble her?" Sabina asked curiously.

"He looks like our father," he said. "A mirror image. Sometimes he acts like him, too. Dad was a passionate man, but he had a core of pure steel, and he used it on everybody. He could send our mother into tears with a look and keep her that way for days if he was angry. She got even, in the most basic way."

She stared at him. "Other men?"

His face darkened. "Other men. Thorn's always hated her for it, and she knows it. I think that's why she stays away. She can't really help the way she is, I suppose, but Thorn never forgave her for betraying Dad." He glanced at her after he'd parked the car behind the Rolls. "Dad caught her with one of her lovers. He dragged her out of the hotel, threw her into his car, and was driving her home in a rage when he wrecked the car. He was killed."

Sabina bit her lower lip. "How old was Thorn?"

"Twenty-four. My age. I'll never forget the way he looked at Mother, or what he said to her. She left the ranch just after the funeral and went to live with an aunt in England."

She shivered. So he knew, too. He knew. Her eyes closed.

"What is it?" Al asked, concerned.

"Nothing," she murmured. "Just a chill." She pulled her coat closer around her. Under it, she was wearing her only pair of cowboy boots, with designer jeans and a bulky gray sweater over a white blouse. The jeans and sweater, like the coat, were from the nearly new shop, and Al just shook his head as he studied her.

"You amaze me," he said. "You always look like something out of Rodeo Drive, but you hardly pay anything for it."

"I know where to look," she said with a grin. "Let's go. I'm just getting warmed up."

"Thorn bites when he's in this mood," he cautioned her. "Don't underestimate him. Stick close to me."

"You can count on it."

The house was misleading. Judging by its front, it was a bastion of quiet elegance. But inside it was a masculine stronghold. The living room was done in earthy tones, with Indian rugs and a strong Mexican influence as well. The walls in the living room and den were pecan-paneled, and hunting trophies and rodeo awards lined the wall of the den.

"Thorn's," Al told her, quiet pride in his voice. "He always took top money. The men still gather around when he feels like a little bronc busting out in the corral. It's quite a sight."

"How big is the ranch?" she asked.

"Not very, by Texas standards. But it's a good place to relax, and Thorn likes to experiment with his purebred Herefords. He's very much into embryo transplants right now, genetic improvement."

That was Greek to Sabina. She'd spent a little time with her grandfather, her mother's father, who had a farm just outside New Orleans. But that was years ago, before the old man died. She had just a few pleasant memories of being allowed to ride horses and breathe clean, country air and gaze toward an uncluttered horizon.

Her fingers lightly touched one of the awards, feeling its cold metal surface. It chilled her, like the man who'd earned it. "He must be very proud of these," she told Al.

"He is," came a deep voice from the doorway.

She turned to find Thorn, long-legged, narrow-hipped, devastating in jeans and a half-unbuttoned blue plaid shirt. He was still wearing dusty boots and the wide-brimmed hat that emphasized his dark complexion. His blue eyes were piercing from across the room, and his chiseled lips turned up in a twisted mockery of a smile.

"The metal is an alloy; they aren't worth much," he told her, oblivious of Al's glare.

"How sad," she sighed, moving away. "You couldn't even hock them if you needed money, could you, Hamilton Regan Thorndon the Third?"

"My name is Thorn," he said in a tone laced with authority.

She looked up, tossing back her long, silky hair. "That's what your friends call you, I'm sure," she said. "I am not, and never will be, your friend. I will call you Hamilton or Mr. Thorndon the Third or Hey, You. Take your pick."

His eyes were flashing with anger, but she didn't even flinch. He pursed his lips. "Declaring war, honey? Watch out. You're on my turf now."

"I don't have a white flag to my name," she returned with deliberate provocation. Honey. She hated that silky endearment that she'd heard so often in her youth. "And don't call me honey, your worship."

"My God, you're brave," he said tartly.

She corrected him. "I just don't like being walked on," she said, never letting her gaze waver.

His blue eyes searched her face for a long, static moment, while he seemed to be trying to read her mind.

She laughed. "Looking for weak links? I don't have any. I'm every bit as hard as you are."

"You'll need to be," he said.

Recognizing the tone, Al stiffened. "Uh, Sabina, let's see the rest of the house."

She turned her eyes away from Thorn, feeling a weakness in her knees. She had had this tingling feeling for a few seconds, but she didn't dare let him know it.

"Sure," she told Al, taking his hand quickly.

"I'm opening up a new oil field out on the western stretch of the property," Thorn told his brother. "Ride out there with me."

"Now? Like this?" Al asked, indicating his gray suit.

"Change first."

"Want to come along, Sabina?" Al asked.

"She rides?" Thorn laughed mockingly.

"*She* sure does," Sabina said with a deliberate vacant smile. "*She* even speaks all by herself, without help."

"I'll just get my suitcase out of the car. Be right back." Al told Sabina with a smile and a wink. As he walked out, she had to fight the urge to run after him.

"You make everything a challenge, don't you?" she asked Thorn after a minute.

His gaze almost knocked the breath out of her. "Honey, you're a walking challenge," he said. "And if you aren't careful, baby brother or no baby brother, I'm going to take you up on it."

"I'm not issuing an invitation. I have wonderful instincts for self-preservation," she replied as lightly as she could.

He drew a cigarette out of his pocket and lit it without taking his gaze off her. "What a hell of an irony," he said with a cold laugh. "That night in Al's kitchen, I'd never touched anything so sweet. And not five minutes later, I had to face what you actually were."

Her temperature was rising. "I'm a rock singer," she told him coldly. "Not a tramp. My profession has nothing to do with my morals."

His breath came deeply, as though he were deliberately controlling it. The cigarette fired trails of smoke between his lean fingers. "I won't let you marry Al," he said forcefully. "I'll do anything I have to do, but I'll stop you."

"Anything?" she challenged.

He nodded slowly. "Within limits," he said quietly, letting his eyes wander slowly down her body. "Don't make me hurt you, Sabina." His voice was deep and as smooth as velvet as he watched her. "You can't help what you are, I suppose. But I want Al married for something more than his bankroll."

Her face dropped. "You think I'm a gold digger?"

"I know you are," he said. "Remember the check for twenty thousand that I gave you?"

She wanted to tell him what she'd done with it. But that would lead to other questions, questions she didn't want to answer. He might get the truth out of her in a weak moment, and where would that leave Al and Jessica?

"If you do what I ask, I'll forget the check," he said. "And I'll get you all the performances you and the band can handle. All you have to do is leave Al alone."

"But, he's such a sweet little feller," she murmured with a wicked smile. "Besides, he turns me on, you know?"

He moved closer, so that she could feel the warmth of his body, and the wild longings it produced tricked her into looking up. His eyes trapped hers. His free hand moved to her face and lightly touched her mouth. The slight sensation made it tremble.

"Stop that. You're no more an experienced woman than I am a monk. I've had women. And if you're not damned careful, I'll have you."

"After I've been embalmed, maybe," she retorted. "And will you please remember that I'm engaged to Al?" she said too quickly.

His fingers were under her chin, sensually tracing the long line of her throat, and she could taste his smoky breath on her lips, feel the strength, warmth and power of his lean body and smell his cologne and faint leathery scent.

"Sure you are. For now." He traced his fingers over her soft cheek, down to the curve of her lips. He drew in a slow, heavy breath. "Skin like milk," he whispered. "Soft mouth, even if it doesn't quite know how to kiss."

Her eyelids felt heavy, her body felt weak. She looked up at him and couldn't look away.

He dropped his hand abruptly as if the contact with her skin was disturbing to him. "I'm not gentle," he said abruptly. "There's never been a woman who could make me gentle. I like it rough, and I don't hold anything back. And that's the last thing you need, cream puff. I won't seduce you. That's not my way. But I could lose my head with you, so keep a few yards away from me while you're here, okay? It would be hell living with myself if I seduced a virgin."

She couldn't even move, the words were such a shock.

"Yes, I know," he said softly, searching her eyes. "It doesn't go with your image, or even with the other things I know about you. But I'd stake my life on your innocence." His eyes fell to her mouth, lingered there. "It would have been so easy, I even had it planned. Now I'll have to find some other way."

"I don't understand."

"I'm ruthless. Didn't Al tell you? I always get my own way. Always." He sighed angrily. "Except with you. If you'd been the experienced little tart I thought you were, I could have seduced you and told Al, and that would have been the end of it."

Her eyes were lost in his. "You'd go that far?" she asked quietly.

He nodded. "He's my brother. I love him, in my way." His gaze silenced her. "He's the only thing I do love, so look out.

You chose to ignore the warning I gave you. You took a bribe and welched on it."

"Did I?" she murmured, staring up at him. "Why don't you tell Al?"

"Not just yet," he replied, his eyes promising dark delights. "I'm going to bide my time. Maybe it will be worth the twenty thousand to have you off the place."

His eyes were the coldest she'd ever seen. If he was vulnerable in any way, it didn't show, but she could almost picture him as a child. She'd have bet that he was a loner from the beginning, a quiet, confident child who wouldn't be pushed by anyone. He'd probably done his share of fighting because of his mother.

"Why are you looking at me like that?" he asked, his tone jarring.

"I'm sorry we're enemies," she said with her irrepressible honesty. "I'd have liked you for a friend."

His face got even sterner. "I don't have friends. Men or women."

"Did it ever occur to you that not everybody in the world is after you for what they can get?"

He burst out with laughter that was cynical and mocking. "You're just the person to tell me about that, aren't you, honey? You, with your eyes like dollar signs!"

"Sabina?" Al called.

She turned and quickly fled from the den without looking at Thorn. "Here I am," she called. "I'll freshen up and meet you back down here, okay?" she told him, as she ran up the staircase. Al followed, frowning thoughtfully.

Remembering what Thorn had said to her made her knees go weak. The threats she understood; he was trying to protect his brother. Ironically, so was she. But in spite of it all, how had he known she was a virgin, when all his imagined evidence pointed in the opposite direction? She turned away from the mirror, forcing herself not to ask impossible questions. All she had to remember was that Thorn was the enemy. If she forgot, he could destroy any hope of Al's marriage to Jessica. She had to keep that in mind. If only it wasn't so difficult to hate him. He was a rich man, like those she'd known in her childhood, like the last one in her mother's tragic life.... She shuddered a little at the black memory, but even that couldn't get the oil baron out of her mind. Somehow, she felt a kinship with him. She understood him. She wore a mask, too, and shunned emotional involvement. What a pity they were in opposite camps.

4

*

Sabina hadn't ridden a horse in a long time, but she sat on the little mare Thorn gave her with grace. It had been a long time, but she remembered very well how to ride. Her grandfather had taken care of her for a year or two, until he died, and he'd been a good rider himself. It had been the happiest period of her life. She'd loved her grandfather dearly, and mourned terribly when she lost him.

The country around the ranch was fascinating. Not too many miles away was the Big Thicket, a fascinating junglelike area where orchids grew wild. Early in the 1800s it had been a trapping outpost. Nearby were the ruins of a French trading post. After that came lumber and rice plantations. And in the early 1900s, oil was discovered in the Spindletop Oil field. Beaumont became the birthplace of three major oil companies. Four, if Thorn Oil was included. The Sabine River, which led into Orange, east of Beaumont, was the origin of Sabina's name. Her father, she understood, had lived on its banks as a boy.

As they were coming back from a look at some land where men were setting up a drilling rig, Thorn had explained it to Sabina with unexpected patience. She had been openly fascinated by it. Al had grinned, watching them, because he'd never seen Thorn so approachable. Al himself looked different in Western gear, except that his jeans were new and had a designer label, and his gray hat was smothered in feathers. Next to Thorn, in his worn and obviously used outfit, he seemed citified. "It's great out here," Al told his brother.

"I'm glad you said that," Thorn drawled, cocking his hat over one eye. "I'll let you help us brand the replacement heifers."

"It's not that great, Thorn," came the quick reply, with a grin.

"So I figured. You need to get out here more often. Sitting behind that desk all the time isn't healthy. Neither is all the partying," he added with a pointed glance at Sabina.

"Al doesn't party." She defended Al, not looking at Thorn. "He has parties."

"Is there a difference?" he drawled.

Al interrupted. "That's all over, anyway. When Sabina and I get married, I won't have the time anymore."

That set the big man off. He reined in his horse and stared at Al until the shorter man visibly fidgeted.

"Marriage is a big step. What about her career?" he asked pointedly. "Is she going to give it all up to stay home with you?"

"So what if she wants to work? What's wrong with a woman being independent?" Al asked.

"Not a damned thing," his brother agreed, "until her independence interferes with your own. Do you like the way other men leer at her in those body stockings she wears?"

"I wouldn't call it leering," Al muttered.

"Well, I would," Thorn said flatly. He crossed his tanned forearms over the pommel and glared at Sabina. "And what are you offering him? Your spare time? I understand you're on the road most of it."

That was a question she hadn't thought about. Her music was part of her life, giving it up was impossible. But she was supposed to be engaged . . . it was time to think fast. "Well, I guess I'll just stay home and have babies," she sighed, and looked up in time to catch an odd expression in the oil baron's eyes. He let his gaze drop down her body, till he was eyeing her midriff. He frowned before he caught her eyes again. Incredibly, she blushed.

"Are we going to see the rest of the ranch now?" she asked quickly. "I'm getting hungry."

"The old timers," Al murmured with a grin, "used to butcher a cow along the way."

"Beef on the hoof," Sabina said with an evil smile in Thorn's direction. "Walking steaks . . ."

"Touch one of my purebred Herefords and I'll take your arm off," Thorn replied with a faint smile.

"Spoilsport," she muttered. "Some host you are."

"They're purebred, dammit!" Thorn laughed reluctantly.

"Okay. Tell you what," she said agreeably. "I'll eat the registration papers with it."

His blue eyes twinkled unexpectedly. Al had to stifle a smile of his own. It had been years since he'd seen Thorn like that. The older man was grim most of the time; he hardly ever cracked a smile. Sabina was working subtle witchcraft on Thorn.

She sighed and shrugged. "Well, if I faint from lack of food, and fall onto a rattlesnake, and get bitten and die, just remember, it's all your fault."

Thorn held back another laugh and turned his stallion. "Come on, for God's sake, and I'll feed you."

He spurred his horse and rode ahead of them to open a gate. Sabina's eyes followed him helplessly, her heart spinning in her chest, a bright new feeling making her light-headed with elation.

"He never laughs," Al said under his breath. "That's a first."

"He's just forgotten how," Sabina said, and her eyes were soft on the tall man's back. "Jess said that deep inside he was a lonely man, and I didn't believe her. Now I do."

"He's lonely from choice," he reminded her, concerned. "Don't go soft on him, Sabina. You never know with Thorn. He'll get your guard down, and then he'll strike. I've seen it happen far too often."

"I'll be careful," she promised. After all, it was just a game, wasn't it? "Don't forget to invite me to the wedding."

Al grinned. "You can give her away, if you like," he teased.

She glared at him. "How did I ever get friends like you?"

"Pure luck," he returned smugly. Sabina laughed and rode after Thorn.

They didn't dress up for dinner that night, although Sabina had halfway expected that they would. Nevertheless, she wore a gray skirt and blue-and-white checked blouse instead of jeans.

Thorn was alone in the living room, brooding over his drink. The white pullover sweater he was wearing with his dark slacks emphasized his own deep tan and black hair. As if he felt her watching him, his head turned and his icy blue eyes met hers.

"Where's your satin, rock star?" he chided.

"I didn't want to risk having your heart stop, Mr. Thorndon the Third," she said with a wicked smile as she joined him.

He caught her arm with a lean, steely hand and held her as she tried to walk past him. "I've told you that I don't like that name," he said in a tone softly laced with menace. "Don't push me. It's dangerous."

She could feel the danger, and she regretted her barb almost as she'd said it. "Mr. Thorndon, then," she said softly. "Will you let me go, please?"

"Did it hurt to ask?" he chided, abruptly releasing her arm. He turned away. "What will you drink?"

"I don't."

He whirled. "You what?"

"I told you at Al's party. I hate alcohol."

He scowled down at her. "A social drink isn't considered alcoholism."

"I'm sure it isn't, and I'm not sitting in judgment," she assured him. "I simply do not like the taste of liquor."

He shrugged. "Suit yourself, tulip."

"What?" she broke out.

"Tulip," he repeated. His pale gaze wandered over her face, down to the deep, full red of her mouth. "Maybe someday I'll tell you why I call you that."

"It must be some horrible reason," she said with resignation, sitting down.

"I'm not a bad man," he said, towering over her as he moved to the side of her chair. "I just don't like opportunists."

Her eyes searched his blue ones. "Or women."

His face hardened. As he took a long drink from the glass he studied her quietly.

For an instant the room seemed to vanish—everything seemed to stand still. She found unexpected depths in those eyes of ice blue and her heart felt jumpy and odd. His lean, dark fingers caressed the glass he was holding, and she felt as if he were touching her. There was something fierce about the way he was looking at her; an odd kind of violence lingered under his thick black lashes. She had to struggle not to remember what they'd shared in that kitchen at Al's house.

"Is Sabina your real name?" he asked quietly.

"Yes." She looked back helplessly, locked to him by a gaze she was powerless to break, while her breath became ragged in her throat.

"Do you know who the Sabines were?" he continued in a voice like velvet.

She did, but she couldn't think; she felt hypnotized.

He bent, moving one hand to her throat. His fingers were cold, and she jumped.

"I won't hurt you," he whispered, misunderstanding the involuntary reaction. His fingers traced the wildly throbbing artery at her throat, and his mouth was so close she could taste the scent of whisky on it. It should have revolted her, but it didn't. Her eyes fell to his hard lips, and she remembered with aching clarity the way they'd felt when he'd kissed her.

"The Sabines," he continued huskily, "were women taken by the Romans."

"Ra...raped by the Romans," she corrected. Her voice sounded odd.

"Sometimes men and women enjoy wild lovemaking," he whispered. "Passion in itself is violent. Like the way I feel with you, tulip, when I touch you and feel you start to tremble. The way you're trembling now. You want my mouth like hell, don't you?"

She wanted to deny it, to rail at him. But she couldn't even speak. Her lips were parted and she wanted his. Wanted his!

"I want yours, too," he whispered roughly, and the hand at her throat slid down to her collarbone, tracing exquisite patterns on her creamy skin. "I want to touch you in ways that would shock you. My skin on yours, my mouth on your body..."

"Don't," she moaned, and her gray eyes, wider than saucers, looked up into his. "I'm...I'm Al's girl."

His nose nuzzled hers and his mouth threatened to come down and take possession of her lips. She could almost feel its texture, exciting, hungry. "Then why," he whispered, "are you begging me to kiss you?"

"Damn you!" she whimpered, swatting at him.

He stood up with a mocking smile on his dark face, his eyes sparkling as they met hers. "You fascinate me, Miss Cane," he said after a minute, fingering his whiskey glass idly as he studied her flushed face. "All that delicious innocence, waiting to be taken. Why hasn't Al had you? Are you afraid of sex?"

She was hardly able to catch her breath. Why did he affect her this way? "You have...a dirty mouth," she muttered, hating that faint amusement in his eyes.

"Yours is incredibly tempting, rock star," he replied, lifting his glass to his lips. "I'd like nothing more than to seduce you, right where you're sitting."

She started to jump at him, out of sheer frustrated fury, when another voice broke the silence.

"Where is everybody?" Al called from the hall. He sauntered in, oblivious of the tense undercurrents in the room. He was wearing a casual denim suit with a patterned blue shirt. It suited his fairness. But he wasn't any match for Thorn.

"You two look so different," Sabina observed quietly, glancing from one to the other.

"Our father was dark-headed and blue-eyed," Al explained. "And our mother was brunette and green-eyed. I guess we got the best of them both."

Thorn's face hardened. "Let's go in," he said, gulping down the rest of his drink. He set the glass down roughly on the desk and strode out ahead of them.

"Ouch," Al muttered, hanging behind. "I never know which way he's going to jump. He and Mother must have really had it out over the phone the other night."

"Don't they get along at all?" Sabina asked.

"Once or twice a year." He led her into the dining room. "Let's eat. I'm famished!"

It didn't help that Thorn kept watching her at the dinner table. He had a predatory look in his eyes, and a rigid cast to his features that was disturbing.

"How did you become a rock star, Miss Cane?" he asked over dessert.

She flinched at the unexpected question. "Well," she faltered, fork poised over the delicious cake Juan had just served them, "I sort of fell into it, I suppose."

His straight nose lifted. "How?"

"I was told that I had a voice with potential," she said. "I tried out in an amateur competition, where the prize was a one-night appearance at a downtown club. I won." She shook her head and smiled wistfully. "I was delirious. I'd been waiting on tables up until then, because it was the only work I could find. I did the one-nighter, and the club management liked me enough to keep me on. From there, I got other engagements. Then I met up with The Bricks and Sand Band."

"Jessie told me about that," Al added. "It wasn't so much a meeting as a head-on collision."

"Ricky Turner and the boys were hired to play for me the first night at a rather sleazy little joint off Bourbon Street," she said, her eyes twinkling. "Somehow, they'd gotten the idea that I was a stripper instead of a singer, and the drummer made a remark that set me off the wrong way." She shrugged and took a deep breath. "Well, to make a long story short, I knocked him into his base drum five minutes before the performance."

Thorn's mouth curled up reluctantly. "But you still teamed up?"

"We didn't have a choice that night." She shook her head. "Ricky laughed himself sick. The drummer had quite a reputation. We did several numbers, and we seemed to score big with the audience. The manager suggested that we stay on for a few more nights. His business boomed. So Ricky and the guys and I decided to team up." She smothered a laugh. "To this day the drummer still avoids me, but now we've got more offers than we can accept."

She didn't tell him that she was trained to sing opera, or that she'd gone hungry a time or two to afford the lessons. Or that all the doors to the Met were closed by her dwindling finances. Or that the amateur competition she'd won had been won with an operatic aria. When the nightclub offer came, it was for quite a sum of money and she'd needed it too much to refuse. She thought about the $20,000 check Thorn had written out so carelessly and could have cried. It was nothing to him, but at one time that much money would have been her mother's salvation.

"Hey, you're a million miles away," Al teased.

"Sorry," she said, forcing a smile as she finished her dessert.

Thorn was still watching her from his kingly position at the head of the table. She couldn't look at him. The luxury of letting her hungry eyes feast on his handsome features was too tempting. It made her remember how she'd felt when he'd kissed her. She'd been shocked by her wild response to him. He appealed to her senses in delicious ways. But he was the enemy, and she'd do well to remember it.

"Our mother also performs on stage," Al volunteered, ignoring Thorn's glare. "She does character parts. Right now she's doing a play in London."

Thorn set his cup down hard. "Al, I'd like to discuss that new field we're considering."

Al's eyebrows shot up. "You couldn't possibly be asking my opinion," he chided. "You never have before; you always go ahead and do what you please."

"You're coming into your majority next year," Thorn reminded. "It's time you took part in board decisions."

"My God, I'll faint," Al said with a little sarcasm. His eyes narrowed as he studied the older man. "Are you serious?"

"Always," Thorn said, with a pointed glance at Sabina. "In every way."

He was reminding her that he'd warned her off Al. She lifted her cup in a mock salute and smiled at him challengingly.

"Let's go," Thorn told his brother, rising. "You'll excuse us, Miss Cane? I'm sure you can find something with which to amuse yourself."

She glared at his broad back as he led Al into the study and closed the door firmly.

Old Juan, the man who kept house for Thorn, came to clear the table, and she offered to help. He smiled and shook his head. "No, *señorita,* but *muchas gracias*," he said charmingly. "Such work is not fit for such dainty hands. I will bring coffee and brandy to the living room, if you care to wait there."

"Thank you," she said, smiling at the dark little man. She'd expected Thorn to have an older woman doing the cooking and cleaning, but it seemed he didn't like any women around him. He had definite prejudices in that direction.

She wandered into the living room and stopped in the doorway to feast her eyes on the interior design. Like the den, it mirrored the personality of its owner. It was done in browns and tans with a burgundy leather couch and love seat and big sprawling armchairs in desert patterns. There was a huge Oriental rug by the ornate fireplace. Over the mantel was a portrait of a Hereford bull. On a nearby antique table stood an elegant chessboard and hand-painted wooden chess pieces. The drapes echoed the color schemes of the furniture, dark colors that gave the room a bold, masculine atmosphere.

There was a piano beyond the chessboard, a Baldwin. Sabina was drawn to it irresistibly. She sat down on the bench, her back straight, and raised the lid over the ebony and ivory keys. There had been a piano at the orphanage, and one of the matrons had taught her painstakingly how to play it, taking pity on her fascination with the instrument. Her fingers touched the keys, trembling with wonder at its exquisite tone.

Slowly, softly, she began to play Rachmaninoff's Second Piano Concerto, a passionate piece of music that mirrored her own confused emotions. Her eyes closed as her fingers caressed the cool keys, and she drifted away in a cloud of music.

She wasn't sure exactly when she became aware of eyes watching her. She stopped in the middle of a bar and stared nervously toward the doorway where Thorn was completely still, spellbound, with Al at his shoulder.

"Don't stop," Thorn said quietly. He moved into the room and sat down on the sofa with a cigarette in his hand, motioning Al into a chair. "Please," he added gently.

Distracted, it took her a minute to pick up where she'd left off. Thorn's penetrating gaze made her nervous. But, as usual, the music swept her away, just as it did when she sang. She finished the piece with a flourish, closed the lid and stood up.

"You play brilliantly," Thorn said, and the words seemed to be forced. "Where did you learn?"

"I was taught by a friend," she said, neglecting to add whom or where. "She wasn't a professional, but she read music quite well. She taught me to sight read."

"She did a brilliant job," he said. "You could play professionally."

"No, thanks," she said with a nervous laugh. "It's too wearing. At least when I sing, I don't have to worry about where my hands are going. On the piano I'd do nothing but make mistakes in front of an audience." She sat down on the arm of Al's chair. "Do you play?" she asked him.

"No. Thorn does."

Surprised, she looked at the older man.

"Shocked?" he taunted, taking a draw from the cigarette. "I enjoy music. Not, however, that noise that passes for it in your world."

It was a challenge. He didn't like her ability; it irked him that she didn't fit the mold he was trying to force her into. Now he was going to cut back; his eyes told her so.

"Noise is a matter of taste," she told him. "I like rhythm."

He lifted an eyebrow and an amused smile turned up his hard, chiseled lips.

She stood up. Well, she might as well live down to the image he had of her. "Say, what do people do for amusement out here?" she asked Al.

"We watch movies," Al told her with a chuckle. "Thorn, want to join us?"

Thorn shook his head. "I've got some paperwork to get through."

Al led Sabina out of the room and down the hall to another, smaller room. "We've got all the latest movies. Which would you like to see?" he asked, showing her the collection stowed beneath the VCR's giant screen.

"I'd really like to sit on the porch and listen to the crickets, if you want to know," she confessed. "But that would bother your brother. He likes me to run true to form."

He ruffled her hair. "Don't let him get to you. Thorn's crafty."

"So am I," she said. "Why does he dislike me so?"

"I think perhaps you remind him of our mother," he said slowly. "She's very much like you, in temperament. Though not in appearance. And there's something else... He really doesn't know how to handle his own emotions, so he pretends not to feel them. You get under his skin. I've never seen him like this."

"Maybe I ought to leave," she suggested hopefully.

"Not yet," he said with a twinkle in his eyes. "Things are just getting interesting."

"You won't leave me alone with him?" she blurted out.

He frowned. "Afraid of him?"

"Yes," she confessed.

"That's a first."

"I suppose it is," she said on a sigh. "He really gets to me, Al."

"Has he threatened you," he asked suddenly.

Not wanting to alarm him, she laughed off his question. "In a way. But I'm not worried."

"I think I am," Al said quietly. "There's a very real hunger in his eyes when he looks at you. I've never seen exactly that expression in them before. He's crafty. Don't let him too close."

"Never mind about me," she reassured him. "I like a challenge. He is a sporting enemy, you know."

"You're incorrigible."

"Not to mention stupid," she teased. "Enough of that. You said you were going to manage some time with Jess. How?" she asked with a wry smile. "He's very sharp. If you invite her here—"

"Yes, I know," he said, checking his watch. "But if he thinks that you and I are watching a movie together, he'll be busy elsewhere, won't he?" he asked with a grin.

"Genius," she said, laughing. "But won't he hear the car?"

"No. Because I won't be driving it. Jessica's going to meet me about a quarter of a mile down the road. When the movie ends," he added, putting in the videocassette, "just go straight upstairs. I don't imagine Thorn will come out of his study for hours yet."

"What if he does? Or if the phone rings for you?"

"Tell him I've gone to the bathroom, and you'll give me the message when I come out," he said, gesturing toward the bathroom in the corner.

"Have it all figured out, hmm?" she teased.

"You have to, around Thorn. Sabina, I'll never be able to pay you back for this," he said gratefully.

She stood on tiptoe and brushed his cheek with her mouth, just as the door swung open and Thorn glared at them. He was wearing a tweed jacket with a white shirt and tan slacks, and looking irritated.

"I have to go to the office for an hour or so," he told his brother impatiently.

"I'll take messages while you're gone," Al promised, struggling not to show his relief.

Thorn glanced from Al to Sabina, and closed the door with a muffled slam.

"He hates it." He chuckled. "He hates the whole idea of my not marrying the oil refinery heiress. Well, I'm off. Hold down the fort!"

"Beat him back home. Please," she pleaded.

"Just go to bed and lock your door, and yell through it if he asks where I am," he said. "Tell him I ran out for coffee or back to my house to pick up something."

"Okay. Have fun."

He lifted an eyebrow. "Never fear."

He darted out the door and she sat down, glancing with no interest whatsoever at the screen. Halfway through the movie she cut the machine off, deciding she needed some fresh air. Borrowing a jacket from the hall, she walked out onto the porch.

The ranch was quiet amid the dark, peaceful night. She sat down in one of the oversized rocking chairs and the wicker squeaked pleasantly as she lazily nudged it into motion. She almost went to sleep, drinking in the night sounds, the distant baying of dogs, the singing of crickets. The stars were out and it was a perfect night for lovers. She was glad for Jessica that Al had finally admitted his feelings. She only hoped that they could all keep Thorn in the dark. Of course, once Jessica and

Al were married, it would be too late. Thorn would have to accept Jess then.

So this was the oil baron's world. Classical music and quiet nights and open country. He wasn't really the sophisticated cynic she'd first met. She wondered if he'd ever really given in to his emotions, if he'd ever been in love. But that kind of thinking was dangerous, so she let her mind wander, lulled by the sounds of the countryside.

The soft purr of an engine startled her. She peered out into the darkness, trying to see who it was. Al should be coming back any minute. But what if it wasn't Al?

She stood up just as Thorn appeared, taking the steps two at a time. He stopped at the post when he spotted her, his face scowling in the scant light from the windows.

"What are you doing out here alone?" he asked curtly. "Where's Al?"

"He had to run back to town to turn off something at his house."

"What?"

"He didn't say," she returned, fighting to keep calm.

"And he left you here all by yourself, songbird? How thoughtless. Why didn't he carry you off with him?"

She held on to the porch railing to keep from giving over to panic. "I didn't want to ruin his reputation," she said with a coy grin.

"You're engaged, for God's sake," he replied, coming closer. "Aren't you?"

"You were the one who had palpitations at the thought that we might want to share a room," she reminded him.

"I'm old-fashioned that way," he replied, his eyes glittering down at her.

"A strange attitude for a womanizer," she challenged.

He stood looking down at her, not speaking, not moving, and she realized belatedly that they were alone and he was the enemy.

"Family is different," he said after a few moments. "Family matters."

"Which is why you don't want me to belong to it."

"There's no question about your belonging to it, honey. No way am I going to let Al be hooked into marriage with a notorious . . ."

"Don't you dare call me foul names!" she warned. "I hit you once and I'll do it again. You really know nothing about me," she added.

His blue eyes narrowed. "What do you see in Al?" he asked bluntly.

She shrugged, dropping her eyes. She was still wearing the borrowed, oversized jacket, and her hair was blowing in the chill breeze. "He's gentle," she said finally.

Before she realized what was happening Thorn was looming over her. The dim light from the house cast a strange sheen in his eyes. "I frighten you, don't I?" he asked quietly.

"Yes." She'd never made a habit of lying. Except with that "engagement" to Al, and it was in a good cause.

"Why?" he persisted.

She smiled slowly. Ironic how safe she felt with him, even as her blood raced and her heart pounded and her legs trembled. She was afraid of everything and nothing when he was near. "I don't know," she admitted. "You wouldn't be a reincarnated ax murderer, by any chance?"

His hard mouth softened into a faint smile. "I hate it when you do that," he remarked. "I'm not used to quick-witted women."

"You aren't used to people, are you?" she asked gently. "I mean, you work with them, and you go to board meetings, and there are social obligations. But you keep to yourself, I think."

"I get the same impression about you," he said warily. He leaned against the post and studied her. "A pity you're wrapped up in ribbon and wearing a tag with Al's name on it. I might have given you a run for that money you want so badly."

"Why do you go around with women you have to buy?" she asked bluntly. This man was so different from her stereotyped impression of a rich man. He was hard and cold, but he would never have raised a hand to a woman. She knew that instinctively.

His eyes searched hers. "They don't get very close that way, Sabina," he said quietly.

Watching him light a cigarette she tugged the jacket closer. "I don't know whose this is," she said. "But I didn't want to go all the way upstairs to get my own..."

"It's mine," he said. "I don't mind."

She felt strange wearing it now, though, and she tingled at the thought of it lying against his hard body.

"How old are you, tulip?" he asked.

"Twenty-two," she returned. "Not quite young enough to be your daughter."

"No, not quite," he agreed with a lazy smile. "I was fourteen, my first time."

"Off with an older woman, I'll bet," she murmured demurely.

"She was an old lady of eighteen," he said, his eyes twinkling as she met his gaze. "The most sought-after girl in the school. When my father found out I got a whipping I'll never forget," he recalled. "My father had strong views on morality, and the fact that I was male didn't make one bit of difference to him."

"He didn't want his son to get a reputation for being easy," she teased. The smile faded then as she looked at him, wanting so much to ask about his parents.

"Yes, my mother loved him," he said quietly, reading the question. "But he was a hard man, Sabina. It wasn't easy for him to love. He thought of it as a weakness. In some ways, I can understand how my mother felt. She was a butterfly, always in the thick of society. He was like me. He much preferred the ranch to the city. They were basically incompatible. But that doesn't excuse her actions. He'd be alive today if she'd been faithful to him."

She was remembering her own mother, the pain of each new man, the horrible night when it all ended....

"What was your mother like?" he asked.

"Like yours," she said under her breath. She looked away, pulling the jacket closer. "I don't talk about her, to anyone."

He lit a cigarette. "Is she why you're still a virgin?"

She nodded. "I don't want that kind of life."

"Are you as passionate with Al as you were with me that night in the kitchen?"

The question startled her. She turned, searching for words. Good heavens, Al had never kissed her at all. She was still trying to come up with some kind of answer when he abruptly tossed the cigarette off the porch and moved toward her.

"No," she said, backing away. "No, Thorn, don't."

"You make my name sound like a benediction," he said in a hot breath. His hands shot out, lean, hurting hands, jerking her against his long, warm body, holding her there even as she struggled. "No, honey," he said in a voice like velvet, stilling her hips. "Don't do that."

She looked up, her hands flat against his chest, her eyes wild, her hair all over her face. "It isn't fair to Al," she said.

"Don't you think I know that?" he said in a grating voice. His eyes were glittering, his face as rigid as steel. His breath came heavily and hard. "I want you," he said huskily. He studied her breasts under the jacket, where they rose and fell with her uneasy breaths. "Are you wearing anything under that top?" he whispered.

"No," she said in a choked whisper. "I'm not."

She felt her knees go weak. Her eyes looked into his and she was lost. Drowning. Her body felt the warmth and power of his. Involuntarily, she brushed against him. Her full lips parted, wanting his mouth.

"I could touch you there," he murmured softly. His lips touched her forehead, open and moist as his hands slid around to her waist.

She trembled as his fingers pressed against her soft skin.

"Has he?" he asked curtly. "Has Al touched you there?"

She swallowed. "He... I'm old-fashioned, too. I've never..."

His mouth moved to her closed eyelids; his tongue tested the length of her lashes. "Untouched," he whispered deeply. "Soft and moon-kissed, and I want you so much, tulip. I've paid for women most of my life, in one way or another. But I've never been the first man." His breath sounded ragged, and the mouth hovering above hers was hard and warm and smoky. His hands were on her rib cage now, and she trembled as the tips of his fingers just brushed the outside edge of her taut breasts.

"This is just the beginning, this hunger. It gets worse." He breathed against her mouth. "I never gave a damn before, but I'm deliberately going to rouse you. I want to watch you. I want to hear those first sweet little gasps of passion when I touch you where no man ever has."

"Thorn..." Her voice broke. She was trembling all over; her hands were buried in his soft white shirt, crumpling it over the wall of his chest. Her eyes were lost in his, and she was more helpless than she'd ever been in her life, completely at his mercy.

He lowered his head, his open mouth touching hers, brushing it with gentle probes that made her own lips part eagerly, so that he could fit them exactly to his.

He was so slow with her, so lazily confident, that she never thought of holding back. His warm, expert mouth pressed her lips apart and his tongue eased inside her mouth, tasting her with a rhythm that built and built and built as his fingers trespassed teasingly under her arms. The smell and feel and touch of him tormented her until finally her breath caught and she moaned, deep in her throat.

He felt her body arch against his thighs and he shifted his dark head to look down at her, at the mouth his had crushed and cherished. Her eyes were wild, shocked, glazed with desire.

"If I touched you now, you'd cry out," he whispered, searching her flushed face.

"Please," she pleaded, hurting, aching for his hands.

"Is it really that bad?" he breathed deeply, fascinated by the expression in her soft eyes. "All right, baby, I'm going to give you what you want."

"So... hungry," she whispered tearfully. "Never... never before..."

"I know," he murmured. His mouth touched her eyelids, closing them. "Shhh. Be still, and I'll be so gentle with you..."

His hands were edging under her camisole top while his mouth threatened hers, poised over it. He found the hem and his warm hands slid up her rib cage, slowly, tenderly.

Her body jerked, trying to lift into his hands, but she was trembling like a leaf.

"Sweet," he whispered, shaken by her ardent response. "Oh, God, how sweet! Here, little one . . ."

He gave her his hands, and she did cry out, a sound that stunned him, shocked him. She threw her head back, her hands pressing against him, her body arched toward him in glorious abandon as waves of pleasure exploded in every cell of her body. His hands were warm and hard and callused, and when they contracted, she almost fainted.

"Thorn," she moaned. "Thorn, it's like fire; it burns, it burns," she whispered.

"God," he breathed reverently, shaken. She was like rose petals in his hands, so soft, so delicate, the skin smooth and warm, the tips hard in his palms. The first time . . . He took her mouth under his and felt his lips tremble as he kissed her and kissed her and kissed her. He was so far gone that the distant drone of a car only barely got through to him. She smelled of gardenias and his body was in agony with its need of hers.

He lifted his head. Her eyes opened, drowsy with passion, hungry for him. Her mouth . . . He had to brush it with his, just once more, to savor the honey of her lips.

"It's Al," he said unsteadily. He took a deep, steadying breath and didn't let go of her right away, because she looked weak enough to fold up. "You're a miracle," he whispered. "A miracle. And you're his damn you! Damn you, Sabina!" Crushing her arms under his fingers as the car came closer, he pushed her roughly away and went into the house without another word.

She couldn't face Al, not like this. She ran into the house and down the hall and back into the VCR screening room. Hurriedly, she shoved the tape into the machine and fell into a chair. By the time Al walked in, she'd just barely gotten her nerves steady and her hair smoothed. She didn't want him asking questions. She couldn't have borne having to answer them right now. She was devastated.

"How did it go?" Al asked, sneaking in the room.

"He came back unexpectedly. I couldn't think fast enough. I told him you'd forgotten to turn off something at your house."

"Good girl! So he won't even be suspicious. That was quick thinking." He grinned. "Any problems?"

She shook her head, avoiding his eyes. "Of course not. Well, good night. See you in the morning."

"We'll go riding. At least, it will look that way," he said with a chuckle. "I'm sneaking off one more time, to get the license."

"I'll be a nervous wreck!" she exclaimed, then rushed off without elaborating.

Behind the door of her bedroom, she collapsed. How had Thorn conquered her so easily? If Al hadn't come back... She blushed wildly, hotly, at the thought of where they were headed. She'd wanted him and it had been obvious that he wanted her, too. Her body still pulsed with the pleasure his hands had taught her. Her mouth burned from his kisses. She felt an ache that wouldn't stop. Tears welled up in her eyes. Oh, Jessica, she thought. If you only knew what I'm going through for you!

She turned out the light and went to bed, hoping the days would pass quickly. She was far too vulnerable to Thorn, and she was dubious about her dwindling strength. He could put her in an impossible situation. And what then? What if he went too far and seduced her? He'd promised he wouldn't, but he'd lost control. She'd felt it. He wanted her just as fiercely as she wanted him, and it could happen. That would destroy her. It would ruin her future. Because there could never be another man after Thorn. Never.

5

*

Tugging on a pair of gray slacks with a pullover V-necked striped top and boots, Sabina went downstairs the next morning, expecting to find Al at the breakfast table. Instead, she found only Thorn.

He was sitting at the head of the table, toying with a napkin, obviously waiting for something or someone. He was in denim today, rugged looking, a cowboy from out of the past. His shirt was half open in front, and she could see dark skin and a feathering of body hair. She remembered her own voice pleading with him to touch her. Her face flamed, her heartbeat shook her. She wanted to run.

His blue eyes jerked up and he found her watching him. "Sit down, songbird. Juan's just bringing breakfast."

There was no way out. She pulled out the chair next to his and sagged into it, turning over the cup in her saucer as Thorn poured hot coffee into it from the carafe.

"Cream or sugar?" he asked.

"I take it black," she said. "Caffeine keeps me going on tour. But I've never had the luxury of cream and sugar."

His eyes wandered over her shoulders, her bare arms. "Is that how you stay so thin?"

"I'm not a heavy eater," she said. Her eyes focused on the coffee cup, until he reached out unexpectedly and tilted her chin up to his probing stare.

"It isn't fair to Al," he said quietly.

"What isn't?" she stammered.

"Wearing that," he said, indicating the engagement ring flashing in the overhead light. "Not when you can want another man the way you wanted me last night."

"I did not—" she began defensively.

"Don't." He touched her mouth with a lean forefinger, and his eyes were stern and narrow. "Don't lie. I could have taken you if he'd waited another half hour to come home."

"Leave me alone, Thorn!" she burst out.

"I won't," he promised. He leaned back in his chair and lit a cigarette. "I can't. You won't take advice. So you can take the consequences."

"What are they?" she returned. "A night in your bed?"

"I'd love that," he said with genuine feeling as his eyes wandered hungrily over her face and made her flush with embarrassment. "It's been a long time since I've wanted a woman the way I want you."

"I'm not like that," she said with quiet pride.

"Yes. That makes it worse." He sipped his coffee. "Where are you from, Sabina?"

"New Orleans. Why?"

"How did you meet Al?"

"Jessica introduced us."

He shot her a piercing look. "Nice girl, Jessica. Did you know that she's in love with my brother?"

Her cheeks burned and the cup almost overturned in her hands.

"I see that you do," he persisted, leaning forward to flick ashes in the ashtray. "Doesn't it bother you, hurting her?"

"What do you care about Jessica's feelings? I didn't think secretaries mattered in your world."

"I don't like that," he said coldly, and his icy, pale blue eyes glittered. "I'm no snob, songbird."

"Oh, but you are, Mr. Thorndon," she assured him bitterly. "You have deep prejudices."

"Only about a certain type of woman, which has nothing whatsoever to do with breeding," he returned.

"Breeding," she scoffed. Her eyes lit up. "You'd probably just as soon breed people the way you breed bulls. You keep a portrait of a Hereford bull over your living-room mantel, but I don't see any pictures of loved ones on your walls. Don't people count with you, oil baron?"

His jaw tightened as he crushed out the cigarette. "You never will, honey," he said in a voice as smooth as silk. "Physically, maybe, but no other way."

"Thank God," she replied fervently.

His temper flared, but at that moment Al chose to join them at the table.

"Morning," he said with an ear-to-ear grin. "Breakfast ready?"

"Juan!" Thorn roared, his voice deep and piercing.

"*Si, señor,* I bring it now!" came the quick reply from the kitchen.

"When Thorn growls, everybody jumps," Sabina murmured dryly, with a pointed glance in Thorn's direction.

"You may learn how, before it's over," he warned her.

"You two aren't arguing, are you?" Al asked Thorn. "Future in-laws ought to get along."

If looks could kill, Al would have dropped dead from the impact of Thorn's angry glare.

"Don't listen for wedding bells too soon, brother," he warned Al. "There's plenty of time. You're young."

"Who made you wait?" Al asked him with a calculating stare. "Remember that stacked blonde you wanted to marry, and Dad threatened to disinherit you? You ran off with her, but he followed and propositioned her, right in front of your eyes. He told her that you wouldn't inherit anything if you married her, but that he had plenty of money, and she switched loyalties on the spot. Is that why you're so worried about me making the same mistake?"

"Go to hell," Thorn said softly. He got up from the table and walked off without a backward glance.

"How horrible," Sabina said under her breath. Her heart ached when she considered the pain Thorn must have endured at such a young age.

"Yes, it was, but he's let it lock him up for life," Al said quietly. "He's hardly human these days, all because of one woman who betrayed his trust. He's got to stop living in the past."

"He'll get even," she said.

He smiled softly. "Not in time," he promised. "Not nearly in time. Let's eat and we'll hit the trail."

They rode so far the ranch was out of sight. Thorn hadn't been seen since breakfast, and Sabina felt oddly sad that he'd gone without it. He must be starving. When they reached the fork in the trail, Al waved and rode on ahead. They'd agreed that if Thorn came looking, she'd say Al had decided to give his roan a workout and didn't want to force her to ride so fast when she was out of practice. She rubbed her arms, wishing she'd borrowed a jacket. It would be cold until the sun rose higher in the sky.

She reined in at the river that cut through the property and sat quietly in the clearing, watching the water flow lazily downstream. She got down to examine a set of tracks, and grinned to herself. Deer tracks. They must have watered at the river. Her grandfather had taught her how to track deer; she'd never forgotten. She felt like one of the old pioneers.

"Are you lost, city girl?" came a sardonic drawl from behind her.

She glanced around, not even surprised to find Thorn leaning over the pommel of his own horse, watching her.

"Nope. I'm tracking deer," she informed him.

He swung down out of the saddle, tilting his wide-brimmed Stetson at a jaunty angle over his eyes, and knelt down beside her. His batwing chaps spread out and his boots made a leathery creak with the motion.

"Tracks," he exclaimed.

"Sure," she told him. "That one's a buck. It's got a pointed, cloven hoof. The other is a doe; it's rounded."

"Who taught you that?"

"My grandfather. He used to take me tracking every fall, before deer season opened," she confessed. "At least, until he died." Her eyes grew sad with the memory. "At that time he was the biggest thing in my life. I worshipped him."

"What else did he teach you?"

"Oh, little things. How to tell when rain was coming, how to make things grow. He was a farmer."

Thorn got to his feet slowly, staring down at her with a confused expression. "You worry me."

"Why?" she asked, rising gracefully. "Because I know how to track deer?"

"Because you don't fit any mold I've ever seen," he said, lifting his chin and scrutinizing her. "Because I want you. I could almost hate you for making me vulnerable, even physically."

That was a shocking admission, but it was like him. He didn't pull punches. She wouldn't have expected it. He was a hard man, and it would have been someone like him a hundred years ago who would have tamed this land where they were standing, and fought off hostile forces, and made the fields green and bountiful.

"You're staring again," he said sharply.

"You're very much a man, Mr. Thorndon," she said, spellbound enough to be honest with him. "I've never met anyone like you before. The men in my world are shallow people. You're solid and honest. I meant it when I said I'd have liked you for a friend."

"No, you wouldn't," he said with a mocking smile. "You'd have liked me for a lover, and that's what we'd be already if you hadn't tangled yourself up with my kid brother."

"I don't think so," she returned. "I'm afraid of you. You take people over, you own them. I couldn't bear to be owned."

"I could make you like it."

And probably he could, but she wouldn't let herself think about that. Her gaze drifted beyond him, toward the meadow behind the banks that stretched to a long line of trees on the horizon.

"It's so lovely here," she said. "So quiet. How can you bear New Orleans after you've lived here?"

His jaw became taut. "I cope—with most things."

She turned back to her horse, but Thorn was in front of her before she got two steps, a solid wall she couldn't bypass.

"It's not that easy," he said, and his hard, lean hands caught her by the arms and held her in front of him. "Where's my brother?"

"He gave the roan its head. He'll be right back," she insisted.

"Not for a little while, Sabina," he whispered, leaning toward her. "Kiss me. I went to bed aching for you; I woke up hurting.... Kiss me, damn you!"

His mouth pressed into hers, and none of the teasing foreplay of the night before was left between them. He lifted her against his lean, powerful body and his arms swallowed her while his mouth taught her new lessons in the art of intimacy. Suddenly, she felt his body harden against her, enticing her. Protesting, she twisted and his hand swept down to the base of her spine to hold her still, even as a groan burst from his lips.

He lifted his head, and his eyes frightened her with their wild glitter.

"Don't move against me that way," he whispered hoarsely. "It arouses me unbearably."

She blushed, but he bent his head again, and his mouth stifled the words she was about to utter.

Her fingers let go of his shirt to slide under it. She sighed as she felt the curly hair covering his muscles, and her fingers tangled in it. She felt his body tauten even more and sensed that he was reacting to the gentle movement of her hands. Her education in sensual things was sadly behind that of most people; there'd been no one to ask except girlfriends, and most of them knew as little as she did.

"Sabina, for God's sake, don't, baby," he whispered, stilling her hands. He drew away slightly, looking more formidable than ever, his eyes glazed, his face taut.

She slid her hands out from under his shirt, shaken by the fierce ardor she'd provoked, and by her headlong response to it.

She could hardly breathe and Thorn's heart was pounding like a trip-hammer. He laughed softly, strangely, and his chest rose and fell in irregular jerks. "You burn me up," he said huskily. "The smell of you, the feel of you ... It's been years since I felt like this."

His words were flattering, but she was getting nervous. They were in a deserted place, where no one would look for them, and Al wouldn't be back for hours. There was a wildness in Thorn that she hadn't expected at the beginning, a reckless passion that matched her own free spirit.

"Thorn," she whispered.

His mouth took the whisper and inhaled it, opening her soft lips to a deep, slow, probing kiss. His hands slid down her sides to her hips and drew them lazily against his in easy, dragging movements. She was so lost in the warm teasing of his mouth that she didn't protest this time. His body and its responses and demands were becoming familiar now. He was like a part of her already.

"I've never made love standing up," he whispered in a voice that was deep and a little unsteady. "You make me wonder how it would be."

A tiny wild sound escaped from her throat, and he smiled against her lips. "I want you," he growled softly. His hands slid to the backs of her thighs and lifted and pressed until she thought she'd go crazy with the sweet, piercing pleasure. He laughed again, roughly. "I want you. I want to lay you down in the grass and let my body melt into yours. But that would be playing right into your hands, wouldn't it, witch woman? You'd love that, making me lose my head with you. You'd hold it over me like a scimitar...."

"Thorn!" she exclaimed, dragging her mouth from his. "I'm not like that, I'm not!" Her drowsy eyes sought his and she searched their cool blue depths slowly, remembering all at once what Al had said over the breakfast table about the blonde who'd betrayed Thorn. Her fingers lifted to his mouth, touching it gently, liking the hard warmth of it. "She was crazy, wanting money instead of you...."

His eyes flashed. The whispered words seemed to anger him. He caught her long hair and jerked her face up to his. "She was a tease, too," he said curtly. "A woman with an eye to the main chance."

The words came out like an insult, and she knew that whatever had been growing between them had wilted.

"You're hurting me," she said quietly.

His nostrils flared and his face hardened, but slowly he released his cruel hold on her hair and let her move away from him. His gaze went down to the small fingers still pressed against his chest, and he lifted them away.

He wasn't a man at the mercy of his emotions now, she thought, watching him light a cigarette with cool, steady hands. He'd become as cold as stone.

His mouth curled slowly. "You've got one hell of a lot of spirit. Al may miss you, after all."

"He isn't going anywhere."

"No. But you are." He lifted his head, studying her insolently. "I'm working on a little surprise for you, tulip. Just another day or so, and I'll have everything I need."

"How exciting," she murmured. "I can hardly wait. Does Al know?"

The smile faded. "I don't want him hurt any more than he has to be. Not that you seem to mind playing around with me behind his back."

How could she tell him that the engagement was a bogus one, that Thorn appealed to her senses in a way that left her completely at his mercy? That she loved him, wanted him, needed him. It was a maelstrom of discovery that left her knees weak. It couldn't happen so quickly, could it? He was arrogant and ruthless and narrow-minded. But he was more man, pound for pound, than any male she'd ever run across in her life. Her eyes coveted the very sight of him. And because of that, she turned away and wouldn't let him see her face again.

"I'll leave you to your work, oil baron," she said as she mounted her horse. "I'm going to find Al."

"Enjoy his company while you can," he returned, mounting his own horse with lazy grace. "You haven't got long."

"What was your father like, Thorn?" she asked suddenly, curious.

"Like me," he said shortly.

"No wonder your mother is the way she is," she said sadly. "She must have been devastated when he died."

He frowned. "What a hell of a way she has of showing it!"

"Al showed me a picture of your father; he's told me things about him." Her hand lifted to shade her eyes from the sun. "He must have been a strong man. There aren't a lot of strong men in the world. I imagine she's been looking all this time for someone who halfway measured up to him, without the least success. She's relatively young, Al said. What a pitiful way to live.''

He glared at her, but he was listening. "She might have showed him she cared while he was still alive. He'd be alive, but for her."

Her soft eyes wandered all over him, loving every rippling muscle, even the stubborn set of his jaw. He'd changed her whole life so quickly. "Perhaps he made it impossible for her to show it. Perhaps she only wanted to capture his attention. And afterward, after it happened, the guilt would have been terrible. Some men take a lot of forgetting," she said.

"How the hell would you know?" he challenged.

He was back to his old impossible self. She shrugged delicately and rode away without answering. If she'd said anything else, she might as well be talking to the wind. She rode back to the path where she'd left Al, dismounted, and sat on a stump waiting for him to return.

She could hardly believe how fast it had happened. She hardly knew Thorn, for heaven's sake! But he'd worn on her nerves and her emotions and her heart more in the past few days than most men had in months, even years. She wanted him, and it was oddly comforting to realize that he felt the same hunger for her. It was a dead-end street, of course. There was no possible future in it. But while she could see him and be near him, she took a terrible pleasure in her growing love for him. There was a lot of man under that cruel, cynical exterior. She was only sorry he was her enemy, that he'd never let her see behind his mask. It would be sheer heaven to be loved by such a man.

Al appeared a few minutes later, grinning. "We got the license," he said, giddy with excitement. "And we decided to set the date. We're getting married the day after Easter."

"That's Monday!" Sabina exclaimed.

"Yes! Oh, God, I'm so happy," he burst out, and danced her around the clearing in a mad little waltz.

Sabina laughed and danced, and tried not to think of how soon her bubble was going to burst. When Al broke the news to Thorn, it would all be over, and she'd never see the oil baron again.

"How about the ring?" she exclaimed.

"You can give it back when we drive to New Orleans Monday morning," he explained. "We want you to come along and stand up with us at the service. Okay?"

"I'd love to! Jessica and you. It's been my fondest dream."

"Mine, too, but it wouldn't have been possible without your help," Al said solemnly. "Thorn would have stopped us. This is the only way it could have worked. Has he been at you again?"

"Not really. We just talked," she lied, crossing her fingers behind her back.

"Good." Al let her go and mounted his horse, watching her mount beside him.

"But I've made him mad again, I'm afraid."

"How?"

"I told him your mother must miss your father terribly and be looking for someone who measures up to him," she murmured.

"That's what I've always thought," he replied. "Dad was one of a kind."

"Like Thorn," she said involuntarily.

He studied her, frowning. "Sabina, don't lose your heart to him. He hasn't got one of his own."

"I know that already," she said. "Don't worry about me, I'll be fine. Besides, a few days from now, it will all be a memory." That was a sobering thought. "Hey, I'll race you back!"

"You're on!"

And they galloped back to the house.

Thorn went out that evening, resplendent in his evening wear, and Sabina felt a surge of mad jealousy as she imagined him with some slinky blonde like the one he'd brought to Al's party.

"He does draw women," Al muttered later as they watched television. "He always has. But not one of them touches him emotionally. He says he'll never let any woman have a hold on him."

"I imagine he must have reason, don't you?" she said. "Can I play the piano?"

"What? Sure!" He turned off the television. "If you don't mind, I'm going to take advantage of Thorn's absence and go call Jessica."

"Mind? Get out of here and do it! I'm delighted to have some time to myself. Not that you aren't good company," she added.

He chuckled. "Don't wear out the keys."

"Not me."

He left and she played late into the night, her fingers touching the keys that Thorn's fingers had touched. It was a wildly exhilarating thought, and made her hungrier than ever just for the sight of him. But when she finished and went to bed, he still hadn't come home.

He wasn't at breakfast, either, but Al looked disgruntled as they dug into the hearty egg and bacon platter that Juan had prepared.

"Thorn's having a party Saturday night," he muttered. "And he's invited Jessica."

"Uh, oh. Think he's suspicious?" she asked quickly.

"I don't know. He says the party is being held to announce our engagement. But it's all a rushed-up job, with telephoned invitations. And it's not like Thorn to give in so easily. I think we've been discreet enough, but he's made some long-distance calls, and I overheard something that worries me." Al lifted his head, and his eyes were narrow with concern. "Listen, what could he find out about you if he dug really deep?"

She stared at him blankly. Her mind whirled, grasping. No, she thought wildly, no he couldn't find out anything after all these years. "Well . . . not much," she faltered. "Why?"

"Because he's in a good mood this morning. And that makes me suspicious."

She glowered at her toast. "Maybe it was just good humor left over from his night out," she said.

Al looked at her long and hard, but he didn't say a word.

A visiting cattleman stopped by after lunch, and Al went to show him around the ranch while Thorn took care of business in his study. Sabina sneaked out the door and went around the back of the house into the woods, beyond the little gazebo that so beautifully matched the house and faced the distant pastures. It was an unseasonably warm day. In her jeans with a green knit top, she looked younger than ever, with her long and soft hair blowing in the wind.

Her mind drifted as she watched a bird circle and soar toward the top of a huge live oak near the small stream. She wished it was warm enough to paddle in the creek.

"You look like a wood nymph."

She whirled to find Thorn standing behind her. He was clad in a white shirt and dark blue slacks with a suede blazer, all sleek muscle and dark tan. A feathering of crisp, curling black hair peeked out of his shirt. He was wearing his wide-brimmed creamy Stetson, and he looked suave and very Western.

"I'm just getting some air," she said defensively.

"Why aren't you with your intended?" he asked, leaning back against a tall oak, his boot propped behind him, his arms folded.

"Al was talking business; I didn't think I'd be welcome."

"Al doesn't know anything about the cattle business," he said. "He's buying time with Bellamy until I get there." He smiled faintly as he studied her. "The longer I take, the more Bellamy will worry. By the time I get there, he'll sell at my price. That's business, tulip."

"You said you'd tell me why you called me tulip," she reminded him. He was almost approachable today. She even smiled at him.

"There's a song about a yellow tulip and a big red rose," he murmured.

The song was one her mother used to sing, and she knew the words quite well. It was an old song—and one of the lines was something about it being heaven "when you caressed me" and "your lips were sweeter than julep...." She stared at him and went as red as the rose in the song.

"I see you know the song," he remarked, smiling insolently.

"I'm engaged to Al," she told him.

"Give him back the ring."

"I can't," she growled.

"That's the last chance you'll get from me," he said, his face grim. "You'd better take it, while you still can."

"Is that a threat?" she asked with a laugh.

"It's much more than a threat." He was looking at her as if he'd never seen her before, an odd expression in his blue eyes. "You're unique, Sabina," he said. "And if you hadn't proven to me already that you're just after Al's money, I might be tempted to forget everything else. But I can't stand by and let Al make this kind of mistake."

"Are you going to spend your life running interference for him?" she asked quietly, not making a challenge of it. "He's twenty-four. Eventually he'll have to stand on his own. And what if you aren't there to prop him up?"

"You're missing the point," he said flatly. Tugging a cigarette out of his pocket, he lit it, inhaling deeply. "I've spent the past ten years of my life building up the company. I've made sacrifices...." He took a draw from the cigarette and let the smoke out roughly. "I'm not going to let him throw away his inheritance. It was hard bought."

She looked at him openly, seeing the lines of age in his face, the wear and tear on him. "Al was fourteen when your father died," she recalled. "You had all the responsibility then, didn't you?"

For an instant he looked vulnerable. Then as if the shutters came down, his expression was masked. "I didn't break under it."

"I don't think you can be broken," she said, searching his eyes. "I even understand."

"Oh, yes, I'm sure you do," he said, eyes narrowing as he held her gaze. "Your own life hasn't been easy street until now, has it?"

He couldn't know, she assured herself. She shrugged. "What do you mean, until now?"

"Designer jeans," he remarked. "Designer gowns. Expensive coats. You live well for a struggling singer."

If only he knew! She smiled inwardly. "I do okay," she said.

"How many boyfriends have you had in your young life?" he asked.

Her shoulders rose and fell. "None, really," she admitted, letting her eyes fall to his shiny boots, oblivious of the momentary softening in his face. "Guess I never had much time for all that. I've worked all my life."

His jaw clenched. "Yes. So have I."

"Not like I have, rich man." She laughed, throwing back her dark head. All her tiny triumphs glittered in her eyes. "I've waited tables and scrubbed floors. I've worked double shifts and fended off roaming hands and smiled over the nastiest kinds of propositions. I've worked in clubs so rough they had two bouncers. And I've done it without any help at all, from anybody!"

He didn't speak. His firm lips closed around the butt of the cigarette as he took another draw and then crushed it under his boot. "Did you get tired of the climb up? Is that why you've decided to marry Al when you're not in love with him?" he asked bluntly.

"Why do you say that?" she stammered.

"You never touch each other." He moved away from the tree and loomed over her, tall and threatening and unbearably masculine. "You smile at him, but not with love. You don't even kiss him."

She shifted backward restlessly, and he followed, too close. "I'm not demonstrative in public," she insisted.

"You're not demonstrative in private either, are you?" he demanded. His hands shot out and suddenly drew her close, so that his breath was on her forehead and his body threatened hers from head to toe. Her heart seemed to stop beating at the unexpected proximity. "You even freeze up with me, until I start kissing you, tulip."

"Thorn, don't," she whispered.

"I can't help myself," he said on a hard, contemptuous laugh. "I can't stand within five feet of you without losing my head. Haven't you noticed? My God, I hate what you do to me!"

She looked up into his deepening blue eyes and shivered with apprehension. Could he sense the secret, dark pleasures that she felt from the tautening of his body against hers, from the crushing strength of the hands gripping her arms?

Around them came the sound of birds, and the faraway rippling of water in the creek. The wind was stirring the limbs of the trees, and leaves crunched underfoot as she shifted in his embrace. But she was more aware of her own heartbeat, of the fleeting nature of her time with him. Just a few more days . . . after that she'd never see him again, she knew it. Once Al was safely married, the oil baron would put her out of his mind. This, all of this, was just a means to an end, an attempt to make her break the engagement. But she was getting involved in ways she'd never meant to. She looked at him and loved him, bad temper, ruthlessness and all.

"It will all be over soon," she said softly.

"Sooner than you realize," he replied sharply. "Break off the engagement, while you can. Don't make me hurt you. I don't really have any taste for it now. But I have to protect Al."

Involuntarily, her fingers reached up, hesitated, and then touched his thick, dark eyebrows. Incredibly, his eyes closed, he stood very still, not moving at all. And that response made her bold. She traced all the hard lines of his bronzed face, learning its patrician contours, touching high cheekbones, his straight nose, his broad forehead, the indentations in his cheeks, the firm, warm line of his lips, his jutting, stubborn chin. His breath stirred as her fingers lingered beside his mouth.

She felt an answering hunger. Was it so much to ask, just one more kiss? One more passing of lips against hers? One kiss to remember, to live on? She rose on tiptoe, her hands behind his strong neck, and touched her mouth to his chin. It was as high as she could reach, but not nearly enough.

"Thorn," she breathed huskily. "Thorn, please . . ."

He was breathing as roughly as she was. "What do you want from me, Sabina?" he whispered back.

"Memories," she managed to get out.

His eyes opened, dark and very soft. He reached down and picked her up in his arms, holding her while he searched her hungry eyes. "Memories," he said gently, in a tone he'd never used with her before. "Yes, I can give you those. In another time, another place—I could have given you a child as well."

She trembled, her eyes filling with tears, and he buried his face against her throat as he carried her deeper into the woods.

"I want you," she told him, whispering it, her voice torn with hunger and pain.

"Me, and not Al?" he asked.

She drew in a breath and looked up into his eyes, wanting only to explain, to tell him everything. But she didn't dare.

His face hardened, even as his eyes blazed with open desire. He laid her down under a big oak tree, on a pallet of leaves, and slid alongside her. "I'm richer than Al is," he said under his breath. "If money is the big draw, why not set your sights on me, tulip?"

"It isn't money," she said hesitantly.

"Well, it damned sure isn't love," he shot at her. His eyes kindled as they wandered the length of her body and back again, hungry on her breasts, her lips, her face. "Beautiful," he whispered. "You're so beautiful you take my breath, my will, my mind. I hold you and want nothing more from life than the taste of your mouth on mine."

"We're enemies," she whispered sadly.

"If it weren't for Al, and your innocence, we'd be lovers," he said. He ran his hand slowly over her shoulder, her collarbone, holding her eyes as he slid it onto her breasts and traced the hard tips.

Her lips parted with the unexpected movement, and he bent and took the sound from them with his own. She closed her eyes and the kiss got harder, deeper, hungrier. She moaned. His breath came heavily. He moved a hand to his suede jacket, unbuttoned it, and tossed it aside. He opened his shirt and tugged it free of his trousers, and drew her hands against his hard, hair-feathered chest. His mouth became more demanding, and she felt herself getting weaker by the second, done in by her own consuming love for him, by the pleasure she'd never known before. She sighed, nuzzling her face against him while his warm, deft fingers made quick work of buttons and hooks, and suddenly smoothed over her with exquisite delicacy, petal-smooth, feather-warm.

She gave a high-pitched little cry and tried to curl up, but he eased her onto her back and smoothed the fabric completely away from her body.

The breath he took was audible as he stared down at cream and mauve contrasts, lifting gracefully with her sighs. "Oh, God," he whispered reverently, poised over her.

Her wide, gray eyes searched the hardness of his face, looking for vulnerability, but it only grew harder as he looked at her. She could feel a sudden, helpless reaction as he stared blatantly at her breasts, and it embarrassed her. She tried to cover them, but he brought her hands to his mouth, shaking his head.

"Don't be shy," he said gently. "I'm just as aroused as you are."

His eyes glittered as he suddenly moved down, shifting so that his whole body covered hers, with his elbows taking the brunt of his formidable weight. "See?" he murmured as his hips moved in a slow rotation against hers, and she felt the blatant proof of the statement. "My God, I want to take you," he said huskily. "I want to strip you and grind your body into the leaves under mine, and make you cry out when the moment comes...."

Her face felt hot. She pressed her fingertips against his hard mouth as the pictures flashing in her mind embarrassed her. "You...mustn't."

"Watch," he whispered, drawing her eyes down to his chest. He moved, shifting so the thick hair over it teased her breasts. The abrasive contact shocked her with pleasure, and her body suddenly jerked, arching helplessly against his, while her eyes told him how helpless she was to stop it.

"Your mind may want to stop, but your body can't. You want me. It must be pure instinct, because we both know you've never known the full intimacy of a man's body."

"I want to," she moaned, touching his chest helplessly. "I don't care if it hurts, I want you..."

"Sabina," he whispered. His mouth opened on hers and he gave her the full weight of his body, holding her, devouring her eager lips. She whimpered, and the sound made him shudder. Her body trembled as the warmth and strength of his burned into it, his chest pinning her soft breasts, his legs tangling in hers.

His hand edged between her breasts, his thumb stroking her, his fingers tracing her. His breath quickened, and he suddenly shifted, his mouth moving from hers down to one creamy breast.

She cried out, arching, her body shuddering with unbelievable pleasure, and her glazed eyes met his as he lifted his head. His hand stroked her, warm and confident and soothing.

"This is what passion is all about," he said softly, holding her gaze. "Total, absolute loss of control. Sensual oblivion. A few minutes of this and you'd kill to have me end the torment."

Her eyes stared up into his, through a fog of hunger and need and love.

He sat up, holding her down by the waist, studying the visible tremor of her body. He was none too calm himself, but he fought for self-control. He sighed heavily then, smiling ruefully at the expression on her face.

His lean hands shook her gently. "Virgins are hell on the nervous system," he murmured.

Her mind was only beginning to focus. "I would have begged you," she said numbly.

"Yes. But even then I wouldn't have gone any further." He drew the front of her bra together and fastened it, then her blouse, with slow, steady hands. "A casual relationship isn't for you. I don't think it ever would be, despite the offer."

"Thank you," she whispered.

He studied her quietly. "Now tell me you're not really marrying Al."

Was that why he'd made love to her? she wondered miserably. To make her break the engagement? Her eyes closed. "I still am."

He glared down at her with pure hatred. "You have until tomorrow night to give him back the ring. If you don't . . ."

She fumbled for words. "I'm sorry," she said. "I can't."

He got to his feet angrily, buttoning his shirt and snatching up his jacket and hat while she sat and watched him curiously.

"My God, you're something," he said. It was no compliment. He glared at her openly. "I've never known a woman to be so damned mercenary!"

That hurt, but she didn't let him see how much. "And you're as unprincipled yourself, oil baron," she shouted back. "You made love to me just to make me break the engagement, didn't you?''

His face went rock hard. "Sure," he said coldly. "I'm ruthless, remember? I thought you might be persuaded to settle for me."

"For how long?" she asked with a bitter laugh. "A few weeks, until you sated yourself?"

"That would depend on how much you wanted," he said with deliberate cruelty, as if he knew! "Most women will sell themselves for the right price or the right reason."

Her face paled, and she could have sworn there were traces of regret in his expression. She turned away. "Thanks for the lessons."

"You're an apt pupil. But school's out now."

"Just as well," she said. "The tuition is too high."

"You're paying for experience," he said tauntingly.

Her head jerked around, her eyes revealing hatred for all the other women he'd had before her. "Did you pay them?" she asked.

His eyes narrowed. "Sure. A diamond here, a mink there. Trinkets."

Trinkets. The price of survival. Her eyes grew wild, her face blanched as she saw her mother's face at the end of life, heard the pitiful words come torturously out of that frail throat.

"Oh, damn you!" Sabina cried, hating him for being that kind of man, hating him for what others had done to her mother, for what they had made of her. "Damn you, damn you . . . !" She sobbed.

"Sabina, wait!" There was an odd hesitation in his deep voice when she turned and began to run. But she didn't stop. Instead she let the wind cut into her face, let the tears cloud her vision as she ran on, lost in her own hell of memories.

6
*

After she washed her tear-stained face and calmed down, Sabina changed into a soft, clinging brown-and-cream dress that suited her dark hair and eyes. Gathering her courage, she smoothed her hair and went back downstairs. She'd purposefully taken her time, so that the Thorndon brothers and the visiting cattlemen were just coming back into the house when she reappeared. She wouldn't look straight at Thorn; she couldn't. Instead she went to Al, who immediately gathered her to his side—a movement that Thorn watched with cynical eyes and a mocking smile.

"Want to ride over to Houston with us?" Al asked her. "I'm going to show Mr. Bellamy the city on the way to the airport." He indicated the heavyset, smiling man nearby.

Sabina nodded.

"Take your time," Thorn told the two men, but his brooding gaze never left Sabina. "I've got a business meeting in New Orleans in an hour. I'll go alone."

Relieved, Sabina was glad of the opportunity to escape from Thorn's sensual pull, even for a little while. She went with Al and the cattleman and was delighted when the outing kept them away from the ranch until late that evening. By the time they got home, it was bedtime, and Sabina was only too glad to have avoided another confrontation. *Oh, Thorn,* she thought miserably, *why did it have to be this way?* Why couldn't they have met under different circumstances? He wanted her so much, there had to be a glimmer of feeling for her under all that ice. Perhaps he might even have loved her, if she'd had a chance to be herself with him. The one time they'd really talked, there had been a rare rapport between them. And in the woods, he'd whispered, "Another time and place, I might have given you a child...."

It reminded her of the taunt she'd made the first day at the ranch, about having babies, and Thorn's eyes had gone to her stomach with a wild kind of hunger. Her eyes closed as a soft moan rose in her throat. How could he be thinking of children with her if there was no emotion in him? A man interested in a body would certainly be thinking of ways to prevent that from happening, wouldn't he? She almost groaned aloud. If only she knew more about men. But Thorn hated what he felt for her, and made no secret of it. As far as he was concerned, she was only the gold digger his brother wanted to marry, a heartless flirt, a woman with her eye to the main chance. She sighed bitterly. None of that was true, but he'd never know. Because in two days, she'd be out of his life for good, and only the memories would remain. At least, she told herself, she had those, as bittersweet as they were.

The next day at breakfast, Thorn reminded them about the engagement party, which was being held that night. The way he said it sent chills up Sabina's spine.

"It will be formal," he told Sabina, his blue eyes challenging.

"I have a gown," she replied. "I won't disgrace you." She didn't look straight at him. She hadn't been able to since their confrontation in the woods, and she'd avoided him every minute she could—a fact of which he seemed angrily aware.

"Of course you won't," Al replied, studying his brother. "You look smug. Any particular reason?"

"I'm holding some good cards," the older man replied with a narrow glance in Sabina's direction. "What are the two of you planning to do today?"

"We're going down to New Orleans to get me a new dinner jacket," Al said smoothly. "My old one is getting a bit tight."

"Don't stay there too long," Thorn cautioned.

"Wouldn't dream of it," Al promised him.

They did go into New Orleans, but while they were there, they held a council of war with Jessica.

"I'm scared," the redhead confessed as they lunched in a small outdoor cafe. "What if Thorn sees through the act? We don't get married until the day after tomorrow!"

"He doesn't suspect anything," Sabina assured her, patting her hand. "Trust us. We'll handle it."

"It's just that it's so risky, even now," Jessica bit her lip, her eyes worshipping Al. "I'm afraid of Thorn."

"He does inspire those feelings," Al said with a chuckle. "But not for much longer. Once we're actually married, there isn't a thing he can do."

"And I'm taking good care of your ring," Sabina told her, grinning as she held it out. "How fortunate that we wear the same size!"

"There's no one I'd trust with it more," Jessica said warmly. "I feel that we're imposing on you, though. You're the one taking all the risks. And all the contempt. I can imagine what Thorn's put you through."

"He hasn't bothered her," Al said with blessed ignorance.

But Jessica, watching the expressions that crossed her friend's face, wasn't fooled. A minute later, when Al went to the men's room, Jessica urgently leaned forward.

"Don't let Thorn hurt you," she pleaded. "Not even for our sakes. I don't want you to suffer."

Sabina searched her friend's eyes. "Jess, I'm in love with him."

Jess's eyes widened. "In love?"

"What do I do now?" Sabina whispered miserably. "It's the first time, and it hurts. And he thinks I'm nothing but a gold digger." She hid her face in her hands. "Oh, Jess, if he found out the truth about me, he wouldn't even soil his feet by walking on me."

"Stop talking like that," Jessica said with genuine concern. "You're every bit as good as he is."

"No," Sabina said. "Not in his mind. For all my small bit of fame, if he knew my background he wouldn't let me through the front door, and you know it."

"Oh, Sabina, what can I say? I feel so guilty!" Jessica said, frowning.

"I'll get over it," Sabina said. "All I have to do is live through the next couple of days. I'll grit my teeth. And then I'll be on the road. Maybe then, when I'm away from him, it won't bother me so much."

"And Thorn?" Jessica said probingly. "How does he feel?"

"He wants me."

Jessica sighed. "Oh, I see."

"Here's Al back. Don't give me away, please. I couldn't bear to have him know how I feel about his brother," Sabina pleaded. "Thorn would chew me up like candy if he knew!"

"I won't say a word." Jessica smiled as Al came back. "Hi, pal," she said, leaning over to give him a peck on the cheek.

"Hi, yourself," he said lovingly.

Watching them, Sabina felt like crying. If only Thorn could look at her that way, talk to her that way, just once. But that was a pipe dream. She'd learned to her sorrow that reality was painful. Thorn would never be hers. The most she could hope for was that she might linger in his memory as the one woman who got away.

That night, the house was filled with guests enjoying a catered buffet supper and dancing to a live band. It was the Saturday night before Easter Sunday, and Sabina thought she'd never seen such elegant clothes before. Her own strappy gown looked simple by comparison, which was probably what Thorn had intended. She might buy one expensive used dress, but her budget didn't allow her to buy several. This was the one she'd worn to Al's party, and she wondered if Thorn recognized it. He gave her a mock toast from across the room, and she turned away, hurt.

"He did that deliberately, didn't he?" Jessica asked. They escaped for a minute alone in the ladies' room.

"Baiting me," Sabina said with a sigh. "You can't imagine what it's been like. If I didn't like you so much..."

"I love you," Jessica said fervently, and hugged her. "Someday, somehow, I'll make it up to you."

"Are you happy, my friend?" Sabina asked with a tiny smile.

In her black satin dress, with her flaming red hair cascading over her shoulders, Jess was a vision. "Deliriously. I only hope it happens for you, too, one of these days."

"It would be a pity if it did," she replied carelessly. "I don't want marriage, and an affair is out of the question."

"But, Sabina, one day you'll want a family."

She winced. "No."

"With the right man, it would be different," Jessica assured her. "Your children would be wanted, loved."

Sabina's soft gray eyes widened as she thought about having a little boy with dark, waving hair and ice-blue eyes. Her heart skipped wildly. It was pure unadulterated stupidity. She had to stop thinking about Thorn that way.

"Are you all right? You're very pale," Jessica said softly.

"All right?" She was remembering the way it felt to kiss Thorn and she burned all over. "Yes. I'm all right. Let's go back."

Al came up to them, fighting the urge to stare at Jessica. "Well, let's see if we can throw the wolf off the track, shall we?" he asked Sabina. "Jess, I wish there was some other way."

"We could leave the country," Jess murmured. "There wouldn't be an easier way, with Thorn."

"Miss Cane?"

Thorn's deep, slow voice rang out and all at once Sabina noticed that the crowd had stopped dancing and everyone was looking at her. She felt like a criminal being fingered, not like an up and coming celebrity in the entertainment world. But despite her modest dress, she held her head high and moved toward him gracefully. His eyes followed her movements with a tangible hunger and something oddly like pride.

"I've told our guests that you have quite a talent with music. How about doing something for us?"

"I'd be delighted," she said, approaching the small combo, which boasted two guitarists, a drummer and a pianist. They were much younger than The Bricks and Sand Band, but the pianist had style. She went straight toward him.

Thorn was expecting some raucous tune, so that he could embarrass her in front of his elegant guests. But the joke was going to be on him. She smiled secretively as she told the pianist what she wanted. And, fortunately, his training enabled him to provide the accompaniment she needed. Otherwise, she'd have had to sing a capella.

She turned to face the group. "I don't think I have to introduce this piece," she said with a faint smile in Thorn's direction. "I'm sure most of you will recognize it immediately." She nodded toward the pianist.

Thorn settled back against the door with a brandy snifter in his lean hand, his face mocking, challenging. *Conceited little girl,* he was saying without words, *you expect these very elite people to know your pitiful rock songs?*

She nodded toward Thorn then smiled at Jess and Al, who were almost jumping up and down with glee.

The pianist began, and she drew in a deep breath and suddenly burst into the exquisite aria from Puccini's "Madama Butterfly." The crowd stood completely still in the large room, as if every breath was suddenly held. Eyes widened as the piercingly clear voice rang out, as the sweep and flow and dramatic intensity of her voice told the well-known story in classic operatic style. When the melody broke into the high, achingly sweet notes near the end, tears were rolling down the cheeks of two of the women listening. And as she held the final note there was a shattering as if of glass. She finished. As she was bowing, she looked toward the back of the room, where Thorn had been standing. Only a tiny pile of broken crystal attested to the fact that he'd even been there at all.

"Bravo!" came the cries from the guests. *"Bravo, bravo!"*

"My dear," one tall matron said as she rushed toward Sabina. "I understood Thorn to say that you were a rock singer!"

"Yes," Sabina said with a smile. "You see, I couldn't afford to go to New York to study. It was my dream, but I'm finding a niche for myself in pop music. At least I can still sing the arias."

"And beautifully," the matron said, tears still in her eyes. "So beautifully. It was a privilege to listen to you."

"Thank you." With a final smile for the older woman, Sabina joined Al and Jessica as the band started up again.

"He broke the glass," Al said quietly, nodding toward the crystal on the floor.

"Did he hurt himself?" Sabina asked, concerned.

"I don't know."

Without thinking she rushed out the door and down the hall toward his study. The door was ajar. She pushed it open and walked in, her eyes searching for Thorn. He was at the window, smoking a cigarette.

"Thorn?"

He turned, his eyes dark and threatening, his face hard.

"Your hand..."

"Hand?" He lifted the free one and stared at it. He seemed not to have noticed that it was cut.

"I'll dress it for you," she said quietly. She went ahead into the half bath beyond the desk and riffled through the cabinet for antiseptic and a bandage.

He joined her, filling the small room, glaring down at her. His presence overwhelmed her, but she didn't speak. She bathed his hand, loving the calloused feel of it, the dark beauty of its leanness, its flat nails. She washed away the smear of blood and checked the cut for slivers of glass.

"I've never heard anything so beautiful," he said absently. "Your voice is a gift."

She laughed. "Yes, I suppose it is. I wanted a career in opera, you see. But I never had that kind of money. Training is expensive. I scrimped and saved to get what I could, but... circumstances made it impossible for me to continue."

"I knew you were penniless. I didn't know about the operatic aspirations, though," he said blankly.

"Don't try to cut me up, please," she said quietly. "I'm not nearly the threat you seem to think I am." She looked up as she put the bandage in place. "My life hasn't been easy. Don't make it any harder for me."

He reached out and gently touched her cheek, and his eyes narrowed. "Then get out, while you can. I've got a trump card. Don't make me play it in front of Al."

She smiled gently. "Trump card? You make me sound like a public enemy."

"You are," he said under his breath. His jaw tautened. "You're the most dangerous woman I've ever known."

She sighed as she put away the bandages and antiseptic. "Well, I'm glad to know that."

"Give Al back the ring, now, and we'll call it quits."

"Why?" she asked, her eyes searching his.

"Because you'll be cheating him. And me." He tossed the cigarette into the sink, where it hissed going out in the residue of water. "Sabina, we can't live under the same roof without sleeping together. Al's my brother. I love him. But I want you. And, God help me, wanting you is a fever I can't put out. One day, one night, it will be the way it was in the woods," he said huskily, watching her blush. "Except that I won't be able to stop in time. You know that, damn you!"

She searched his eyes. "You really care about Al, don't you?" she asked.

"Yes, I care," he said harshly. His eyes were devouring her face. He started to touch her and then drew back. "Sometimes I almost forget what kind of woman you really are, for all that soft innocence that drives me mad." He drew in a sharp breath and turned away from her. "Forget it. I must be going soft in my old age. Let's rejoin the rest. I'll even announce the engagement for you."

He strode ahead of her with his face set in rigid lines, his long legs making short work of the hall. Cutting straight through the crowd, he poured himself a glass of whiskey. When he turned, with a reckless, do-it-or-die look on his face, Sabina knew immediately that the war wasn't over. It was just beginning.

"Ladies and gentlemen, I'd like to make an announcement," he said, lifting his glass to get everyone's attention. "My brother, Al, has chosen a fiancée. May I introduce to you his choice, Miss Sabina Cane," he said, toasting her, his smile deliberately cruel as he concluded. "Sabina Cane, the illegitimate daughter of a New Orleans lady of the evening and one of her many paying admirers."

Sabina felt the blood drain from her face, but she didn't falter. She merely stared straight into Thorn's eyes. She didn't glance over her shoulder, where Al's expression was murderous, or to her side, where Jessica's face was contorted with pity.

The crowd split, clearing a path for her as she walked toward Thorn. She didn't miss a step. Her face was white, her eyes dark with pain and hurt, but she faced him bravely.

She didn't know where the courage was coming from, because inside part of her had died. All the long years she'd kept her secret, held it back, forbidden Jessica even to mention it aloud. And here the oil baron was, producing it like an incubus, taunting her with it in front of his elegant guests.

"Congratulations," she said unsteadily. "You've found me out. But let me tell you all of it, oil baron. My mother was in love with a boy who went away to Vietnam and didn't come back. He left her pregnant and her family threw her out into the streets. She wasn't eligible for welfare because she made a few dollars too much in tips from a waitressing job. Her earnings were just enough to pay the rent, but not much more. When I was born, she took on a night job as well, to support us. But after a few years of that, her health gave out." She straightened, aware of the hush around them, aware of the frozen expression on Thorn's dark face.

"The one thing she had in abundance was beauty. So when she couldn't get any other kind of job, she accepted a date with a wealthy merchant. He was the first. He bought my first pair of shoes, and other trinkets," she added, watching the word register in his narrow eyes. "The second was a shipping tycoon, a friend of the merchant. He paid off the overdue rent and bought us a whole week's worth of groceries as well. We'd been getting scraps from the butcher to make soup until then, because we didn't have enough money for anything more." Thorn's face was so drawn by now that it looked pasty. "There were other men after that. She'd discovered the luxury of having enough to eat and warm clothes and necessities for her little girl. Then she met Harry. Harry was rich, but he had this one little idiosyncrasy. He liked to beat her until she couldn't stand up...." Her voice was beginning to tremble now, as it all came back. She swallowed and straightened again. "She loved him desperately, and when he was sober, he seemed to love her, too. But one night, he had too much to drink. And he beat her to death. Right in front of me."

"Oh, God," Thorn whispered, his voice tormented, his eyes wild.

She drew in a slow breath. "So I was sent to the local orphanage, where I learned how to work for a living. I've been doing it ever since. And trying to live down the past. Ironically, until tonight, there was only one other person in the whole world who knew it. Now," she turned to the guests, who

were staring helplessly at her, "I suppose I'll be dragging it behind me like a chain as long as I live. There's just one other little thing. This is what you wanted, I believe, Hamilton Regan
Thorndon the Third."

And she tugged off her ring and turned to hand it to Al.

"Just a minute," Al said, coming forward. He faced his
taller, older brother with venom in his eyes. "That was unwar-
ranted, and unworthy of you. And if you don't apologize, I'll
knock you down, big brother."

Thorn gave him a considering look and nodded. "Yes, it was
unworthy," he said in a subdued tone. "And damned cruel.
Miss Cane, I apologize for my lack of manners," he added,
looking straight at Sabina.

Her eyes were so clouded with unshed tears, she was unable
to see the lancing pain in his icy blue eyes. She only nodded,
turned and left the room.

Thorn hadn't apologized for his insolence, only for his lack
of manners, she thought hysterically. She packed quickly,
dragging clothes from drawers and stuffing them into her
carryall. She felt poleaxed. Devastated. Apparently, he'd done
some checking into her past and come up with this—what had
he called it—his trump card.

She laughed through tears as she finished packing. It was so
cruel to throw that in her face, in front of all those people. So
cruel!

The door opened and he was standing there. His eyes were
dark, his face unsmiling, his posture stiff and strange.

"Did you bring a knife?" she asked. "I can only assume you
intend to finish me off in private."

"I shouldn't have done that to you," he said in a tone she'd
never heard him use. He had one hand deep in his pocket, the
other holding a cigarette. "It was like tearing the wings from a
butterfly, and about as satisfying. I had no right."

"Why bother about rights?" she asked, smiling bitterly.
"Nobody else ever did. I wasn't even a person when I was little. I was that love child down the street, Bessie's yard child. At
the orphanage it was a little better. At least I didn't have to
watch her with men." Her eyes clouded at the memory and
Thorn actually flinched. "I knew she was doing it for me—I

even understood—but that didn't make it any easier." She ground her teeth in an agony of remembrance. "I hated her for a long time. Until he killed her." Her eyes closed and she shuddered, trying to blot out the memory. "It took years to get over that, and I was so alone. I missed her then," she whispered. "But I hated what she had to become, and I hated rich men dangling expensive gifts to lure her in, to tempt her. If her health had held out, maybe it would have been different. But she had to support us, and that was the only way she could find. Still I'll hate what she became until the day I die, and I'll hate rich men who made her that way. I won't be like her, I won't, I won't!"

She was crying openly, and Thorn's face had gone white. Absolutely white.

Her lower lip trembled and she fought for control. "This isn't much, is it?" She nodded toward the dress. "You wanted to show me up in front of your wealthy guests down there, and you did it, too. I don't have money to throw away on designer gowns. The clothes I wear are all secondhand, but I need to have them to perform in. Al says I'm the best bargain hunter around."

His eyes were fierce and the cigarette had to be burning his fingers, but he didn't even seem aware of it. He looked tormented. "I gave you that check . . ."

"I gave it to Al," she said wearily. "He's building a new wing for the hospital, a wing for disadvantaged children. The project we wanted your support for was a benefit to help build it. I endorsed the check and signed it over to him, to be donated in your name."

She turned away from his white face, which was drained of emotion, and life, and picked up her carryall. "As for the engagement, you'll find out soon enough that it was a sham, and why. Now go away, Mr. Thorndon the Third. Get out of my sight, before I get sick."

He stared at her, trying to find words. "I'll drive you home."

"No, you won't," she said sharply. "After what you did to me downstairs, you won't drive me anyplace. I'll walk."

"Sabina," he whispered in anguish.

"Congratulations, you won," she said, her hot eyes glaring at him. "Aren't you proud of yourself, oil baron?"

"No," he growled. "I'm ashamed." His eyes searched her face one last time before he turned and went out the door, closing it gently behind him. Sabina glanced around the room slowly and went out behind him.

She met Al and Jessica as she started down the staircase.

"We'll drive you home," Al insisted. "I'm sorry. God, I'm so sorry!"

"Regrets don't accomplish anything, dear friend," she said with a wan smile. "Just get me out of here, please."

"I'll stay with you tonight," Jessica said firmly. "And no arguments. I won't leave you alone. Al, he may be your brother, but he's a monster."

"He's going to be a lonely one from now on," Al promised her. "We're getting married. All out in the open. And I'm forming my own company. We'll talk tomorrow. Thorn's really fixed things tonight."

Sabina didn't say a word. She was in love with Thorn, and he'd shown her graphically that he didn't give a damn about her. She wondered if the pain would ever stop. She felt eyes watching as she went out the door, but she didn't turn. She couldn't have borne the sight of him. She still cared. Damn him, she still loved him.

7

_____ * _____

Jessica's pale eyes narrowed with concern as Sabina sat huddled in her gown and robe drinking the coffee they'd brewed.

"Are you going to be all right?" Jess asked, breaking Sabina's trance.

"Of course I am," Sabina said coldly.

Jess saw right through the mask behind the stiff lip and the determined rigidity. "You really love that man, don't you?"

Sabina took a slow breath and a sip of the hot black coffee. "He doesn't deserve to be loved."

"I'm tempted to agree," Jessica said, watching the taller girl. "But I got a look at his face as we were going out the door. If I were old Juan, I'd hide all the guns tonight."

"Did he look as if he might follow me home and shoot me as well?" Sabina laughed hollowly, but there was curiosity in the question, too. She looked up, searching Jessica's face. "Did he?"

"He looked as if he might blow his own brains out, if you want to know," she replied quietly. She wondered if she ought to tell her anguished friend the rest as well, that there had been a kind of loving anguish in Thorn's blue eyes.

"He'll get over it," Sabina said, leaning back in her chair wearily. "When he's had time to reason it out, he'll decide that it was all my fault and he'll pat himself on the back for his brilliance. He saved Al from me, you know."

"Al told him the truth." Jessica bit her lip. She hadn't meant to let that slip.

Sabina's face went stark white, her eyes as big as saucers. "And what did Thorn say?"

Jess shifted restlessly. "He didn't say anything, but Al had to call his dentist. Thorn knocked two teeth out."

"Then what?" Sabina asked.

"Thorn stormed off to his study and locked the door." Jessica sighed. "Al figured he deserved the punch, and I think I deserve one, too, for what we've done to you and Thorn with this stupid deception," she added tearfully. "If we'd had any idea..."

"Thorn and I live in different worlds," Sabina said quietly. "You mustn't blame yourselves. It would never have amounted to anything. I would have been just another notch on his belt."

Jessica shook her head. "I'm afraid not. If it had only been that, Sabina, he wouldn't have minded hurting you. Al said he was like a wounded bear. Even the ranch foreman wouldn't go near him. He went to Al, and that was a first."

"All those people," Sabina said under her breath, closing her eyes. "All those exclusive people, knowing everything about me." She shuddered. "I don't know how I stood there and said those things to him."

"I was so proud of you," Jessica said. "So proud! You were every inch a lady, and it was Thorn who was getting the killing glances, darling, not you. No one's ever beaten him before."

Perhaps she'd beaten him, but at what cost? "Everyone will know now," she said dully. "We'll never get another job. I'll have to leave the band—"

"Stop that!" Jessica said firmly. "I won't let you feel sorry for yourself. You're just not the type."

"I could turn into the type right now," Sabina laughed bitterly.

"Can I fix you something to eat?"

"I'd like Thorn's heart, fried," she said with pure malice.

"Yes, I imagine so. How about some steamed liver, instead?"

Sabina laughed in spite of herself. "No. I don't want anything." She huddled closer in her robe. "Al was terrific, wasn't he?"

"Absolutely." Jessica's eyes warmed. "That was the first time he's ever stood up to Thorn, you know. I don't think it will be the last, despite the loss of his teeth. He didn't duck. He said he figured Thorn had the right."

Sabina hardly heard her. Her mind was drifting in and out of the past, shivering with the force of the memories. For years she'd fought to suppress them. Now they wouldn't be suppressed anymore.

The phone rang and Sabina stiffened.

Jessica soothed her. "It's probably Al." She got up and answered it. "Hello?" Her face went rigid, and she started to speak, but whoever was on the other end apparently said something that got her attention. She paused, glancing warily at Sabina. "Yes. Yes, I think so." She bit her lip. "I don't know if she'll listen, but I'll tell her. Yes. Yes. Good night."

She put down the receiver and turned. "Thorn," she said quietly.

Sabina's eyes grew as hard as diamonds. She averted her face.

"He wanted to make sure you had someone with you tonight," Jessica said, feeling the way. "He . . ." She hesitated. "He sounded odd."

"I don't care," Sabina said brutally. "I'll never care again. Let's get some sleep."

Jessica watched her friend walk out of the room. Sabina was too hurt right now to listen, but if his voice was any indication, Thorn was hurting, too. That concern had been real. Perhaps he hadn't quite realized it himself, yet, but he'd destroyed the one thing of value in his life. Sabina had gotten closer to him than anyone else, and he'd lashed out at her with a fury. Al had said that. But the cruelty had backfired. It had cost him dearly. Jessica felt like a traitor to admit it, but she felt sorry for her future brother-in-law. Sabina and Thorn were so alike, both trapped in shells of their own making, keeping the world at bay so that it couldn't hurt them. She shook her head sadly and went to bed. Long after she had lain down, she heard Sabina's sobs.

Al and Jessica were married early Monday morning. It turned out to be more of an ordeal than Sabina had expected. She'd thought that, under the circumstances, Al would get one of his employees to stand up with him, but when she got to the small church, Thorn was there.

Sabina, in a neat beige suit, hesitated at the back pew. Jessica, in an oyster-colored street-length dress, came to meet her.

"He won't bother you," Jessica said gently. "Al made him promise."

Tears threatened to overflow Sabina's eyes. She was still vulnerable, afraid of what he could do to her right now. She hesitated. "I almost didn't come," she confessed softly. "I . . . Dennis, our road manager, got an offer this morning for a gig at a fabulously well-known club in New York City. Right out of the blue, at a fantastic salary. We jumped at it, of course. We needed the job really bad, and I'm . . . not known in New York." She choked on the words.

"Nobody will know!" Jessica said firmly. "For heaven's sake, those people aren't going to run to the nearest newspaper and have it all dragged out on the front page! Even Thorn wouldn't do that to you!"

"Wouldn't he?" Sabina asked unsteadily. She stared at his back in the dark business suit he was wearing, at the dark hair that her fingers had stroked. So they'd dulled his fangs, had they? She still felt savaged, and her pride was in tatters. The humiliation he'd heaped on her was fresh enough to burn. She'd stood up to him before, and she wasn't going to run. But her heart pounded wildly with every step she took with Jessica to the front of the small church, where the minister, Al and Thorn waited.

Thorn turned as she came down the aisle. He watched her with an intensity that almost tripped her up. His face was pale and drawn. There were deep, harsh shadows under his haunted blue eyes. So you can't sleep either, she thought coldly. Good! I'm glad you can't sleep!

She edged around him without actually meeting his searching gaze and stood on the other side of Jessica for the brief ceremony. All through it, as the minister spoke the age-old words, she felt her heart aching for what she might have had with Thorn in another time, another place. Tears blurred her vision of the minister and she bit her lip to keep the tears at bay. As he spoke the words "with my body, I thee worship," her eyes went helplessly, involuntarily to Thorn, and found him staring at her. She quickly dropped her gaze to the carpeted floor.

Thorn, she whispered silently. Thorn! How much he must have hated her, to be so cruel. His conscience was bothering him. He was guilt-ridden, but she had to remember that it was only that. He'd never cared. He'd only wanted her. And now he pitied her. Her eyes closed. That hurt the most, that all he felt was pity. She'd rather have his contempt.

It was all over in minutes. Al kissed Jessica with gusto, and then turned to be congratulated by the minister and Thorn. Sabina brushed Jessica's flushed cheek with cool lips and grinned at her.

"Be happy," she said softly.

"We'll see you soon, when we're back from Nassau."

"Not unless you don't go at all," Sabina said with a forced laugh, aware of Thorn's deep, slow voice behind her. "The band and I have to leave for New York tonight. We'll be at the club for two weeks, and Dennis said something about a video we may film there. Some agent heard us in Savannah and thinks we may have video appeal, how about that?"

"Things are looking up," Jessica grinned. "I'm so glad for you."

Sabina nodded. "Yes, I'm looking forward to it."

Jessica stared at her uneasily. Sabina was as pale as Thorn, and she seemed subdued, haunted. Of course, Thorn's presence here was enough to do that to her.

"I thought you still had a week to go at the club here," Jessica said under her breath.

Sabina shifted from one foot to the other. "Al let us out of it, with no argument from the other partner," she said, refusing even to say Thorn's name.

"Where can I write to you?" Jessica asked.

"Send it to the apartment house, in care of Mr. Rafferty," Sabina said, her voice dull and lackluster. "He said he'd hold my mail for me until I got back. I packed this morning."

The two women embraced warmly and Sabina turned to kiss Al, gently and with genuine affection. "Congratulations, pal," she said with a hint of her old brightness. "Take good care of my best friend, will you?"

"You bet," Al said. He looked radiant, but his green eyes were narrow with concern. "Take care of yourself, you hear?"

"Of course."

He kissed her cheek. "Thanks. I'm only beginning to realize just how much Jess and I really owe you for today," he added quietly.

"Just be happy. See you," she said with a forced grin. She turned, trying to get past Thorn without speaking, but he wouldn't move. Al and Jessica discreetly moved off with the minister, deserting her. She clutched her purse convulsively and stared at his striped tie.

"Well?" she asked tightly.

His quiet, darkened eyes studied her, memorized her. His hands slid into his pockets. "I'd like an hour with you."

"I don't have an hour. I don't have five seconds for you, oil baron," she said curtly.

"I expected that you'd react that way. Maybe I can condense it. I didn't know the truth. Does that count for anything?"

She finally lifted her eyes and had to fight not to throw herself into his arms. He looked and sounded genuinely sorry. But if she'd hoped for more than a surface regret, it wasn't there. Or he was hiding it well.

"Should it?" she asked. "You savaged me!" Her lower lip trembled, and he looked violent for an instant. "I never told anyone about my past, not a soul, except Jessica!"

His face hardened. "Didn't anyone ever tell you it's dangerous to keep secrets? I tried to make you give the ring back without going that far, but you wouldn't do it."

"I couldn't," she returned hotly. "I'd promised to divert you until they could get married."

He ran a rough hand through his dark hair. "Al could have leveled with me at the outset! I like Jessica, I always have. I wouldn't have fought him if I'd known he was that much in love with her."

"He was afraid of you," she said, her voice short. "He said you'd put an end to it. They're the only friends I've ever had, so I agreed to help them. I wanted to pay you back for the way you'd treated me...." She had to stop as the rage threatened to choke her. She could barely see the shadow that darkened his eyes. "And you...trying to buy me for the night—" She laughed shakily. "My whole childhood was one long procession of men with money. You can't imagine how I hate rich men and desperate women who let themselves be bought!"

"Maybe I understand better than you think," he said. "We talked occasionally. You might have told me. It would have saved a lot of grief."

"And give you the perfect weapon to use against me?" she burst out. "Wouldn't you have loved that! An illegitimate orphan with a tramp for a mother, from the back streets of New Orleans."

"Stop it," he said roughly. "I never would have hurt you—"

"What would you call stripping my soul naked in front of Beaumont's finest?"

He looked around the church uncomfortably. "I've apologized," he said tersely.

"Some apology," she returned. "I told Jessica that you'd find some way to put the onus on me. You don't make mistakes, do you, oil baron?"

His eyes darkened as they looked down into hers, and his jaw clenched. His chest rose and fell heavily with each breath. "You don't know me."

"Oh, yes, I do," she said fervently. "I know you inside out. You're so warm and safe in that shell you wear that you'll never let anyone else in it with you. You'll keep the whole world away, and tell yourself you're satisfied. You'll grow old, with no one to love or be loved by. You'll have that fortune you've made, and you'll have all the women you can buy. But you'll be alone until you die."

His breathing was audible now, his eyes cutting. "Are you through?" he asked.

"Almost." She searched his face, feeling her will cave in, her body tremble with remembered pleasure, with the bittersweet agony of loving him. "I came too close, didn't I?" she asked quietly. "You didn't just attack me to save Al. You hated me because I saw too much. I saw beneath that mask you wear."

His eyes flashed anger, his tall body tensed. "Get out of my life," he said in a harsh whisper.

"I thought I'd already done that," she said lifting her chin. "You win. You always win. You even told me so. I should have listened. Goodbye, Hamilton Regan Thorndon the Third," she said with a forced, broken laugh. "I hope you and your money will be very happy together."

"If you're going, go!" he said icily.

She knew she'd never forget that hard face, not as long as she lived. She turned away, turning her eyes down. Her steps quickened as she started back down the aisle.

"Al . . . Jessica . . . see you!" she called. And Thorn watched her every step as she ran blindly from the church.

The next few weeks seemed to pass like slow motion. Sabina wasn't even aware of being tired, of pushing herself as she and the band gave one performance after another. But she did, exhausting her body and soul, as if to purge herself of the painful memories.

They filmed the video their first week in New York. It was exciting, and Sabina's head reeled when she heard about the thousands of dollars it had cost. All Dennis told her was that they had a backer, but he kept changing the subject when she asked who. Not that it mattered, she supposed. It was the newest way to break into the recording field, anyway. One video on the music channel could make or break a new group, and she was almost sure that theirs was going to be a sensation.

The young production crew that filmed it for them was wildly supportive, impressed with the quality of Sabina's voice and the throbbing rhythm and harmony of the song Ricky had written. It was titled "Ashes and Wind," and they decided on a rooftop fantasy, with Sabina wearing black tattered chiffon and being chased across rooftops with smoking chimneys by a man in a top hat carrying a white cane. It was funky and wild, and a lot of fun.

Ricky Turner was overwhelmed with the finished product. It was in the can days later, and in a month it would be released on the cable music channel.

The group was getting advance publicity, too, with ads on television and radio and in the print media, and their opening at the New York club netted them some flattering reviews. The advertising would surely boost sales of "Ashes and Wind,"

Ricky told them smugly. And if Sabina hadn't been so involved in performing and trying to get over Thorn all at once, she might have wondered about the amount of money all this was costing. And where it was coming from.

"The advertising is drawing big crowds," Dennis mentioned one afternoon, excited about the fact that the club had already booked them for two additional weeks. "And next week, the video will be out. We're going great, people. Just great."

"Yes, we sure are," Ricky murmured. "I just hope nothing goes wrong."

"Worrywart," Sabina said accusingly. "You just sit and brood on things to worry about, and nothing ever goes wrong."

"That's what worries me."

She threw up her hands and walked away.

The New York club was an exclusive one, over fifty floors up near Rockefeller Center, and the city spread out below in a jeweled fantasy at night. Couples held hands at their tables while the band performed the soft rock music it was growing famous for, and Sabina felt a twinge of envy. It had never bothered her before. But then, she'd never known what love was until Thorn walked into her life.

The memory of him made her sad, bruised her heart. It had been a tragic thing all the way around. If she'd had good sense, she'd never have agreed to run interference for Al. But then, he and Jessica wouldn't be married now and looking forward to any kind of life together.

Her eyes misted over as she thought what it might have been like if she and Hamilton Regan Thorndon the Third had met under normal circumstances. If, that first night at Al's party, they'd been strangers altogether and could have started from scratch.

But just as quickly, she remembered his harsh accusation that last night, about her illegitimacy, her mother, and she went hot all over with rage. She wasn't good enough for him. Eventually, he'd have found it out even if they'd started dating and Al hadn't been in the picture. He'd have found out about her past, and he'd have walked away. When Hamilton Thorndon married, it would be a society ingenue, a Houston oil heiress or a

New Orleans society woman. It certainly wouldn't be an illegitimate child and orphan.

As long as she lived, she'd remember his face at the church. If only it had been something deeper than a guilty conscience, she might have been tempted to throw herself into his powerful arms and take up residence. But, of course, it hadn't been anything deeper. Because he wasn't capable of it. Especially with a woman like her.

Bitterness replaced her frustration and she pushed harder, rehearsed longer, put her whole heart into her performances. She'd show him. Her past wasn't going to hold her back. She'd make a name for herself, have the whole world at her feet. And then he'd see what he'd passed up; he'd be sorry.

She looked at herself in the mirror, sighing. Sure. Look what Thorn passed up, she thought miserably, seeing dark eyes dominating a white, drawn face. Even her hair was lackluster, and she was losing weight rapidly. She turned away from her reflection, demoralized.

When she got back to the club, Ricky was glaring as the technicians finished the set and adjusted the heavy lighting.

"I don't like the way that light's hanging," he muttered, pointing to one of the small, low-hanging spotlights.

"You're just overanxious, as usual," she said accusingly. "Come and have some coffee with me. I want to ask you about that new number we did in the video."

He shrugged philosophically as she dragged him away. "Okay," he said. "Maybe it won't come crashing down on your pretty head."

"If it does, I'll remember that I told you to leave it alone," she promised.

The words were prophetic. That night, as they started into their routine, the small spotlight swiveled and came loose. It crashed down onto the stage to the hysterical screams of the packed audience, hitting the side of Sabina's head.

She was knocked out as the hardware still attached to it cut into her shoulder. It wasn't a big light, fortunately, but it was heavy enough to do some damage.

Sabina regained consciousness in the hospital, her eyes unfocusing, her body hurting. The last thing she'd remembered was singing a song and hearing a yell from the door of the club, a tormented yell in a voice she'd thought she recognized. But then the spotlight made impact. She'd thrown up an arm and felt shattering pain in her head and shoulder. And then, darkness.

"Come on, come on," came a harsh, commanding voice. Her hand was being restrained, gripped in something rough and warm that wouldn't let go. "You're tough, tulip. You even beat me. Now come on and fight your way back. I'm not letting go until you do. Come on!"

Her eyes blinked. It had been warm and comfortable in her oblivion and now she was hurting like hell. She moaned.

"That's it," the voice continued, softer now, coaxing. "That's better. Open your eyes, honey, let me see your eyes."

Weren't they open already? How odd they felt. She struggled and her heavy eyelids slowly lifted. There was someone bending over her. She blinked and her eyes opened a little wider. A man. An older man, with a stethoscope. She glanced around numbly and saw the maze of machines connected to her body, in a tiny room whose window faced a nursing desk. She tried to move, but there were wires everywhere. She blinked again.

"Miss Cane, do you feel any discomfort?" the elderly man asked.

She had to lick her dry lips before she could answer. "Hurts," she managed. "Head. And...my...my shoulder." She tried to move, but the pain was too great. She was gently pressed back into the pillows.

"You've been in a coma, but you're going to be all right now. We're going to give you something for the pain," he said. "You'll be fine."

Her eyes closed again. It was too much of an effort to keep them open.

The next time she opened them, it was to find herself in a hospital room. Her mind still felt foggy, but the pain had lessened considerably. She glanced toward her right shoulder and found it bandaged. It felt odd when she moved, stiff and sore. There was something tugging uncomfortably at her temple, too.

She reached up slowly with her left hand and found something like thread there, and raw skin. Stitches!

"Hello."

That voice.... She frowned drowsily, turning her head. Even half unconscious and full of painkillers, she reacted to the sight of him. She lay there helpless, looking, staring, loving.

"Thorn," she whispered.

He leaned over her, his face looking tired, his blue eyes soft. Sabina couldn't believe her eyes. She had to be dreaming.

He was wearing a dark suit and he looked rumpled. The white shirt had blood on it. She frowned. Blood? Where had he gotten that? And it was a dinner jacket, not a suit. Her eyes went back up to his.

"Are you in pain, darling?" he asked softly.

She was delirious. He wouldn't call her darling. Anyway, he wasn't there. She closed her eyes. "Sleepy," she mumbled, and it was the last thing she remembered.

Daylight streamed in through the blinds, disturbing her sleep. She brushed at it, as if it were a fly she could shoo away.

"No," she muttered. "Go away. Too bright...."

"I'll close the blinds."

Had somebody spoken? She heard a chair creak and hard, heavy footsteps. She turned her head on the cool pillow and saw him again. The pain had returned so this time she knew she wasn't dreaming. It really was Thorn.

8

_____*_____

Sabina stared at him with eyes that wouldn't quite focus. Painkillers and weariness had made them foggy.

"How do you feel?" he repeated, his voice deeply textured and slow.

Her eyes searched his face blankly as she tried to fit the pieces together. He hated her. He wanted her out of his life. He'd shamed her and humiliated her and told her to go. Why was he here?

"Terrible," she said, her voice thin and weak. Restlessly, she turned her disheveled head against the soft white pillowcase. She felt numb discomfort. "That light...." She tried to get up.

"Settle down. You'll tear something loose," he said curtly. Firm but gentle hands nestled her back down into the pillows.

"My shoulder...." She tried to move it, but there were bandages. And the other arm had a Styrofoam pad under the forearm and a tube leading to a needle in the wrist. "What—"

"An IV," Thorn said. He sat down in the chair beside the bed and leaned back. "You've got a nasty concussion," he said quietly. "And a bruised shoulder, and some cuts and bruises. But your doctor says that if you keep improving, you'll be out of here within five days, and back at work in about a month."

She blinked. None of this was making sense. And why was he here? Her eyes went to his stained shirt. He was still wearing the dinner jacket, and the same shirt.

"You've got blood on your shirt," she faltered.

"So what?" he asked. His eyes were anything but soothing.

"How long have I been here?"

"Three days," he said, and there was a world of meaning in his tone.

"Were you...at the club when it happened?" she persisted.

He sighed roughly, grabbed an ashtray already half full of stubs, and lit another cigarette. "No," he said a moment later. "I was at a dinner party in Manhattan. I'd planned to stop by later. Dennis phoned me as soon as he'd called for an ambulance." He laughed shortly. "The ambulance and I got there at the same time. I rode in with you."

She didn't understand any of it. "Why are you here?" she asked, confused. "You hate me."

His angry glare seemed to underline her statement. "Who else have you got?" he asked bluntly. "Al's in Saudi Arabia, with Jessica, on a business trip for me. Dennis and Ricky and the guys were willing to stay with you, of course, but they had to finish off the club engagement with another vocalist."

"Another singer? Who?" she asked, her ears perking up.

"Does it matter?"

She sighed, feeling uncomfortable and confused and thoroughly miserable. Her big chance and someone else was taking her place, while Thorn sat there glaring at her as if he despised her. Her eyes closed. Tears welled up and spilled out.

"Oh, for God's sake, not that!" Thorn growled.

Her lower lip trembled, too, and she bit it to keep it still. "I'm being taken care of, obviously," she said, forcing her eyes open. "Thank you for all your concern, but why don't you go home? I can take care of myself now. I'm good at it. I've had years of practice."

He got up, looming over her, with one hand in his pocket and the other holding the cigarette. The blue eyes that glittered down at her were impossible to read.

"What do I have to go home to?" he asked bluntly.

That threw her. She dropped her gaze to the sheet. She wanted to tug it up and wipe her wet eyes, but both hands were immobilized. "You've got your women, oil baron." She laughed coldly.

"I'm alone," he said. His eyes studied her up and down and returned to her face, where a stark white bandage was taped around her temple and her neck. "I have no one."

Unable to meet his gaze, she stared blankly at the needle in the back of her hand. "Join the club."

He drew in a slow breath. "You're going to be out of commission for a while."

The implications were just beginning to get through to her. She looked up at him in a daze. Yes, she'd need looking after, and a place to rest. Since Jessica wasn't around now, what would she do?

"There's no need to panic," Thorn said, lifting the cigarette to his mouth. "You're coming home with me. I'll take care of you until you're back on your feet."

"Like hell you will!" she burst out, horrified at the thought of being completely at his mercy for weeks.

He lifted his shoulders and let them fall. "I expected that," he said absently, studying her. "But what else can we do, tulip? God knows, you can't be left alone."

"Get me back to New Orleans," she said. "I can stay in my own apartment. Mr. Rafferty will look after me."

His face hardened. He turned away. "Rafferty thinks you're a cross between a saint and the good fairy."

She stared at him nervously. "How do you know?"

His broad shoulders shifted as he stared out through the window blinds. "I wanted to see where you lived."

She shuddered. "Why?"

When he turned, his face was expressionless. "It's a hovel," he said coldly.

Her eyes blazed. "It is not! It's a decent, economical place to live, and I have good neighbors! They'll take care of me!"

He took a final draw from his cigarette and crushed it out angrily. "Mr. Rafferty is hardly able to take care of himself. How do you think he'd manage those stairs to your apartment several times a day?"

Tears threatened to come again, as she realized how right he was, how helpless she was.

"Yes, I know, you're proud and you hate being obligated to me in any way," he said quietly. "But you don't have much choice."

But being near him, living with him . . . how would she bear it? Especially knowing how he felt about her, how he hated her.

"You said that I was afraid to let anyone come close to me. That I was afraid of involvement. Aren't you the same way?"

She felt trapped. "Yes, but . . ."

He reached down, drawing his fingers softly against her cheek, her mouth, holding her eyes with his. "I've hurt you more than I ever meant to, Sabina," he said gently. "For God's sake, let me make amends in the only way I can."

"To salve your conscience?" she asked unsteadily.

He stared at her mouth, running his lean finger sensuously around its perfect bow shape. "If that's what you want to believe."

"It was only desire. You said so."

"I did, didn't I?" he murmured.

"Thorn—"

"I'll take care of you."

"But, the band—" she moaned.

"They can live without you for a few weeks," he said. "Once that video hits the market next week, you'll be a legend in your own time, anyway."

That hardly registered. Between her foggy mind and his devastating nearness, she wasn't thinking straight. "How did you know about the video?"

He tilted her chin up a little more. "Never mind how I knew." His voice sounded oddly strained. "Listen, I need to go back to my hotel and change. Will you be all right now?"

She blinked, suddenly realizing that if she'd been here for three days, he had, too. She knew because he was wearing the same clothes he had on when she was brought in.

"You've been here all this time?" she burst out, aghast.

He brushed the unruly hair away from her pale face. "Yes."

"But why?"

"I like hospitals," he growled. "I love sitting in emergency rooms and watching people in green uniforms pass by, and sitting in waiting rooms in the intensive-care unit begging to see you for five damned minutes three times a day! And there's nothing quite as comfortable as a straight chair in a waiting room."

"You didn't have to—" she began.

"How could I leave you, for God's sake?" he said, and his eyes wandered hungrily over her face. "You were in a coma when we got you here!"

"Coma?" she parroted.

"Until you opened your eyes and started grumbling at me early this morning, I wasn't sure you'd come out of it at all, despite what the doctor said."

"You can't pretend you cared whether I did or not," she said coldly.

"You can't imagine how I felt," he said in a rough undertone.

"That's right," she replied abruptly, giving him a burning look. "Remember me? The illegitimate kid from the wrong side of the—"

She suddenly stopped as a lean, hard finger settled over her mouth.

"Don't," he said, regret forming a mask of strain over his handsome face. "I tried to tell you at Al's wedding how deeply I regretted that. You might not believe it, but I hurt myself as much as I hurt you."

Her face turned into the pillow as it all came back, a bitterly vivid memory.

"I disgraced myself, you know," he said after a long pause, sounding ironic and self-mocking. Her eyes came up to meet his and he smiled. "That's right. None of the people who came to that dinner party will even speak to me now. And the matron who cried when you sang even went so far as to sell her stock in my company. How's that for revenge?"

She showed a hint of a smile. He seemed to be more amused than angered by the reaction. "You don't mind?"

"Of course I mind," he murmured. "I'm never invited to luncheons or formal dinners these days. I'm having to survive on old Juan's cooking, and he's mad at me, too. He burns everything he sets before me. Juan is another of your instant conquests," he added ruefully.

She flushed, lowering her eyes to his stained shirt. Odd where that stain was, just about where her bleeding head would have rested if he'd held her.

"If you'll come home with me," he said, "Juan will have to cook good meals, and I'll gain back some of the weight I've lost. So will you. You've lost a bit yourself."

"I've been working hard," she said.

"Yes. Dennis told me." He stuck both hands in his pockets. "Come on. I dare you."

Dare. The old word from her childhood brought her eyes up. She stared at him, taking in the mocking smile, the challenge in his blue eyes. "All right," she said. "I'll go with you."

He smiled slowly. "Think of it as a crash course in human relations. You can teach me to be human, and I'll teach you how to be a woman."

Her body tingled. "I don't want to become a . . ."

"Hush." He bent and kissed her mouth tenderly, barely touching her. "I won't seduce you, even if you beg. Okay?"

She could hardly catch her breath. "You could make me beg," she whispered with painful honesty.

"I know. Is that what frightens you?" he asked gently.

She nodded. Her eyes were so close to his that she could see their dark blue outline, the wrinkles beside his eyes.

After a pause, he said, "You aren't the only one who's vulnerable. I'd better let someone know you're awake." He said it as if the weakness irritated him. He pressed the call button and before she could get her mind together enough to question him, he was out the door and the nurse was inside making a condition check.

"How lucky you are," the young nurse said with a smile as she took Sabina's temperature. "The ICU staff bent the rules a little for Mr. Thorndon when they saw what his presence was doing for you. He sat and held your hand and talked to you all the time. You kept having seizures and he sat there like a man possessed, watching us work on you." She shook her head with a sigh. "We were all afraid you wouldn't come out of it. Comas are so unpredictable, and we're helpless to do anything about them in circumstances like these. We just have to sit and wait."

The thermometer came out and Sabina stared at the nurse. "Thorn stayed with me all that time?"

"He sure did," She sighed. "What a heavenly male. Lucky, lucky you." She grinned, finished her tasks, and breezed out again.

Thorn was back less than an hour later, still worn but a little more relaxed. He had an attaché case with him, and after sitting down in a chair beside the bed, he opened it and took out a sheaf of papers.

"Go to sleep," he told her. "I'll sit here and work."

From his pocket, he pulled out a pair of reading glasses, tinted ones that looked more like pilot's sunglasses. She smiled faintly at the way he looked in them as he bent over reams of paper. He was wearing a white turtleneck sweater with a blue blazer and dark blue slacks, highly polished boots and a cream-white Stetson. She looked at him with adoration.

He looked up, smiling warmly at her. "Go to sleep," he repeated gently.

"Aren't you tired?" she said drowsily. "You need some rest, too."

"I can't rest away from you," he said quietly.

If only she wasn't so sleepy. But her head had been throbbing and she'd asked for something to kill the pain. The injection of Demerol was just beginning to work.

"Don't . . . leave me," she whispered sleepily.

"Never again," came the soft reply, but she was past hearing.

A week from the day she'd entered the hospital, Thorn took her back to Texas. She was weak, and she'd suffered some vertigo and nausea those first days out of intensive care. But now she was on the way to recovery, and it felt wonderful to be outside again, even in the bitter cold.

Christmas was barely a week away. So was the band's new video. She smiled, remembering the brief visits the guys had made to her room, when they could get past Thorn. He was determined that she should rest, and ran interference like a professional. Ricky and Dennis managed a few minutes, long enough to tell her how well the club engagement was going, despite the fact that their stand-in vocalist was male. Anyway, they said, the video was going to be the big thing, and it would be on the music channel within days. She was to look for it. Thorn's ranch was beyond the limits of the cable company, but he had a satellite dish, so they'd be able to get it anyway.

She was surprised to find the ranch fully decorated for Christmas, all brightly lit and an enormous fir tree loaded with decorations, and a kitchen full of baked delights. Under the tree were dozens of presents. Sabina had a downstairs room, so that she wouldn't have to risk climbing stairs.

"Is your mother coming for Christmas?" she asked Thorn once she'd settled in. She was sitting in the living room with him during their first evening at home.

"No," he said quietly, filling a glass with whiskey. "Maybe after the New Year, though, when Al and Jessica get back."

"There are only the two of us for Christmas?" she asked hesitantly.

He turned, watching her in the blue velour robe he'd brought her. "Just the two of us," he agreed quietly.

"But, all those presents—!"

He looked uncomfortable. He sat down beside her, putting his glass to one side while he lit a cigarette. "I invited a few people over on Christmas day."

Her face went white, and his jaw tautened. "No," he said quickly. "Not anybody from that damned crowd!"

She swallowed, and clutched at her robe. She still felt vulnerable. "Sorry."

"You'll learn to trust me," he said putting the cigarette to his mouth. "I don't make promises that I don't keep. I'll never hurt you again."

She forced a smile. "Okay."

"I invited your Mr. Rafferty and a couple of twins and their mother, and that elderly woman who lives on the first floor in your building . . ." he began.

Her face froze in mid-smile. "You what?"

"They're your friends, aren't they?" he said.

"Yes! But, I never dreamed—"

"I told you I wasn't a snob," he reminded her. "I thought it was about time I proved it to you."

"But, what about your friends?" she asked, concerned.

He took the whiskey glass in his lean hand and sipped at it, laughing mirthlessly. "I don't have any," he said, and sounded so alone that she felt tears sting her eyes.

9

_____*_____

She stared at him hungrily. "You met my friends when you picked up my things at the apartment?" she asked, after a minute.

"That's right," he said, turning. His eyes swept over her thin body in the deep blue velour robe. The robe was one of hers, old and worn, and his face hardened as he saw the worn places. "I looked for nightclothes, but that robe and a couple of cotton gowns were all I could find," he added.

She lowered her eyes, embarrassed. "They're all I have," she confessed. "I had to spend most of my money on stage costumes."

"You mean 'what was left.' After all, you gave away most of what you had to your neighbors," he said.

She looked up and saw a surprising look on his face, which she was helpless to decipher. "You saw how they live," she faltered.

"Yes." He lifted the whiskey glass to his mouth and took a sip. His broad shoulders rose and fell with a heavy breath. "I suppose I've had money myself for so long that I'd forgotten what it was like to be without it." He dropped down beside her. "Not that I ever lived the way your neighbors do. My father always made good money."

She curled her feet up under her and leaned her head back against the sofa, watching him. He was good to look at, she mused. So handsome and big and vibrantly male. She smiled softly. All the bad memories faded as her heart fed on him.

He glanced at her and saw that searching look, and smiled back gently. "Feeling better?"

She nodded. "Will I have to go all the way to New York to have the stitches out?" she asked, voicing a question that had worried her for two days.

"Of course not," he said. "I've had my doctor call yours, and I've made an appointment for you on Friday. I'll drive you in to Beaumont."

"What will they do to me, do you know?" she asked, frowning.

He reached out and touched her hair lightly, tracing its sheen to her shoulder. "Just an office checkup, that's all. They'd never have let you out of the hospital if they'd had any doubts about your recovery."

"Of course." She lifted her shoulders and winced as the bruised one protested.

"How does it feel?" he asked, nodding toward her arm.

"Sore." She laughed.

He put down his whiskey glass and moved closer, opening her robe with such deft assurance that she didn't think to protest the intimacy. The gown underneath covered her of course, but it was old and worn thin. When he drew the robe away from her body, he smiled wickedly at the flush on her cheeks.

"You can't possibly be self-conscious with me?" he teased. "Not after that day in the woods."

Her eyes widened, as they looked into his, and the smile on his face began to fade. His long fingers drew a pattern down her throat, tracing the madly throbbing pulse, lingering just below her collarbone where the loose gown had sagged.

"I wanted you," he breathed. "Never more than that day, when you let me open your blouse and look at you, and touch you, and taste you." His jaw tautened as he sighed wearily. "I was so wrong about you, Sabina. I knew it then, but things had gone too far. I was afraid of what was happening to me. I hated you for leading me on, when you belonged to Al, for keeping us both on a string. I couldn't be sure you weren't the gold digger I thought you were. I didn't trust my instincts. It never occurred to me that you could have been pretending. But it should have. Everything was wrong about that engagement. A blind man could have seen through it."

"You were trying to protect Al. I realized that, although it didn't help a lot at the time," she said quietly. "I've been so ashamed of my past, you see."

"Why?" He brushed the dark hair away from her face. "None of it was any of your doing. Your mother did what she could for you. I can see that it would have left scars, but it was never your fault."

Her eyes fell to his chest. "I was there the night my mother died—" she closed her eyes "—that last night, when he hit her..." Her voice broke.

"Darling, don't." He pulled her gently into his arms and held her and rocked her, his hand smoothing her long hair, his deep voice soothing her. "It all happened a long time ago. It's over."

She dabbed at the tears, shifting and moaning as her shoulder began to ache again.

"Did I hurt you?" he asked softly. His hand moved to her face and touched it hesitantly, learning every soft contour, as hers had once done to his, delighting in its vulnerability.

"Thorn," she whispered.

His breath became audible. His mouth was poised just above hers and his eyes looked deep into her own as his fingers passed slowly down her throat to her collarbone and still further. She tensed, but he shook his head.

"No," he whispered. "Let me touch you."

She bit her lower lip as his lean hand eased under the fabric, and he watched her as the tips of his fingers teased softly around the edges of one perfect, creamy breast.

He moved, easing her down onto the couch, and she heard the springs shift under them. But what he was doing was so delicious that she didn't even protest. She trembled with sweet anticipation, wanting him so much that it was almost painful. His arm made a pillow behind her head, and he smiled softly as her body jerked toward his fingers.

"Wicked, wicked...man," she whispered brokenly, watching his face.

"Indulge me," he whispered back. "You can't know how it was, seeing you in that hospital bed."

It was hard to think. "The nurse said...that you talked to me and...held my hand...oh!" she gasped as one lean finger brushed the hard tip of her breast.

"Did she tell you that I sat by you when they told me you might not come out of the coma, and that I cried like a boy?"

He put his hard mouth slowly, warmly on hers. "Because I did. Open your mouth."

"Cried . . . ?" She couldn't think. His tongue was working sorcery on her parted lips, and his hand had eased down completely over her bare breast, so that she could feel not only his slightly calloused fingers, but also the wrinkly moist warmth of his palm. "Thorn," she moaned, and her body arched.

"Open my shirt, and do that to me," he whispered into her mouth. "Let me teach you how to arouse me."

Her breathing became short. Her hands shook so much she could hardly fumble the buttons of his shirt open. To be allowed free license with his body was overwhelming.

She eased her fingers down against the thick mass of hair and over the warm muscles. She searched for his skin, finding taut peaks that might have been the mirror image of her own. Her eyes found his.

"Do men . . . too?" she whispered.

"Yes." He held her head gently in his hands. "Open your mouth, and put it against me, there," he whispered, guiding her down his chest. She did as he told her, and he groaned harshly, a sound that made her head lift so that she could see his face.

"Don't you moan when I put my lips on you?" he whispered, smiling.

Her eyes were full of wonder. "Oh, Thorn, I never knew—!"

"Thank God." He moved, peeling the gown to her waist, and she let him, lying pliant in his arms, watching his face as he saw what his stroking had accomplished. "I like knowing that you're a virgin," he said unexpectedly, touching her lightly. "You aren't afraid of the first time with me, are you?" he asked quietly.

Her face reddened. "I can't . . ."

"Not now, little tulip," he said with a laugh. He bent and eased his bare chest down over hers, and smiled at the way she trembled. "Yes, I like that, too. I like the way it feels to have you half nude against me. You're a sexy woman."

"Thorn, I won't be—" she tried again.

"Where would you like to be married?" he asked.

She stared at him as if he'd gone crazy. "What?"

"Where would you like to be married?" he murmured against her mouth. "Beaumont or New Orleans? Mr. Rafferty can give you away, and Jessica can be matron of honor."

Her palms flattened against his chest. "I can't marry you," she said.

His face went expressionless. "Why not?" he said.

She drew a breath and tried to get up. Surprisingly, he let her, watching as she drew her gown back up and shouldered gingerly into her robe again. "I just can't, that's all."

"Is it your career?" he persisted. "Because I'll compromise."

She shook her head. She wrapped her arms around her waist, dying inside because he'd just said the one thing she wanted most in the world to hear. She loved him, would have died for him. But she couldn't marry him.

"Then why?"

"How would you announce it?" she asked with a bitter laugh, and ran an unsteady hand through her hair. "My parents were never married, you know. There was a front-page story when my mother was killed. Inevitably, people would find out. In the circles you move in, I'd be so much of a liability—"

"Liability, hell! That's no excuse at all." He sighed wearily and got to his feet. "It's because of what I did to you, isn't it?" he asked in an odd voice. He wouldn't look at her. He lit another cigarette, took a few draws and, as quickly, put it out. "It's because I humiliated you. You think I might do it again."

"No!" Her head came up. "No, it isn't that, truly it isn't! It's just that you'd—oh, Thorn, you'd be so ashamed of me."

His eyes closed. "The only person I've been ashamed of in recent weeks is myself." He moved restlessly toward the door. "I need to do some paperwork, I'll see you later."

She stared at his broad back, half puzzled, half certain. Did he care? Could he care that much and still not believe her reasons for rejecting his proposal? Her heart raced wildly.

She took a gamble, the maddest gamble she'd ever taken in her life. If he rejected her, she'd never get over it.

"Thorn!" she called.

He paused with his hand on the doorknob. "Yes?"

She gathered all her courage and held out both her arms to him.

He hesitated for an instant, and her heart began to throb. She feared that she'd misread the entire situation. Then his face changed. He moved back toward the sofa and suddenly dropped to his knees and clasped her hard enough around the waist to hurt her, burying his face in her breasts.

She held him, feeling the tremor in his body, her hands tangling in his dark hair. She sat disbelieving, trembling with new emotions, with shared emotions.

"I love you," he managed in a broken tone. "Oh, God, I love you, and I didn't know it until that night, until it was too late, and I wondered how I was going to live if I'd caused you to do something desperate. I called to make sure Jessica was with you because I was afraid. After that, I could never get close to you again. I knew I'd lost you. I knew I had..." His arms tightened and he caught a savage breath, while Sabina stared down at his dark head in shocked delight. "I kept up with you, I followed your career, I even paid for that damned video," he added, stunning her. "But nothing compensated me for you. I haven't been near another woman since you left. I've hardly eaten or slept...and then that damned light fell on you, and I paid for sins I haven't even committed yet. I sat by your bed and held your hand and knew that, if you died, I might as well lie down beside you, because I wouldn't have had a reason left to stay alive myself."

"Oh, Thorn," she whispered, pulling his head closer. "I love you so much..."

His head lifted, his eyes unusually bright. "Do you? Even after all I've done to you?"

Her fingers touched his face wonderingly. "I understood even then, you know," she whispered. "I knew you so well. It frightened me sometimes, especially when I was pretending to be engaged to Al, because you were like the other half of my soul. I even knew what you were thinking."

"Yes, I felt that," he sighed. "At the church, when you said I never let people come close, you hit a nerve, darling. I hated having you know that, hated being so vulnerable, so readable.

If it's any kind of compensation, I've paid for what I did to you. Being without you was more than enough punishment."

She bent down and kissed his mouth tenderly. "I want a child with you."

His breath held, and his eyes were gloriously loving. "I want one with you. I did even that first day you came to the ranch. You mentioned having babies, and I looked at you and wanted to see you big with mine. It scared the hell out of me," he said with a chuckle. "After that, all I could think about was getting you pregnant. That was when I realized how committed I was." His smiled faded. "Marry me, Sabina."

"There'll be gossip," she cautioned.

"Darling, there'll always be gossip. I love you. What else matters?"

"You're hard to argue with," she murmured.

"So they tell me." He kissed her gently. "Marry me. Give me some children. I'll buy you a new bathrobe and let you sing in my nightclub."

She laughed at his phrasing. "How can I sing when I'm pregnant?"

"Listen, lady, you can even sing while you're getting pregnant, for all I care."

"Thank you," she murmured demurely, batting her eyelashes at him. "Thorn, I hear that new vocalist is doing great with the band. And if you'd let me study opera in my spare time, and let me teach voice . . ."

He looked shocked. "What are you offering to do?" he asked. "Give up everything you've ever worked for?"

She slid down onto the floor in front of him and linked her arms around his neck. "I have everything I ever wanted right here," she said solemnly. "There is nothing I want more than you, and that includes a career. Later, when the children are older, perhaps. But being on the road was already beginning to pale, and I'm terrified of large crowds. I want to live with you and travel with you. I love you."

"Darling," he breathed, searching for words.

"Shhh," she whispered, putting her mouth against his. "Lie down, darling," she murmured wickedly.

"Like hell." He chuckled. He got up, smoothing his hair. "You're not getting me into bed without a wedding ring."

"Tease," she said accusingly.

He made a mock bow and helped her to her feet. "We'll set a wedding date. Meanwhile, don't you want to know who all those presents are for?"

She stared past him at the tree. "Who?"

"I got Mr. Rafferty a warm coat, and the twins some new shoes, and their mother a coat..."

Tears welled up in her eyes. "My friends...."

"The whole world is your friend," he whispered. "But I'm your best one. Between us, we'll spread a little comfort, okay?"

She reached up and pressed a warm kiss against his chin, her eyes brimming with love. "Okay."

He smiled at her. In his eyes, she saw the sweetness and laughter of the years ahead. And she laughed, softly, wonderingly, just before he lifted her in his arms and carried her back to the sofa.

"I thought you weren't going to let me get you into bed until we were married," she chided.

"I didn't say one word about sofas, did I?" he murmured with a roguish smile. He put her down on the couch and let his eyes wander slowly from her toes up over her legs and hips to her taut breasts. His hand went to the buttoned cuffs of his shirt and he flicked the buttons out of the holes with deliberate slowness while she looked up at him, lips parted, body aching.

"The door's open," she whispered.

"For your sake, we'd better leave it that way," he murmured. His lips curved in a smile. "On second thought, to hell with it." He closed the door without looking out, locked it, and went slowly back to the couch. "Now," he said in a breathless, laughing tone. "Aren't you too hot, with all those clothes on?" he murmured, easing down beside her. "Hmmmm, your skin's hot, darling," he taunted, watching her as he lazily disposed of the robe and put it aside. His mischievous eyes went down to the taut outline of her breasts, which were moving with the torturous raggedness of her breathing.

"Thorn," she whispered in a tone that throbbed with hunger.

"I want you, too," he said in a whisper. "But I'll stop before we go too far. Lift up, darling, and let me get this gown out of my way.... Yes, yes!"

Old Juan, who'd been on his way to tell them dinner was ready, had watched the door close and simultaneously turned around on his heel, smiling, to go back to the kitchen. Time enough to eat, he told himself. There were more important things. He put the plates aside and began to hum.

* * * * *

DREAM'S
END

1

*

Eleanor Perrie peeked up from her typing. The distinguished man in the gray business suit had begun shifting restlessly on the luxurious couch. He seemed to be checking his watch every minute. She permitted herself a tiny smile before she touched the intercom button between the living room, where she worked, and the stables down below the big ranch house.

"What is it?" came the impatient reply.

"I think your souffle is done," she said, purposefully vague. "It's very puffed and browning off on top."

There was soft, deep laughter just for an instant on the other end of the line. She could almost see the grin on that swarthy face. "I'll be right up, Miss Perrie."

"I sincerely hope so, Mr. Matherson," she replied with sugary sarcasm, and cut off the connection. She glanced at the man in the gray suit and smiled. Her creamy complexion lit up and emphasized the odd pale green of her eyes, hidden by oversized round eyeglasses with black frames. Her jet black hair was coiled and pinned on top of her head.

"Mr. Matherson will be right up," she said courteously, raising her voice now so that he could hear her from across the room.

"Thank you," the impatient man said stiffly.

"One of our prize Appaloosa mares was foaling this morning," Eleanor added for effect. "Mr. Matherson wanted to see about her."

"I understand," the older man nodded, with a polite smile that didn't reach his eyes.

Oh, no, you don't, Eleanor thought with amusement as she dropped her eyes back to the letter she was typing. Curry Matherson knew how to get what he wanted from people, and this poor little fish was about to find it out. Curry had planned

to build a very sophisticated office complex on land that belonged to this annoyed speculator. The whole deal hinged on
whether or not Durwood Magins, sitting nervously on the very
edge of the big sofa, could be persuaded to sell at a fair market price—not the exorbitant figure he was demanding.

Tired of bargaining with him, this morning Curry had called
Magins to tell him he was dropping the whole project and had
found another site. Fifteen minutes later, Magins had been sitting on the same sofa he was glued to now. And Curry, who was
only looking at the new foal, not helping to deliver it, had allowed him to sit there and sweat it out for two solid hours.
Eleanor watched the greedy little man with mingled compassion and amusement. His own avarice seemed to her to be his
worst enemy. And he should have had the sense not to tangle
with Curry in the first place. This was really one of her boss's
nicer tactics.

Seconds later, Curry Matherson walked into the room. There
was a half smile on his lean, tanned face that was at variance
with the glittering, quite dangerous look in his silvery eyes. He
towered over most people, and since Magins wasn't tall anyway, Curry made him look like a dwarf. Her boss's athletic
body was built with hard riding and ranch work, as well as
sports, at which he excelled. Curry excelled at everything.

She tried not to look at him too hard as he shook Magins'
hand with a grip that probably bruised it, but her eyes kept
going back to him, tracing the hard lines of his face, the thick
dark hair that was just a little unruly from the wind. She'd
loved him forever, it seemed. Since the day she applied for the
job as his private secretary three years ago....

He hadn't been in a good mood at all on the morning of her
interview, and Eleanor had been a little bit afraid of the tall,
dark man. If she hadn't just lost her parents, and suddenly
discovered how badly off she was going to be financially, and
needed a job in such a desperate hurry, she'd probably have
walked out the door.

Looking back, she couldn't help but smile at her own deter-
mination. She was fourth in line to be interviewed. The three
women who preceded her had been experienced and neatly
dressed—one of them was a raving beauty. All were older than

her very nervous eighteen years. And there were four more waiting to be interviewed, equally equipped with brains and beauty.

Eleanor had been wearing a simple mint green cotton shirt-waist dress with white sandals. Her hair was coiled on top of her head because she thought the severe style made her look older, and her eyes were surrounded by a pair of unstylish black eyeglasses that made her look owlish. She only needed the glasses for close work, but they were a kind of security blanket and she wore them all the time, like camouflage. She'd never tried to emphasize her looks—she didn't believe she had any, thanks to the effort of her devoutly religious mother to keep her "un-painted." She'd never dated a man, or been kissed by one, and her evenings at home had been filled with chores numerous enough to make dating impossible even if she'd been interested in it.

Curry had barely spared her a glance when she walked into his office and sat down in the chair across from his massive, polished oak desk. He sat there with his eyes on what presumably was her résumé, and she wondered at his powerful physique, at the black hair threaded with gray, the dark complexion, and was knocked for a loop when he looked up directly into her eyes and she saw that his were silver. Not gray, not blue—silver, polished and glittery. She didn't even hear his first question, she was so fascinated by him.

"I said," he repeated with a calm that did nothing to disguise his impatience, "what kind of experience do you have? It isn't listed here," he added, waving the sheet of paper at her.

She straightened her thin shoulders. "I was my father's secretary at home after I finished school," she recalled, the memory making her sad. "I kept his books and handled all his correspondence."

He leaned back in his swivel chair, lighting a cigarette as he studied her through narrowed eyes—disapproving eyes, she thought suddenly.

"You're not even out of your teens, are you, Miss..." he looked at the résumé and back up at her, "Perrie?"

She lifted her chin proudly. "I'm eighteen, Mr. Matherson."

"Eighteen," he murmured, his eyes sweeping what was visible of her about the level of the desk. "Got a boyfriend, Miss Perrie?"

She shook her head.

"Why not?" he asked nonchalantly, leaning forward on his elbows to pin her with those strange eyes. "Don't you like sex?"

She drew in a shocked breath, and her pale eyes widened.

His face relaxed suddenly, and his silvery eyes danced as he smiled at her. "I won't have to chase you out of my bed, will I, Eleanor Perrie?" he asked. "Or dodge from having you throw yourself at me?"

"That sounds like conceit to me, Mr. Matherson," she replied with a cool, steady tone despite her screaming emotions. "You're not *that* attractive, with all due respect, and you're years too old, anyway."

His eyebrows went up. "My God, little girl, how old do you think I am?" he exclaimed.

She studied him for a long moment, her eyes touching, for some inexplicable reason, the fine, chiseled line of his mouth. "Oh, at least thirty," she replied with irrepressible honesty.

His brows collided and he scowled. "I'm thirty-two, as it happens. But until now, I didn't know that put me on the waiting list for the local old age home."

She smiled shyly and dropped her eyes.

He laughed again, softly. "Spring flower," he murmured. "Little jade bud. How can I turn you down?"

She looked up. "I'm hired?" she asked incredulously.

"We all have moments of unexplained weakness," he replied. "You do realize that a private secretary lives in? I have a passion for dictation at one o'clock in the morning while I watch the Johnny Carson show."

"That's all right," she replied. "I like staying up late."

"Most children do," he told her with an amused smile, and laughed outright at the look that chilled her face.

It had been the beginning of a long, rewarding partnership. Eleanor knew him as few other women ever got to. She saw him tired, angry, happy, playful, bored, even rarely discouraged. She saw him as only a wife would ordinarily, in all kinds of conditions, at all times of the night and day. And gradually, so gradually that she wasn't even aware of it, she grew to love him. Despite his women, and he had them, plenty of them, she never looked at another man. With her hair still in its coil, her glasses still in place, with new frames identical to the old ones every year, the same simple country girl kind of dresses, she was no threat to any of his heartthrobs. They didn't see Eleanor as any kind of competition, and they confided in her, hoping it would get them close to Curry. But, of course, it didn't. At the end of the affair, Curry would have her send a dozen yellow roses from the florist. It was an unspoken thing, a quiet rejection, that was as final as death. And a few weeks later, he'd be off in pursuit of someone else.

He liked sophisticated women. Beautiful, sleek, well-groomed women who knew it all. She'd never seen him date anything less. Oh, Eleanor went with him to an occasional party in the line of duty—but it was always in something simple, she never wore makeup or changed her hair or took off her glasses. Whether or not that was intentional, she didn't stop to ask herself. The relationship she had with her boss, while platonic, was satisfying and delightful. She didn't want to rock the boat by admitting how deeply her feelings went. She'd learned long ago never to want very much. Disappointment had taught her the dangers of caring too deeply.

Her mind came back to the present just as Curry finished talking with Magins, shook his hand, thanked him for his cooperation and shoveled him out the door.

"You are," she told Curry, "a pirate. You'd have been right at home on the Spanish Main, hanging people from yard-arms."

He raised an amused eyebrow at her. "Probably," he admitted, lifting his lighted cigarette to his lips. "What's wrong, Jadebud, your conscience bothering you?"

"Thanks to you, I don't have one," she shot back at him. "I've been corrupted."

He laughed outright. "No doubt. How about calling Mandy for me? Tell her I'll be a little late picking her up tonight. Jack Smith's ready to talk terms on that prize filly I've been after for two months."

"How's Amanda going to take that?" Eleanor asked dryly. "I mean when I tell her she's been stood up for a horse?"

His eyes narrowed sensuously. "I'll soothe her ruffled feelings later," he said in a soft tone.

Eleanor felt ripples of jealousy wash over her, but she was too practiced to let any emotion show. She smiled instead. "I'll call her. What time do I tell her to expect you?"

He turned and started for the door. "Make it seven," he called over his shoulder.

She glared after him, at that dark, masculine arrogance he wore like a cloak around his muscular body. He'd been going with Amanda Mitchell for well over six months, a new record for one of his relationships, but if he felt much of anything for the gorgeous titian-haired model, it didn't affect him in any obvious way. He could leave her hanging like this, and had, many times, without a single qualm. He took her for granted, just as he took Eleanor and everybody else around him for granted. Arrogance, and Eleanor wondered how Amanda put up with it. The model could have had any of a dozen men by snapping her fingers, but the only one she wanted was Curry. And by being cunning—and probably by holding out—she'd landed him. Temporarily, at least. Eleanor didn't take the affair seriously. It was just one more conquest for Curry, that was all.

She dialed Amanda and gave her the news.

"Just like a man," came the musical reply, and Eleanor could almost see the amused look on Amanda's thin face. "Honestly, if Curry could forget horses for just five minutes..." She sighed. "Eleanor, how do you stand it?" she asked sympathetically.

"I have a nervous breakdown once a week, religiously." Eleanor laughed. She couldn't help liking the red-headed model; everybody did, she was so vivacious and open-hearted.

"I believe it. All right, tell the incorrigible brute I'll wait. Not," she added, "that he deserves it."

"I'll tell him that, too." Eleanor laughed.

"I dare you," Amanda teased. "Don't you know Curry would faint if you ever talked back to him? Why do you let him walk on you the way he does? It's outrageous what you take!"

"It goes with the job, I've been doing it a long time. Besides, what would his ranch hands say if he fainted?" Eleanor replied.

Amanda sighed. "I give up. See you."

"'Bye."

Eleanor sighed, shaking her head. It was true; Curry could be hard to get along with. But sometimes, he could be charm personified. Especially when he wanted her to work overtime.

Curry had already gone to see the filly when a late model Buick drove up the front steps.

Jim Black was a head shorter than Curry, just about Eleanor's own height, burly and just a little overweight, with a leonine face and dark eyes. He was smiling, and his eyes twinkled as they met Eleanor's.

"I thought you might feel like having supper," he said.

She laughed. "As a matter of fact, Bessie had a church meeting tonight, and I'd be eating alone," she replied.

"When I get through stealing you," Jim told her gaily, "Bessie Mills is next on my list. Of all the cooks in the county, Curry has the best one."

"Curry always has the best, didn't you know that?" Eleanor laughed.

"You're the best, too, Norie." Jim grinned. "Why won't you come work for me? I pay better than Curry, and I'd even give you two days a week off. That's two more than you get from Curry."

"Don't tempt me," she said with a smile. "Are we going out, or do you want me to cook you something here?"

"Out, woman, of course," he exclaimed. "You work hard enough as it is."

"I don't really," she protested.

"Will you go and get dressed?" he sighed.

She held out her arms, gesturing toward the pale yellow dress. "Why can't I go like this?"

"Because I'm taking you to the Limelight Club," he replied patiently. "And I'd love, just once, to see you dressed to the hilt."

She stared at him. "Me?"

His dark eyes narrowed. "You. Why not try a night out without your camouflage? Curry won't see you, I guarantee it."

"You're asking a lot," she murmured. "Why?"

"Just curiosity. Aren't we friends enough for me to be a little curious, Norie?" he asked gently.

"Well . . ."

"Be daring! Think of yourself as Mata Hari, feverishly pursuing state secrets!"

She laughed in spite of herself. "Well, maybe . . . I do have a gown I've never worn."

"You could let your hair down, too, and take off those horrible glasses you don't need."

She gaped at him. "What are you up to?" she asked suspiciously.

He looked vaguely uncomfortable. As long as she'd known Jim, he'd never been able to keep a secret from her. They were only friends, but it was a close kind of friendship, and she genuinely cared about him.

"Jim, what is it?" she probed softly, her green eyes holding his intently.

He smirked. "All right, I need a little help. Just a little, just this once," he said quickly.

Her eyes widened and she smiled. "Why you old rooster," she laughed. "You want to make someone jealous!"

He turned beet red. "Well . . ."

She laughed. "Jim, my friend, for you I'll do the very best I can. But don't expect miracles," she called over her shoulder. "For that you need good raw material to start with!"

She had gowns and she kept makeup, but tonight was the first time in her life she'd ever tried deliberately to look attractive. It was new, and a little frightening, and she had a sudden premonition that things would change beyond recognition if she went through with it. But after all, Jim had never turned his back on her when she needed help. He was every bit as rich as Curry, but so much more approachable. And she owed it to him. She began to take down her hair.

2
*

She took out the long, white chiffon gown she'd been saving for a rainy day. It was low cut in a V-neck, sleeveless and fell seductively around her slender figure. Her feet were encased in white high-heeled sandals with a beading of rhinestones on the straps.

She sat down in front of her mirror, looking curiously at the stranger she saw there—her long, waving hair tumbling down around her shoulders, her eyes bigger and more feminine without the protective glasses. She applied just a touch of eye shadow and lipstick. And when she was through, she stared at herself with astonishment. Remembering her mother's valiant efforts to keep her from using "paint" or emphasizing her assets, she felt a pang of pure guilt at the way she looked. There was a sensuous air about her that had never been apparent before, and the white chiffon left a lot of soft, honey-colored skin bare. Before she could change her mind about it, she grabbed her lacy shawl and pearl clutch bag and hurried downstairs.

Jim turned when he heard her footsteps and froze where he stood at the bottom of the staircase, looking up at her as if he'd never seen a woman before.

"Well," he said finally, on a hard sigh. "Well, well! I don't think I've ever seen anything that could top that transformation," he said, shaking his head. "Norie, have you always looked like that, or do you have some magical device upstairs?"

"A fairy godmother," she whispered conspiratorially. "But don't tell anyone."

"Cinderella, is it?" He laughed. "Come hop into my horseless carriage, you gorgeous thing, and I'll take you to the ball!"

She did feel like Cinderella, even if Jim's sleek blue convertible wasn't exactly a golden coach. He took her to the Limelight Club, one of the better restaurants. They sat in a private alcove surrounded by live plants.

Looking at her, Jim shook his head and sighed, his dark eyes still disbelieving. "I knew you were pretty," he said with his usual candor, "but I didn't know you were a potential Miss World. Why the rags and cinders all this time, Cinderella?" he asked.

She shrugged. "I've never wanted to impress anyone," she admitted with a tiny smile. "My mother was devoutly religious. She felt that vanity was the greatest sin, and she taught me to underemphasize my assets."

"Does it embarrass you to look pretty?" he asked.

She blushed. "I didn't know I did."

He laughed. "I'm glad I had this idea," he remarked, letting his eyes trace her lovely features, her smooth shoulders.

"Who are we working on?" she asked as the waiter left their menus and went away.

"Her," he said quickly, nodding toward a woman who'd just come in on the arm of a much older man.

Without being obvious, Eleanor half turned in her seat and got a glimpse of a lovely young blonde, as delicate looking as a rosebud, with a knockout figure.

"Who is she?" she whispered.

"The daughter of the man who owns the club—that's her father with her." He grinned suddenly and turned his attention back to the menu. "I think we've been spotted. Don't look, but she's really giving you a green-eyed look."

"Aha, that's why you brought me here, to be stabbed in the back." She smiled.

"In a sense. You're a real pal, Norie. I'll do you a good turn one of these days," he promised faithfully.

"No need. I love playing cupid. Is she still glaring?"

"Sure is . . . oh, my gosh!" His face drew up.

"What's wrong?"

"Hide behind your menu for a minute, quick!" Jim said.

"Why?" she whispered.

"Because Curry and Amanda just walked through the door!"

She felt herself sinking down in the leather booth. Frightened suddenly, for no good reason, she quickly pulled the menu up to conceal her face, leaving her shoulders and a glimpse of her long hair visible.

"Hello, Jim!" came Curry's deep voice. "Haven't seen you in a long time."

"You're never home when I call at the ranch." Jim laughed. "I get over a good bit to see Norie."

"Norie," Curry scoffed. "My God, what a name. She looks like an Eleanor; pet names don't suit her."

"You call her Jadebud," Jim countered.

"In my good moods, when I want something," Curry said darkly. "Eleanor's not much to look at, even though she's a damned good secretary. I flatter her a little now and then. It doesn't hurt and," he added with a heartless smile, "it helps keep her efficiency up."

"Curry, how can you talk like that about her?" Amanda scolded gently and Eleanor, listening helplessly, hurting, blessed her for it. "After all, she's been with you for three years!"

"She'll be with me forever," Curry said nonchalantly. "Where else does she have to go? No man will ever want her, that's for damned sure, and I pay good wages. What else does the little spinster need?"

"Someone better than you to work for," Jim said with sudden, hot anger, and Eleanor knew without looking that those dark eyes would be narrow with it. "She's never had a vacation, did you notice? She never takes time off at all, she just bows down to you as you pass by her. Someday she won't be there for you to walk all over, Curry, and what will you do then?"

Curry's voice deepened as it always did in anger. "Are you still trying to steal her, Black?"

"Any way I can, Curry," he replied gruffly. "I may not be as colorful to work for as you are, but I'll treat her decently and that's something you've never done!"

There was a short, tense pause. "How would you like to step around back with me?" Curry asked huskily.

"Any time," Jim replied tightly.

"Now, boys," Amanda said gently, "this isn't the time or the place. Let's just enjoy the meal, okay?"

Eleanor felt the tension slowly relax, and she knew her fingers were trembling where they held the menu.

"Let it pass," Curry said roughly. "But, Black, you stay the hell away from my spread."

"With pleasure," Jim ground out. "Watch your nose, while you're about it, Curry. If it rains, you'll drown."

Jim waited until Curry and Amanda were a few steps away before he took down the menu Eleanor was using as a shield. His face grew tighter when he saw the tears misting her soft green eyes.

"Let's get the hell out of here," he told her. "I've lost my appetite."

She only nodded, throwing her wrap around her shoulders as she stood up. She felt a strange tingling at the back of her neck as she and Jim started out of the Club. It wasn't until they were outside that she dared dart a glance backwards to see Curry staring after them. She kept her face carefully averted and followed Jim to the parking lot.

"The damned high-handed son of a . . ." Jim was muttering as they pulled up in front of the ranch house after a light supper at a restaurant smaller than the club.

"Don't strain yourself," Eleanor said with forced lightness. "Curry isn't worth it, he really isn't."

"Now will you come work for me?" Jim asked flatly.

She nodded. "Just give me a day or two to work out the details and give Curry his two weeks' notice."

"All right. Norie, I'm so sorry you had to hear that," he said gently, brushing the hair away from her flushed cheeks.

"I'm not. I only wish I'd known three years ago," she said miserably. "Goodnight, Jim."

"Goodnight, Cinderella. I hope the ball wasn't too bad."

She kissed him on the cheek. "The handsome prince wasn't bad at all," she teased as she got out of the car. "I hope your young lady gets jealous enough to call you up and propose."

"She might at that, you lovely creature. Goodnight!"

She watched him drive away with a feeling of loss, of sweeping aloneness. With a sigh, her dreams shattered, her hopes in

ruins, she turned and went into the house and up to her room.
And she cried herself to sleep.

In the morning, she put the camouflage back on and went down
to breakfast. Curry had already had his coffee and toast and
headed out to wait for Smith to deliver the new filly, Bessie told
her.

The buxom housekeeper sat down at the table with Eleanor
and sipped her own coffee.

"Came in late last night, he did, must have been four in the
morning," Bessie remarked. "I barely heard him and looked
at the clock. Out with that redhead again, I'll bet."

"With Amanda? Yes, I think so," Eleanor said vaguely.

"She's no country girl," Bessie sighed, cupping her reddened hands around the mug of coffee. "If he marries her, he'll
be sorry. Won't want kids, either, if I don't miss my guess. Too
proud of that slim figure."

"You have to admit, she's the nicest one so far," Eleanor
said tightly, wishing Bessie could talk about something else.

"That isn't saying much."

"She loves him."

"Like fun," Bessie scoffed. "She loves his money, and
maybe she likes the way he is in..." She stopped, flushing.

"Bed?" Eleanor finished for her.

Bessie shrugged her heavy shoulders. "None of my business."

"None of mine, either," the younger girl said with a smile.

She went into the living room and sat down behind the desk.
She was sorting the correspondence that needed answering
when Curry came into the room.

"Good morning, Jadebud," he said brightly, looking younger than he had in weeks.

She spared him a glance, feeling the wound open up at the
sight of him, and wondered how she was going to break the
news to him. Her heart began to race nervously.

"Good morning," she replied nonchalantly.

His eyes narrowed. "Is something wrong, Eleanor?"

He rarely called her by name. It made her tingle when he said her name like that, but she stiffened and held onto her resolution. "I . . . I wanted to ask you . . ."

"I've got something to tell you, too." He drew out a cigarette and lit it. "Now's as good a time as any. I asked Amanda to marry me last night. She said yes."

3

————— * —————

It was like dying, Eleanor thought suddenly. Just exactly how it must feel to die. The quick, sharp blow vibrating through her body and all of life and love and color draining out in an invisible pool on the floor beside her chair. The cruel words she'd heard last night were nothing compared to this. Nothing!

She knew her face would be pale, but she kept her eyes from showing anything, hoping he was far enough away that he wouldn't see the sudden wounding in her quick pulse and unsteady breathing.

His eyes narrowed. "Didn't you hear what I just told you?" he asked curtly. "I'm getting married."

Her eyebrows went up. "I heard you," she said carelessly, and forced a smile onto her lips. "Give me time, I'm trying to think up some condolences to send to Amanda."

He made a half smile at that, but something was troubling him. It showed in the turbulence of his silver eyes as he studied her through wisps of gray, curling smoke.

"Eleanor," he said quietly, "you won't leave me?"

She licked her pink lips nervously and dropped her eyes to her typewriter. "I . . . I've been trying to find some way to tell you," she faltered, "that I've had . . . another offer."

"You've had other offers ever since I brought you here," he said roughly. "From Batsen, Boster, even from Jim Black. Which one is it? Black?" he asked ominously.

"Yes," she replied calmly, lifting her face to catch the flare of anger in his dark eyes. "Please," she said softly, "I've been here three years. You can't really expect me to stay forever. There's a whole world out there, Mr. Matherson, and all I've ever seen of it is my parents' home and then yours. I've never been out on my own, I've never had the kind of freedom that

you and other people take for granted. I've got to decide what
to do with my life. I can't do it here!"

His eyes narrowed, and she saw his square jaw lock and she
knew she was going to be in for a fight. "You've been doing
it," he snapped. "What's the matter, honey, don't I pay you
enough? Do you think you're worth more?"

He studied her insolently, his eyes whipping over her slender
body in the shapeless dress as she rose to stand unsteadily beside the desk. "My God, you wouldn't bring five dollars on
auction, you little chicken! What do you think you're going to
find out there, some man blind enough to want you?"

Nothing, ever, had hurt her as much as those last cold words.
It was just Curry, furious and meaning to hurt, to get even. But
that didn't register, not on top of what she'd overheard last
night. She felt as if he'd put a knife into her and twisted it. She
couldn't stop the tears that welled hot and flooding in her eyes.

She turned and walked toward the door, not looking at him,
not speaking.

"Where are you going, you scrawny ostrich?" he growled,
"to hide your head in the sand?"

She opened the door and walked out into the hall, blind to
the appearance of Bessie, who stood there as if she'd been
struck dumb. There had never been a cross word between
Eleanor and Curry, not in three years.

"What about those reservations for my Miami trip, Miss
Perrie?" he said from the doorway of the living room, his voice
harsh and unpleasant.

Eleanor had her hand on the banister and she turned, with
tears running down her cheeks, her slender body shaking with
mingled rage and humiliation.

"If you want the damned reservations, you call for them,"
she told him fiercely. "And you've got my two weeks' notice
right now!"

She whirled, ignoring the shock on his face, and ran upstairs.

She stayed in her room for the rest of the day. All day, without moving from the chair by her window, from which she
could watch the Appaloosas dancing in their paddocks, the

prize black Angus cattle grazing on the meadows that stretched flat and green to the horizon.

She wanted to go downstairs and throw something heavy at the arrogant cattle rancher. Three years of putting up with his temper and his tirades, of standing between him and the whole world, of smoothing his path, making his stupid reservations, sending flowers and cards and gifts to his women, keeping up with his correspondence, being dragged out of bed at two in the morning to write a letter about a bull he wanted to buy. All that, for three years, and in five minutes he'd forced her out of his life. Perhaps, she thought miserably, he'd even done it on purpose.

With his uncanny knack of reading her, it was possible he'd guessed how she felt and was making it easier for her to go. She'd rather have thought that than to have thought he'd cared so little about her that he could insult her so easily.

Chicken. Ostrich. Wouldn't bring five dollars at auction. Find a man blind enough to want her. Her eyes closed on the painful words. He'd never spoken to her like that before. He'd ranted and raved, and lost his gunpowder temper, and growled at her slowness when he was pacing the room waiting for some typing. But he'd never made his remarks personal, he'd never touched her, or tried to. It had been a non-physical relationship from the very beginning. It had been a comradeship. Until today, when he finally decided to tell the truth and let her know what he really thought of her as a woman.

Fighting tears, she reached for the telephone and dialed Jim Black's number.

When he answered, a sob involuntarily tore out of her throat. "Jim?" she asked huskily.

"Norie, is that you?" he asked incredulously, and she remembered that he'd never seen her cry. Very few people ever had.

She fought to control her voice. "It's me. I . . . I've just had an awful blowup with Curry. Could you . . . I shouldn't ask you to come here after what he said last night, but . . ."

"Give me five minutes," Jim said curtly. "He's welcome to try to throw me off the place if he wants to."

The line went dead. With tears still in her eyes, Eleanor sat down at her vanity table and tried to do something about her face. What she saw in the mirror made her angry. The same owlish face, the same screwed-up bun of hair, the same pale and lifeless look. It made her hungry for the different person she'd been last night, when men looked at her and smiled. She'd never known what it was to be admired before, and she found that it was like a drug. She put her mother's scoldings in the back of her mind and went to work.

She tore the pins out of her long hair and let it fall around her shoulders, brushing it vigorously until it began to shine and bounce back in perfect waves. She took off the unsightly glasses and put them aside. She fixed her face with a hint of makeup, the way she had for her date with Jim.

Then, riffling through her closet for something that looked leisurely, she found a patterned green skirt with a solid green terry top that just matched her eyes, and changed into them.

She slipped her feet into a pair of white sandals and went downstairs to wait for Jim, all traces of tears removed, her heart pounding hard because she was unsure of herself, of what she'd say if Curry...

Before she could finish the thought, the door to his den opened and he walked out into the hall, his face hard and lined, his stride uncompromising. She stood there like a slender young statue, dreading the confrontation she knew was yet to come.

Just then, he looked up and saw her, frozen there against the banister, and an expression she'd never seen before swept across his arrogant face.

He looked at her as if he'd never seen her before, at the slender young body whose gentle curves were no longer hidden in shapeless dresses, at the waving dark hair flowing around her shoulders, the green eyes so pale and wide that looked back at him like those of a frightened kitten.

"My God," he whispered in a voice that barely carried to her ears.

She'd never seen Curry shaken, not in all the time she'd worked for him, but he was shaken now. It puzzled her. It even frightened her a little. Her hand clenched on the banister as all the hurtful things he'd said came flooding back all at once.

"Jim's coming for me," she said in a strained voice. "I...I'll make up my time, later," she added unsteadily, "but I've got to go somewhere...." She bit her lip to stem the tears rising in her eyes.

"Eleanor..." he began hesitantly. His eyes glittered over her again, like quicksilver. "I didn't mean what I said to you," he growled, as if the words came hard, and she knew they did. "God knows, I never meant to... Will you come in here and sit down? I've got to talk to you."

She swallowed down the hurt in her throat. "There's nothing left to say," she whispered huskily. "You've already said it all."

"It was you with Black last night, wasn't it?" he asked suddenly. His eyes narrowed as they traced her young face. "I knew there was something familiar about that ramrod-straight little back, but I couldn't place it. My God, why the camouflage all these years? What was it for, Jadebud?" he demanded.

She stiffened at the familiar nickname as she recalled what he'd told Jim last night. "What do you want, Mr. Matherson? Or is it just to... keep my efficiency up?" she added bitterly.

Realization clouded his eyes and he scowled. "You heard every damned word, didn't you?"

"As you say, every damned word," she bit off. "You might tell Mandy I appreciate her taking up for me. She's better than you deserve."

"No doubt," he said quietly, and still he watched her, as if he'd never seen her before. "You never answered me. Why the disguise all this time?"

"You know what my mother was like," she said bitterly. "I don't have to remind you what she thought of painted women who flaunted their bodies. But last night was special, and Jim asked me to... I did it for him because..."

"Never mind," he said curtly. "I can guess. So that's why you're going to work for him. The little girl's got a crush," he sneered, making it sound like a sin. "My God, he's old enough to be your father!"

"You're nearly old enough to be Amanda's!" she returned fiercely.

"There's a difference..."

"I'll bet there is," she retorted, her eyes contemptuous. "If I slept with Jim, there'd be a difference there, too."

"You little tramp!"

She raised her hand and moved forward, but he caught her wrist in a steely grasp before she could connect with his firm, arrogant jaw.

Her pale eyes blazed at him like chips of Colombian emerald. "Don't you ever call me that again," she whispered furiously. "I may deserve some names, but I don't deserve that one, and you keep your foul mouth to yourself, Mr. Matherson!"

His eyes flashed at the green glitter of her own, at the little figure so tense and battle-ready, defying him, and he almost smiled. "You little hellcat," he breathed. "Do you really think you're up to fighting me?"

Something in the way he said it, in the look he was bending down at her, made her go trembly inside.

"I...I'm not afraid of you and a dozen like you!" she said with false bravado.

His darkening eyes dropped to her mouth. "Yes, you are," he murmured. "You were afraid of me the first day you came here. You still are."

"Words don't frighten me, Mr. Matherson," she replied tightly.

"You aren't afraid of anything I might say, or my temper," he agreed. "But," his voice dropped, low and caressing, "you're terrified of me in a physical sense. Or didn't you think I could feel you trembling, Eleanor?"

With a start, she realized that she was, and her cheeks blistered red. With a cry, she tore away from him, and he let her escape, standing there like some proud conqueror, confidence glittering out of his eyes as he pinned her with them.

What might have happened then, she never knew, because the sound of a car purring up the driveway claimed their attention. Eleanor turned and went quickly out the door with Curry right behind her. Jim got out of his big Buick and faced the taller man, his eyes blazing.

"I'm taking Norie out for the day," he told Curry flatly. "If you've got any objections, I'll be glad to listen."

Curry glanced back. "I told you last night that I didn't want you near this spread!" he said in a low, dangerous tone.

"Then I'll send one of the hands after her from now on," Jim replied, "but until she works out her notice, I'll see her every damned day if I want to."

"Then you'd better send one of your boys," Curry replied hotly, "because I'll have you shot if you drive through the gate!"

Eleanor gaped at her boss, barely able to believe what she'd just heard. She'd never seen Curry in such a temper before, nor had she ever heard him make an irrational threat.

"What's the matter, Curry?" Jim probed sharply. "Jealous?"

Curry's eyes caught fire and burned. Eleanor got in the car and slammed the door, her eyes pleading with Jim to let it go before something violent happened. She didn't recognize Curry in this strange mood, and she was afraid of his unpredictability.

"Jim, let's go, let's go now, all right?" she pleaded softly.

With insolent slowness, he slid in beside her. She didn't dare look at Curry as they drove away.

Halfway down the long driveway she breathed a sigh of relief. "I didn't think I was going to get away with it for a minute there. I've never seen him like that!"

"Because he gets his own way most of the time," he said tightly. "Not this time, though. Don't let him put the pressure on you, Norie. He's so damned underhanded, I wouldn't put anything past him."

"Curry's not . . ."

"He's dangerous," he repeated. "I don't think he'd ever hurt you physically, but we both know what his temper's already done to you. Just take it slow and easy, all right? Don't press your luck."

Eleanor wasn't sure that she believed him, but she nodded to be agreeable. She was too tired to argue.

"Norie," he said gently, catching her eyes as she glanced toward him, "what did he say to you?"

She shifted uncomfortably and gazed out the window instead of looking at him. "Too much, and I'd rather not talk about it now, okay?"

"Sure, hon," he agreed quietly. "If you'd rather not go back at all . . ."

"I would, but I gave my word, Jim." She sighed. "I can't go back on it, no matter how much I might like to. It's not my way."

"Stubborn little Texas mule," he chuckled. "Tough as old boots, aren't you?"

On the outside, at least, she thought, but she laughed anyway and saw the light come back into his grim face.

They rode around looking at crops for a while—it was one of Jim's favorite pastimes, and Eleanor enjoyed the feel of the big car as it took the bumps almost imperceptibly. She felt good as she looked out at the green young cotton and peanuts scattered over miles and miles of flat land spreading out into the horizon. She loved this land, from its cities to its bastions of history. It was in her blood like a silver thread.

It was almost dark when Jim took her back to his ranch, the Rolling B, and ushered her into the sprawling one story frame house. His 13-year-old son, Jeff, was sitting at the kitchen table with Jim's sister, Maude, who doubled as housekeeper and looked as if she could outdo any two men with her big frame and piercing dark eyes.

"About time you got back, we've been waiting supper," Maude told Jim with a sly wink at Eleanor. "Sit down, both of you, and we'll dig in."

Jim sat down grimly and picked up his napkin. He said grace with a strange curtness and started to fill his plate with mashed potatoes, steak, green beans, tomato slices and fresh corn.

"Last time I saw him look like that," Maude observed, "Ned King had outbid him for a black stallion he had his heart set on."

"It's my fault," Eleanor explained. "I had an awful fight with Curry and he rescued me."

"About time," Maude grinned. "I'm proud of you."

Eleanor blinked at her. "Why?" she asked bluntly.

"You've been letting that man walk all over you ever since I first met you. It's time he found another carpet. That Amanda person ought to do nicely," she added tartly.

"You had a fight with Curry?" Jeff asked excitedly, and Eleanor noted with a smile that he had his father's dark eyes and prominent nose.

"I did," Eleanor admitted.

The boy's eyes widened. "Did you paste him one?"

"Jeff!" Maude scolded.

"Well, I just wanted to know, I never saw anybody hit Curry who didn't end up with his nose rearranged." Jeff laughed.

"Boys!" Maude burst out. She paused, peered curiously at Eleanor, and leaned forward. "*Did* you hit him?"

"No, but I tried to," Eleanor admitted with a tiny grin.

"I wanted to hang one on him, myself," Jim broke in, as he swallowed down a gulp of his iced tea. "Damned, hard-headed bull! He ordered me off the place and threatened to shoot me if I ever set foot on it again."

Maude's eyes popped. "Curry Matherson said that? The man's sick! I've never known him to threaten anyone!"

"Oh, we've had our rivalries," Jim admitted, "but it was always friendly until now. You know, I think he's jealous of me taking Eleanor out. He acts like she's his personal property."

Eleanor blushed furiously. "He just hates not getting his own way," she protested.

"You didn't see the way he was looking at you when you got into my car," Jim countered. "I did. I know that look in a man's eyes, and I don't like it in Curry's. He's too damned underhanded when he wants something, and right now, he's got his mind set on keeping you. God only knows what he might do...."

"I can take care of myself," Eleanor returned.

"Like Bambi," Jim growled, and his big, dark eyes narrowed as they looked into hers. "Curry's dangerous."

"I promise you he won't poison me," she said with a half smile.

"Poison is the least of my worries. Norie, we're friends, aren't we? Then from one friend to another, get out while you can. Let me go get your bags...."

"Jim," she said, stopping him mid-sentence. "You're my friend, and I appreciate your concern. But I promised to work out a two week notice, and I'm going to do it if it kills me. I'm not afraid of Curry."

"I'm afraid for you," he persisted. "You're just a babe in the woods."

Her pale green eyes fixed on him. "You're serious, aren't you? But, Jim, you can't possibly think ... after all, he's engaged to Amanda."

"Curry? Engaged?" Maude broke in. "He must want that redheaded scarecrow pretty bad to marry her."

"Watch what you say in front of the boy," Jim growled.

"Why? He's almost fourteen," Maude replied, "and he probably already knows more than you want him to."

"Curry's fond of Mandy," Eleanor said, taking up for the girl.

"But he doesn't love her," Maude came back hotly. "I've heard him say a hundred times that he'd never let any woman tangle up his heart the way his mother tangled his father's. The old man killed himself when his wife divorced him, you know."

Eleanor nodded, sipping at her tea. "It's something he's never talked about."

"Probably because it hurt too bad. No, Miss," Maude said with set lips, "you'll never see Curry in love with a woman. But if he wanted one bad enough and couldn't get her any other way, he'd marry her. And don't you think that redheaded hussy doesn't know it! She's got about as much place on a ranch as I have in Saks Fifth Avenue!"

"Doing what, scrubbing floors?" Jim teased. "By the way, did Anderson call me back about that auction over in Alabama?"

And with the shifting of conversation, Eleanor was able to sit back and relax and stop thinking about her incorrigible boss. For the time being, anyway. And she dreaded going back to the ranch more with every second that passed.

4
*

She stayed at the ranch with Jim and his family until late, and when Jim suggested that they stop by the local disco for a drink, she was all eagerness.

The music was loud and throbbing and made her bones go weak. Around them people were laughing and enjoying themselves, and Eleanor felt some of their gaiety chasing her grimness away. She'd never had more than a sherry before, but she persuaded Jim, against his better judgement, to buy her her first whiskey sour. The strong taste and smell of it was dampening at first but she found that the more she drank of it, the better she liked it. Her face began to brighten up. Her muscles began to feel loose. And all at once, all her cares and worries dissolved into music and laughter.

By the time they left the bar, Eleanor was singing the "Yellow Rose of Texas" at the top of her lungs.

She was still going strong when they reached the ranch house. Jim pulled up in front of the two-story white structure, with its lights blazing ominously.

"Eleanor, I can't let you go in there like this," Jim said grimly.

"Sure you can!" she exclaimed with a hiccup and a smile. She struggled with the door handle and spilled out into the night with a little laugh. "Oh, I'm *soooo* relaxed!" she told him.

He got out, too, and, taking her arm, escorted her up the steps onto the porch, just as Curry came out the door. His silver eyes were blazing, his hair was rumpled by his restless fingers, his tie was off, his shirt was unbuttoned—he was the picture of impatient waiting.

"It's about damned well time you got home," he growled at Eleanor, who grinned at him.

"She wanted a whiskey sour," Jim explained wearily. "I never should have . . ."

"Hell, no, you never should," Curry cut at him. "Did you bring her straight here?"

Jim's lips compressed. "One more remark like that and I'll deck you!" he said flatly.

Curry reached out to take Eleanor by the arm. "I'll have Bessie look after her," he said. "Don't let your engine get cold."

Jim glared at him. "Lose your shotgun?" he challenged quietly.

Curry took a deep breath and his eyes narrowed. "We both know you got to her in a moment of weakness or she'd never have agreed to leave me. Don't expect any favors. And I wouldn't make any dates with her, she's going to be damned busy for the next two weeks," he added meaningfully.

"All the same," Jim replied with a cool smile, "If she calls me to come after her, I'll come, and you can damned well do your worst. Goodnight."

Without a word, Curry pulled Eleanor into the house and slammed the door behind them.

Eleanor pulled weakly against the lean brown hand that was strangling her wrist as Curry dragged her up the stairs.

"Let me go!" she protested, coming out of the stupor the unfamiliar alcohol had caused.

"When I get you sober," he agreed curtly. "You're going to get a bath, little girl."

"I had a bath already," she replied haughtily.

"Not the kind you're about to get. Bessie?" he called loudly. When there was no answer, he yelled louder, "Bessie!"

"I'm coming, I'm coming, I only have two legs and I'm using both of them as fast as I can!" Bessie grumbled as she ambled up the stairs behind them, finally catching up in Eleanor's blue and white bedroom.

"Lord, what's the matter with her?" she burst out, when she got the first look at the younger woman's tousled hair and glazed eyes. "She don't look like Eleanor. Where's her glasses? Her clothes look . . . Are you sure that's Eleanor?" she asked in a low, curious voice. "Where'd you find her?"

"Crawling out of Jim Black's car like a misbehaving pup," Curry said gruffly. "Put her in a cold tub and get her sober," he added with a malicious glance at Eleanor, who was hanging onto a bedpost for dear life and glaring at him.

"But the poor child will freeze!" Bessie protested.

"If you don't do it," he said with a flash of intent in his silvery eyes, "I will!"

"Of all the unconventional things!" Bessie caught Eleanor by the arms and shuffled her off toward the bathroom. "Come on, child, I'll save you."

"Couldn't you save me," Eleanor asked dizzily, "without the cold bath?"

Bessie only laughed. "You know Mr. Curry doesn't make threats. Besides, it'll all be over in just a few minutes and I'll tuck you in and bring you some aspirin and a cup of nice, hot chocolate."

"What," Eleanor mumbled, as Bessie started unzipping the terry top, "do I need aspirins for?"

By the time Bessie got her numb body into a gown and into bed, she knew with painful clarity what the aspirins were for. Her head was throbbing and she felt vaguely nauseated just at the thought of the whiskey she'd put away. She knew without being told that she really was going to hate herself in the morning.

Curry came in just as Bessie went out, after leaving hot chocolate and aspirin by Eleanor's bedside. He leaned nonchalantly against a bedpost to stare at the white-faced little ghost in the big bed, her black hair swirling untidily around her shoulders.

"Feel bad?" he chided with a straight face, but his silver eyes sparkled with amusement.

"I feel terrible," she said in a whisper, managing to take a sip or two of hot chocolate. She felt dizzy, and sick, and her head pounded.

"How about another whiskey sour?" he asked.

She glared at him with narrowed green eyes. "I hate you," she said levelly.

"Why? I didn't get you drunk."

"Neither did Jim, so don't you blame him," she told him.

"Why, baby?" he asked quietly.

She glanced up at his dark, somber face, and let her eyes fall to the white coverlet. "Do I need a reason?"

"I think so. I've never seen you drink before." He jammed both hands in his pockets. "Was it what I said to you, Eleanor?" he asked, his eyes darkening. "God knows, I've got a hair trigger temper, but I never meant to say those things to you. Damn it," he growled, running a hand through his dark hair, "I don't want you to go! There's no reason in the world why you can't stay on, even after Mandy and I get married! The two of you like each other."

Men, she thought, miserably, were the densest substance God ever created.

"I'd still rather go," she said stubbornly. "Jim needs me more than you do, now."

His eyes narrowed even more, dangerously glittering. "What for? To do his typing, or to..."

"Don't you say it, Curry Matherson!" she dared, knowing what would have come if she hadn't interrupted him.

"You little prude," he taunted, his eyes studying her slender body outlined under the bedclothes. "Hasn't the relationship progressed to that stage yet? My God, how has he been able to keep from dragging you off into the woods? The way you look with your hair down like that, and those ridiculous glasses off..." He frowned. "Or is all that sensuality just on the outside?"

She blushed at the look in his eyes. He made her feel threatened, uncomfortable.

"Why did you threaten to shoot him?" she asked.

He shook his head. "I don't know," he said honestly.

She dodged his piercing eyes and took her aspirins, swallowing them down with the sweet, rich hot chocolate.

"Stay, Eleanor," he said quietly, his hands jammed into his pockets.

She looked up. "I can't," she said simply. "Not after what I heard you say. I'd never be able to forget it. Not when I know what you really think of me," she added in a pained, husky young voice.

"Do you know?" he asked, and there was something dark and quiet and unfamiliar in his eyes. "Do I?"

She felt a kind of electricity burn between them as she noticed for the first time that the coverlet had slipped down to reveal the wealth of bare, silky skin where the thin spaghetti straps of her pink nightgown clung to the soft curves of her breasts. His eyes had traced those straps down, and he was looking at her in a way he never had before—a look so adult and masculine that it made her fingers tremble as they jerked the coverlet back up.

He met her shocked eyes levelly. A slow, sensuous smile tugged at his mouth and the glitter of his eyes made her feel vulnerable and weak. He laughed softly.

"You lovely little creature," he mused.

She bristled. "I thought I was a chicken," she said curtly, remembering.

He shouldered away from the bedpost nonchalantly and paused with his hand on the doorknob to look back at her. "Baby chicks are soft and downy and sweet to touch," he observed, grinning at the quick, hot color that poured into her face as he went out and closed the door behind him.

She puzzled over the remark, over the look he'd given her for a long time before she finally slept. It was just as Jim had said, Curry wanted his own way and he wouldn't stop at anything to get what he wanted. He might try flirting, or even something more to keep Eleanor from leaving. She shuddered, remembering that dark, strange flame in the eyes that had traced her body, and wondered if she could resist Curry, loving him as she did. If he ever touched her... She put the disturbing thought out of her mind and rolled over.

She overslept for the first time in three years, and ran downstairs to see if Bessie had kept anything out for her.

"Think I'd let you go hungry because you didn't wake up?" Bessie teased. She took a covered plate out of the oven and put it in front of Eleanor where she sat sipping her hot coffee at the kitchen table. "Here. Saved you some sausage and eggs and grits. Want a hot biscuit to go with it?"

"Yes, please." She looked up at the older woman sheep-ishly. "My head hurts."

"No doubt. Tied one on, did you?" Bessie teased.

"Not exactly. I just wanted to see what a whiskey sour tasted like."

"Found out, didn't you?" she laughed.

"Boss gone out to the field?" she queried.

"No, he's waiting for you to get yourself together enough to take some dictation," came a disapproving voice from behind her.

She flinched visibly as Curry came into the kitchen, wearing his jeans with a blue checkered work shirt half unbuttoned. He poured himself a cup of black coffee and sat down next to Eleanor at the table.

His eyes traced what he could see above the table of her trim figure in a white knit shirt and matching slacks. Her hair was left loose because she didn't have time to put it up, and her glasses were pushed casually on top of her head, giving her a sporty look.

"Looks young, doesn't she?" Bessie smiled, nodding to-ward Eleanor as she set a plate of hot biscuits and some jam on the table.

"Like spring time," Curry agreed. His eyes were warm on Eleanor's slightly flushed face. "Jim's influence, no doubt," he added with a contempt he didn't try to disguise.

"No doubt," Eleanor agreed sweetly, reaching for a biscuit.

His eyes flashed at her. He leaned back in the chair, sipping his coffee, and she braced herself for a storm, because it was building in his eyes.

Bessie must have felt it, too, because she dried her hands on a dishcloth, muttered something about dusting the flowers, and made a dive for the back porch.

"I meant what I said," Curry told her quietly. "I don't want Black on this property again."

"Or you're going to shoot him?" she asked carelessly, dart-ing a nonchalant glance at him.

"I don't have to shoot him," he said quietly. "If you're de-termined to walk out on me, there's a lot of work I need to get through before you pack, and that won't leave much time for socializing." His jaw set and locked. "You can save your plans for when you're on his time. I'm not paying you to play."

Her own eyes narrowed. She glanced back at him. "Since when," she demanded, "have I ever shirked my responsibilities?"

"Since you got yourself tangled up with Jim Black!" he returned.

"I'm not tangled up with him!"

His eyes lanced over her contemptuously. "Aren't you?" he asked insinuatingly.

Her face went dark with anger. She wadded up her napkin and threw it down next to the plate with her half-eaten breakfast, and stood up. "If you'd like to get started, Mr. Matherson?"

"Sit down," he said quietly, "and finish your breakfast. I won't have you passing out from hunger. You're too damned thin as it is."

She tossed back her long, waving hair. "From all my socializing, you know," she shot back. "And I've lost my appetite, thanks to you."

"Keep pushing," he said softly, rising, "and you're going to find out just how far I'll let you go."

"I'm not afraid of you," she said defiantly, turning to leave the room.

"Yet," he said as he followed her out, and the hard spoken word had an ominous sound.

They worked in a strained silence for the next hour. He leaned back in his chair at the desk and dictated letter after letter while Eleanor pretended a calm she didn't feel and managed just barely to keep up with his ruthless, deliberate speed. Every once in a while, she'd feel his eyes studying her, watching to see if he was getting her rattled. It was new, fighting Curry like this. Exciting, but very unnerving. The old comradeship had disappeared forever. Overnight they were adversaries, it seemed.

"Got that?" he shot at her when he finished the last letter.

"Yes," she replied sweetly. "Disappointed?"

His jaw clenched. His face hardened, and he started to rise with a hint of violence that made her heart leap when the door opened suddenly and Amanda breezed in wearing a jaunty gray pantsuit with a white silk blouse.

"Good morning, darling." She smiled at Curry. "Hi, Eleanor!" she added pleasantly.

"Good morning," Eleanor replied, lowering her gaze as Amanda slid her thin arms around Curry's towering neck and reached up to kiss him.

"Eleanor?" Amanda turned abruptly, her eyes wide and disbelieving as they fixed on the young girl who sat in the dowdy spinster's place at the table beside Curry's huge desk. "Is it you?" she whispered.

"It is," Curry smiled maliciously. His eyes narrowed on his secretary's face. "Jim's handiwork," he added.

Something in Amanda relaxed at the words. "Romance in the air?" she teased.

"Maybe," Eleanor agreed cautiously.

Curry turned away. "Let me make a phone call and I'll take you down to the corral with me and show you how we brand the cattle."

Eleanor could have sworn Amanda's complexion went two shades lighter.

"Branding? But, Curry, darling," she purred, following him to place a pleading slender hand on his hard muscled arm. "I had my heart set on driving into Houston today."

"We'll go later," Curry told her inflexibly. "I can't take the time this morning. You know what we go through with roundup."

"No I don't, actually, and I'm not at all sure I want to learn." Amanda laughed nervously. "I don't like all that dust, and, darling, cattle smell so."

Curry's jaw clenched hard. "You'll get used to it."

Amanda looked resigned. "Perhaps. At least, after we're married, I can go to Houston and get away from it," she teased. "I'll keep my apartment and we can spend weekends there."

Curry didn't say anything, but his dark face was stormy. He dialed a number and waited. "Terry? I'm going to need you this afternoon if you can make it. I've got a new shipment of heifers and I want them all checked before I turn them in with the herd. You can? Thanks. See you about one.''

He hung up, and Eleanor knew immediately that he'd been talking to Terry Briant, the local vet. She smiled. Terry was a confirmed bachelor, a little crusty around the edges, but he knew his job and he was well liked in the community. He'd come for Curry, but this was one of the busiest times of the year for him, and he wouldn't have made room for many people in his schedule.

''All right,'' Curry told Amanda, grabbing up his battered wide-brimmed ranch hat and propelled her out the door. He didn't bother to spare a glance for Eleanor, a deliberate omission that cut her. Curry could be the very devil when he wasn't getting things the way he wanted them. And, Eleanor thought doggedly, this was one time he wasn't going to win, no matter how hard he put on the pressure.

For the next two days, Eleanor did her job with robot-like precision, ignoring Curry's temper and impatience with a stoic calm that she was far from feeling. It was on the third day that things seemed to come to a head.

It had been a long day, and Eleanor was sitting in the porch swing with the phone in her lap talking to Jim Black when Curry came in from the fields where he'd been checking on the haying.

''Jim, I've got to go now,'' she said as Curry came up the steps.

''When am I going to see you?'' Jim asked pointedly.

''Maybe this weekend. I'll phone you. Goodnight.'' She hung up before he could answer and got up long enough to put the phone back on the table by the settee before she curled back up in the porch swing.

Curry paused on the edge of the porch, leaning against one of the white columns to light a cigarette. He pushed the hat back away from his dark face and studied her through glittering eyes. The subdued light from the single fixture farther down the porch gave him a faintly satanic look. He looked as if it had been an unusually hard day. His shirt was completely unbuttoned and dark with sweat stains. His khakis were stained with grass and dirt. There was a cut on the back of one lean brown hand where blood had dried. And his face was heavily lined. He looked every year of his age.

"Talking to Jim?" he asked carelessly.

"I am allowed to do that, I suppose?' she asked sweetly.

He glared at her. "When you're on your own time," he agreed. "Did you finish those letters I dictated?"

"Every last one," she said cheerfully. "I did the production reports on the new additions, too."

"So efficient, Miss Perrie," he drawled with underlying sarcasm. "How will I live without you?"

"You could live without anybody." she said quietly. "You're as self-sufficient as a Marine."

"I was a Marine, little girl," he reminded her.

"Poor Amanda," she murmured. "She'll never really feel needed at all."

"She'll feel needed, all right," he said in a caressing undertone, and with a smile full of meaning.

She flushed uncomfortably. "No doubt," she said curtly, "but will it be enough?"

He laughed deeply. "Don't you know the answer to that?"

It was a losing battle, and she knew it. She rocked the swing into motion, turning her attention to the dark silhouette of the trees in the yard, the insistent chirp of the crickets.

"Mr. King called today, by the way," she said carelessly. "He said the plans for your new office complex had been completed by the architect and were ready for approval."

"Has Magins signed the property transfer?" he asked.

"Of course," she replied.

His eyes narrowed as he took a long draw from his cigarette. "You never cared for my tactics, did you, honey? But they work. No man ever got anywhere in big business without being just a little ruthless."

"I can't picture Jim being that way," she said quietly. And it was true, she couldn't. He was a gentleman, a caring man. Worlds away from Curry.

"He'll never amount to a damn, either," he said harshly. "That spread will never be any bigger than it is right now because he doesn't have the ambition to grow. He'll live comfortably, but he won't have much to show for his investments."

"Good for Jim," she flashed, defending him. "It's nice to find a man now and again who's satisfied with what he's got!"

"Just what has he got, Eleanor?" he asked quietly. "Charm? Sophistication? Personality? Or is he just good in bed?"

She'd never felt such rage in her life. She trembled with it as she got out of the swing and walked past Curry toward the screen door.

"I won't take that kind of insult from you or anyone else," she said icily. "You aren't going to grind your heel into me."

His lean hand shot out suddenly, grasping her upper arm so hard that she could feel it bruising, and jerked her around. She felt the heat of his body at his nearness, smelled the fragrance of tobacco mingled with the masculine odor of sweat as he held her there under his glittering eyes.

"You're getting damned sassy, little girl, and I don't like it," he said in a voice that cut. "You may stab Black with that sharp little tongue, but don't think you can get away with it here. Nobody backtalks me, not on my land."

"Oh, no, they wouldn't dare," she returned, even though the effort to talk was choking her. "Mr. God Almighty Matherson doesn't take anything from anybody!"

"As you're about to find out," he said ominously. The half-smoked cigarette went flying out into the yard, and both lean, steely arms went around her slender body, crushing her softness against the length of him.

5

*

The sudden, unexpected contact made her panic, and she fought him, struggling to put distance between them, to escape those arms that felt like steel bands, the crush of his chest hurting her.

"Let me go!" she cried wildly.

"Make me," he said in a voice she couldn't recognize.

She threw her head back and looked up at him defiantly, her pale eyes throwing off sparks as she panted with the unsuccessful effort to free herself. Her body felt like metal, stiff and icy, in the first brutal embrace she'd ever endured.

"Did you expect to win?" he demanded, and his eyes burned with suppressed fury. "I could break your young body like a matchstick."

"All right, I'll admit that you're physically superior," she panted angrily, "now will you let go of me?"

"Not until I give you what you've been begging for ever since I came up those steps," he said in a low, dangerous voice.

Before she could ask him what he meant, his head lowered and she felt the crush of a man's lips against her mouth for the first time in her young life.

She stiffened at the hard, moist contact, at the urgent way he was trying to force her lips apart under the warmth of his, at the brutal way he was holding her so that she felt powerless against anything he might do.

He was making no allowances at all for her innocence, her inexperience. He was kissing her with a violent passion, his tongue running along the edge of her trembling mouth, his teeth nipping sensuously at her lower lip as his hands slid down her back to her hips and arched her against him.

A frightened moan broke from her throat. She pushed against his massive chest with all her might, feeling with a sense of terror the cool bare flesh with its light covering of curling hair against her fingers.

He tore his mouth away suddenly and looked straight into her wide, shocked eyes, dark with the fear she was feeling. Her face had gone white and even as he looked at her he felt the shudder race down the length of her body pressed so intimately against his.

The truth registered with a flash in his silvery eyes. "My God, you've never been kissed before!" he exclaimed, as if he couldn't believe what he was saying.

Her lips trembled as she tried to speak. "No, I haven't," she whispered shakenly, "and if...if that's how it feels, I never want to again!"

His arms loosened and she took advantage of the momentary reprieve to tear loose and run. She didn't stop until she reached the safety of her room.

All through the long night, she lived that kiss over and over again. The first time should have had something of tenderness in it, consideration. She'd dreamed of kissing Curry, of being kissed by him, but that brutal assault was more of a nightmare than a dream.

He'd meant it as a punishment, and that was what it had been. A way to show her how weak she was, how vulnerable she was to his strength. She'd learned the lesson, but in a way that became more painful with every passing second. What had he thought of her? That she was easy, that she was really Jim Black's woman? Her eyes closed on the harsh memory. Perhaps he had thought that, until he kissed her. A man with Curry's experience would hardly mistake a novice's reaction to his passion. She remembered with a tremor just how expert his demanding mouth had been. She wondered what it would have been like if she'd relaxed against his hard body and let him teach her how it could be between a man and a woman. But playing tutor to an inexperienced girl wasn't in Curry's line, and pleasuring her had been the last thing on his mind. He had Amanda for pleasure, and Eleanor, temporarily, for business.

The only thing that didn't make sense was why he'd chosen that particular way to get back at her. Curry wasn't the kind of man to experiment, or amuse himself with an unsophisticated woman. And it wasn't his usual method of revenge, either. But Eleanor had never fought with him until the past few days. She'd always given in with a smile and gone along with whatever ruthless plan he devised with that brilliant, innovative mind of his. Now, things were different. She was fighting back, and he didn't like it, and he was using the only weapons he had.

She turned her face into the pillow, feeling its coolness drain some of the heat out of her face. Why couldn't she have fallen in love with Jim Black? He was so much more her type; gentle and kind and caring. Not at all like Curry. Curry would burn a woman alive and leave her in ashes. It was his nature. And now, more than ever, she prayed that the last days of her employment would go quickly, before he had a chance to wound her even more.

He was already out on the ranch when she finished breakfast and went to work the next morning. It was as if he couldn't face her—a ridiculous thought which she promptly dismissed. Curry never backed away from a confrontation of any kind, and he wouldn't be the least bit embarrassed or self-conscious about what he'd done last night. Before he was through, he'd even find a way to make it look as if she'd tempted him to do it.

Amanda came by unexpectedly at lunch time, looking for Curry.

"He promised to drive me into Houston today," the model pouted when Eleanor said she hadn't heard from her boss. "I'd been looking forward to lunch in a nice, quiet restaurant."

"Bessie never minds setting another place, you know," Eleanor said with kindness in her voice as she smiled at Amanda.

Amanda smiled back, her eyes puzzled at the change in Curry's secretary. "You look so different," she said involuntarily. "Younger, more alive. Is Curry right, are you interested in Jim Black?"

Eleanor shifted uncomfortably. "He's a very nice man," she admitted. "And a lot of fun to be with."

"A lot older than you, though," Amanda probed.

"He's only thirty-four," she reminded the redhead. "A year younger than Curry Matherson."

Amanda frowned. "You never call him Curry, do you? It's always his full name, or Mr. Matherson."

She shrugged with a smile. "He's my boss. I'd feel terribly uncomfortable calling him by his first name."

Amanda shook her head. "How you could work with him year after year and keep it strictly business is beyond me," Amanda said as she perched herself on the edge of Curry's desk and lit a cigarette with long, tapered fingers. "Or is that why you wore that awful disguise, to keep things businesslike?"

That rankled, but Eleanor let it pass. "My upbringing didn't allow for frivolity of any kind," she said. "But when Jim asked me to dress up for him . . ."

Amanda smiled with what looked like relief. "You couldn't resist, I suppose." She laughed. "Curry said that was you with Jim the night we were in the club. How awful for you to have to sit there and hear what Curry said about you."

"It was . . . pretty awful," she agreed quietly. "Thanks for defending me, anyway."

"My pleasure, men can be such beasts. Is that," she probed further, "why you gave him notice?"

"Part of it was. We had a terrible argument the next morning," she admitted. "He . . . he said some pretty rough things about me. I suppose, added to what I'd overheard, it was really the last straw. And Jim's been trying to get me over to his place for over a year. I finally gave in."

"He has a son," Amanda said.

"Jeff. He's fourteen, and the image of his Dad," she laughed. "And Maude, Jim's sister, keeps house for them. She's quite a lady."

"Sounds like a ready-made family," Amanda remarked. She took a draw from her cigarette and blew smoke out of her perfect, red mouth. "Children are the one problem I'm going to have with Curry. I can't risk a pregnancy for quite a few years if I'm to go on working, and I can't give up modeling. I've worked too hard, too long, to get where I am."

"You're very good at it," Eleanor said genuinely.

Amanda smiled lazily. "It's demanding, and it gets rough, but I love every second of it."

"You couldn't take time off for a baby?" Eleanor asked.

"Babies give me goose bumps," the model said drily. "I'm twenty-five, you know. And I've only got a few years left in modeling before the wrinkles start to show too much. Diapers and tears are a poor trade for spotlights and the salary I draw. Curry will understand. We'll both have to make a few compromises, but it won't be a bad marriage."

Curry didn't make compromises, but apparently Amanda hadn't found that out, yet. Eleanor had a feeling she would before very much longer.

"You must love him very much." Eleanor smiled.

"Love, my child, is highly overrated." Amanda laughed. "I'm fond of Curry, but I want him more than I love him. And he wants me. And," she added with narrowed eyes, "the day he puts the right ring on my finger, he'll get me; not before." Her gaze flicked to Eleanor's stunned face. "Shocked, darling? It's the only way any woman's going to land Curry. He isn't the love-forever-after kind. He's a virile, sensuous man who wants a woman to match that volcanic passion of his. I've held him off so far, but it won't take much longer, and I'll have him in the palm of my hand."

"You make it sound . . . cold." Eleanor frowned.

Amanda shook her head. "It isn't. I'll give Curry everything he wants, and in my own way, I'll care about him. But he doesn't really need a loving, possessive wife—he's too damned independent. He needs a woman in his bed occasionally who'll leave him alone the rest of the time, and I can give him that. Very few women could live with him on those terms, and you know it. A woman who loved him would literally smother him to death. I won't."

Grudgingly, Eleanor had to admit that the model was right. Curry wouldn't like possession, or being clung to, or depended on. He was so independent himself that he wouldn't want a woman who wasn't the same way. The thought made her sad. It wasn't really much of a future.

"Oh, darling, there you are!" Amanda said suddenly, crushing out her cigarette as Curry came into the den, freshly showered, his hair still damp. He looked like a fashion plate in the gray suit that just matched his eyes. "I thought you'd forgotten," Amanda teased, hugging him.

"I don't forget much, baby," he said with a half smile. He glanced toward Eleanor, who was avoiding his eyes with a vengeance.

"Have you got enough to keep you busy until I get back from Houston?" Curry asked Eleanor with an edge on his voice.

"Of course," came the calm reply. Still she wouldn't meet his eyes, feeling her heart running wild just at the sound of his voice as she remembered unpleasantly the last time she'd heard it.

"If you run out of work, you can start updating the files, cleaning out old material," he added gruffly. "I'll want to start fresh when I replace you."

"Yes, sir," she said deliberately, her voice quiet, unhurried, efficient.

She could feel the smouldering anger before she flashed a glance at his face and saw it there. Her eyes fell back to the calendar she was studying.

"Do I have any appointments this afternoon?" he asked.

"No. You have an 8:30 appointment in the morning with that feed salesman from Atlanta," she reminded him.

"Cancel it," he told her. "I won't be back. Tell him I've solved my feed allotment problem by trading around with some of the other ranchers, and I won't need any extra shipments."

"What if I can't find him?" she asked irritably.

"Then, you have breakfast with him, honey, and explain the situation," he said with icy patience. "Wear your glasses and one of those damned sack dresses—it'll thrill him."

Her jaw set and if Amanda hadn't been standing there, she'd have told him in no uncertain terms just where to go. He seemed to read the thought in her spitting green eyes and raised his head arrogantly, slitting his eyes down at her as if he was silently daring her to say it.

"I might just do that," she said sweetly. "I need the practice."

The emphasis on that last word wasn't lost on him, and he looked strangely uncomfortable for an instant before his hard face went impassive again.

"Let's get on the road, baby," he told Amanda, sliding a possessive arm around her tiny waist. "It's a long drive."

"Not the way you drive." Amanda laughed. "Bye, Eleanor."

"Bye," came the soft reply. She almost added a bitter "have fun," but she was a little afraid to push Curry any further. His temper was suddenly unpredictable, and Jim's words came back to her with blunt meaning. Curry was dangerous, all right, and even if she had been a little afraid of him before, it was without any substantial reason. Now, it wasn't, and she wondered how she was going to live through the next few days.

At least he wouldn't be in until late tomorrow; that was something of a reprieve. But he'd be with Amanda, and the thought of them together made her want to cry. In just a little while he'd be married, and there'd be a barrier between them that nothing could break. Tears glimmered in her pale eyes. Three years of loving him, only to lose him to a woman who could only give him passion. He'd never have the son he craved, or anyone to care about him if he got sick, or when he grew old, or...

She wiped away the tears. It was none of her business anymore. She had a life of her own to pursue, and it was, she told herself, time to get on with it. She had to make plans. She had to map out a life for herself. And it was going to take some doing to decide if Jim Black was at the end of her path, or if she needed to put more than ten miles between herself and Curry Matherson.

Jim called late that afternoon and asked her out to supper at the ranch.

"Oh, I'd love to," she agreed with a smile. "Curry took Amanda to Houston and they won't be back until tomorrow. A whole night and day of blessed peace!"

"Are things that bad over there?" Jim asked suddenly, and in her mind she could see the set of his square jaw and the darkness in his eyes.

She took a deep breath. "Just about," she admitted finally.

"I'll be over in an hour and a half," he told her. "It'll take that long to scrub off the mud."

"Mud?" she queried.

He chuckled softly. "Remember that sorry old Brahma bull of mine I've been trying to pawn off on the rodeo boys?"

"How could I forget him?" She laughed.

"Well, I finally convinced Bubba Morris that he could shed any rider who was fool enough to climb up on his back, so I was throwing a rope on him while the boys got the trailer back up to the corral."

"There was a mudhole," she guessed.

"From last night's rain," he agreed.

"And the bull pulled harder than you did."

"Lady, you read my mind. Never fear, the headache's gone now, and I hope some mean-tempered cowboy rips his gut open for him."

"Sadist," she teased.

"What did Curry take Amanda all the way to Houston for?" he asked suddenly.

"Lunch."

"Why didn't they go to San Antone; it's closer," he said, abbreviating the name of the well-known Texas city affectionately, because, it was said every Texan had two homes—his own and San Antonio.

"I don't know," Eleanor told him. "I guess she wanted to look in on her apartment or something. She's been staying with a friend for the past two weeks, over in Victoria."

"Bad time for Curry to be away from the ranch, what with roundup coming on," Jim remarked. "He's got a hell of a lot of work ahead of him. It's no easy thing to move that many cattle from winter to summer pasture, and brand them, and check them, and spray them..."

"Don't tell me, I know all too well," Eleanor sighed. "Whose shoulder do you think they cry on when Curry's out of earshot? Sixteen hour days, no time off, hurting feet, no booze because Curry won't let them drink on roundup, machinery breaking down...I've heard it all, and I will again. But I understand Curry to say it was already going on; he invited Amanda down to watch the branding."

"Of those new ones he just bought, probably," Jim reminded her. "I'll bet he called Terry over to check them and give them their shots at the same time."

"That's right, he did," she replied. "Oh, gosh, I knew things were going too smoothly. I've got to live through roundup before I get out of here!"

"If we broke your leg, you wouldn't be any more use to him," he said thoughtfully.

"Oh, no," she returned. "I need both legs to keep out of his way!"

"What's he been up to, Norie?" he asked darkly.

"Just his usual incorrigible temper," she lied calmly. "I'd better get off this thing and get dressed. Want to go back to the club tonight and give the lady another charge?" she grinned.

He paused. "Why not? Let her see what she's missing." He chuckled.

Jim was more outgoing than usual, and Eleanor found herself laughing as she hadn't in weeks. The Club was crowded, but not so much so that she couldn't see Jim's pretty blonde shooting curious glances their way.

"She's hooked," Eleanor told Jim, darting a glance toward the blonde two tables over. "I'm getting vicious green-eyed looks."

"You don't mind?" he asked quietly.

Both narrow eyebrows went up, and she smiled. "If I did, would I be here?"

He smiled back. His dark eyes twinkled. "Isn't she a dream, Norie?" he asked.

"Now, Jim, I'm not that interested in girls," she told him.

"Oh, hell, you know what I mean!"

She laughed. "Yes, she is a dream. For heaven's sake, why don't you ask her out? Are you afraid of her?"

He shifted restlessly in his chair. "I guess maybe I am, a little." He sighed. "I'm not a young man any more, Norie, and I've got a son. There are a lot of women who'd mind that combination."

"And a lot more who wouldn't." She leaned forward. "I dare you."

"Norie, I can't."

"I double dog dare you."

"But, I. . . ."

"I double-double dog dare you."

He threw down his napkin. "That does it, no man alive could refuse a double-double dog dare! But if I come back bleeding, it'll be your fault."

"I'll put on the tourniquet," she promised faithfully.

She watched him out of the corner of her eye as he walked up to the table where the fragile looking blonde was sitting alone and bent over to speak to her. She saw the look on the girl's face, and something inside her relaxed. That beaming, tender look the blonde was giving Jim said more than a volume. Eleanor smiled involuntarily and turned her attention back to her supper.

All Jim talked about on the way back to the ranch was Elaine and how sweet she was and how amazing his luck was that she'd finally agreed to go out with him.

"And what do you mean, finally," Eleanor chuckled. "You never asked her before, you big old shy maverick."

"Thanks, Norie." He sighed. "You'll never know . . ."

"Yes, I do," she protested, "and you're very welcome. What are friends for?"

"To help each other, it looks like." He pulled up in front of the ranch house and switched off the engine. "I only wish there was some way I could help you besides giving you a job."

"I'm fine, Jim, really," she said, twisting her purse in her hands. "Just . . . a little worn, and time will fix that. I may not stay with you for a long time, you know," she added gently. "I'm not sure where I want to go yet. I've never given any thought to a future beyond this place," she said, gesturing toward the Matherson property. "Now, I have to decide what I want to do with my life. You know, I've only just realized that there are things beside ranch work that I could do. I could work for lawyers, or doctors, or I could go back to school. I could even train for an entirely new profession—go to a technical school, or train on the job. The world is opening up for me."

"It won't bother you to leave here?" he asked shrewdly.

She looked down at her darkened lap. "I didn't say that. But time heals most wounds, even the kind Curry Matherson dishes out. I'll live. People do."

He tilted her face up to his eyes in the dim light that came from the front porch.

"Curry's a damned fool," he said quietly. "Amanda will never make the kind of wife he needs. She'll be sick of the ranch in two weeks, and back to Houston to recuperate. Unless I miss my guess, she'll live there and leave Curry here and he'll have to come to Houston just to get to see her. She'll never adapt."

She shrugged. "He loves her," she said simply.

"No, he doesn't. He wants her, which is something you'd have to be a man to understand. It's a kind of burning thirst that usually gets quenched after one good sip. But she'll keep him hanging until the ring's on her finger, and then it'll be too late to go back." He sighed. "Curry's not the kind of man to back out of a deal once he's given his word. That includes marriage. No, he'll stick it out. He's too bullheaded to cry quits."

"It won't be much of a life, will it, Jim?" she asked softly.

"No, hon, it won't. But don't think you can tell him that."

She laughed mirthlessly. "When was the last time *you* tried to tell him something?" she challenged.

"I remember it well, as it happens. It was 1969, and I warned him that if he bought that damned helicopter to use to herd cattle, he'd spend more time maintaining it than he would flying it."

"That was before my time," Eleanor said. "What happened?"

"One of his temporary summer hands got smashed at a local bar and decided to take the thing up at midnight one night."

"Could he fly a helicopter?" Eleanor asked.

"Well, as a matter of fact, he'd only been in one twice. He knew how to start it and how to get it in the air. The only problem," he added with a grin, "was that he didn't know how to get it down. Hit a pine tree, broke off a blade, and came down in the lake. My God, you should have seen Curry when they told him. He hasn't let a drop of alcohol on the place during roundup since. And," he added with a grin, "he's never bought another chopper."

"So that's why he uses the little Cessna," Eleanor remarked.

"That and the old-time ways. They're really better on some ranches." He chuckled.

Eleanor sighed. "Well, I guess I'd better call it a night. It's been such fun, Jim. Thank you."

"Thank you," he said with a smile. "If Curry gives you a hard time, come on over, and hang working out your notice. The Blacks will take care of you good and proper."

"The Blacks," she returned, "are super people—all three of them."

"Now, if you'll help me convince Elaine of that . . ."

"Any time," she promised. "Goodnight."

"Goodnight, Norie."

She went into the house with a dreamy smile, relaxed because Curry wasn't home, content to be alone and decide what she was going to do with herself when the job ended. It wasn't going to be so bad after all. Once she got over the initial jolt of not waking up to see Curry at the breakfast table in the morning, in his den during the hours he had to be inside, on the porch late in the evening when the world was still. . . .

6

*

As she moved through the halls, the grandfather clock chimed twice in a loud, metallic voice. She hadn't realized that it was so late. She'd really enjoyed herself tonight as much from playing cupid as from Jim's company. She had a feeling that Elaine was going to be good for the lonely widower and his family.

"What the hell do you mean coming in at this hour of the morning?" came a loud, angry voice from the doorway of the den.

She froze for an instant, not expecting that, as she tried to decide whether or not she was hearing things. She turned slowly to find Curry leaning against the door, his hair tousled, his eyes glittering like sun on a knife blade, his whole appearance threatening and dark.

"I...we were at the Club," she faltered. "I thought you were in Houston. You said..."

"You don't even look kissed, little girl," he growled, and his eyes dropped to her mouth with its soft traces of lipstick, her hair flowing in soft waves around her shoulders, looking as neat as if she'd just left to go out. "I always suspected he was something of a cold fish. Lida Mae started running around on him barely a year after they were married."

"You don't have any right to talk that way about him," she replied coldly.

"Why not? I'll bet he's been giving me hell behind my back ever since he started taking you out."

Before she could deny it, the flush on her high cheekbones gave her away.

"Come have a drink with me, Jadebud," he said gently, shouldering away from the door facing with a weariness that was so alien it was faintly shocking. "I've had a hell of a night."

She followed him hesitantly into the den and watched him fill two glasses with whiskey and ice, lacing one liberally with water to weaken it. He handed her the weaker drink.

"Sit down," he said, indicating the sofa.

She perched herself on its edge, trying not to cringe when he dropped down beside her and crossed his long legs. The pale brown slacks he wore emphasized the powerful contours of his thighs and he was wearing a cream silk shirt that was partially unbuttoned, and since he never bothered with an undershirt, it left a wide expanse of bronzed chest and curling dark hair uncovered. He looked unbearably adult and masculine, and the sensuality that clung to him like the exotic cologne he wore made her feel like running.

"Don't start tensing up on me," he said roughly, darting a quick glance at her rigid profile. "I've learned my lesson, and I don't have the patience to initiate terrified little virgins into the intricacies of lovemaking. You're perfectly safe, so you can lean back and stop looking like a fawn in the hunter's sights. I won't rape you."

She went red as a beet and sipped at her drink, hating him now as she'd loved him before, wishing she had the sophistication to fight back.

He studied her quietly and a heavy, bitter sigh left him. His lean hand brushed away a thick swathe of hair from her cheek with a tenderness that puzzled her.

"I'm in a hell of a temper. I didn't mean to say that, little girl." He set his drink down and lit a cigarette. "I feel like I've had the floor cut out from under my feet tonight."

She studied her drink, aching with conflicting emotions. "Do you want to talk about it?"

He took a long draw from the cigarette and exhaled a cloud of silvery smoke that almost matched his eyes. "Amanda wants to live in Houston," he said simply.

"She's a top model, Mr. Matherson, her job..."

"Don't call me that!" he said curtly, his eyes pinning her.

"You...you are my boss, what else should I call you?"

"My name is Curry."

She turned her head away from that penetrating gaze, but his hand caught her under the chin and turned her right back to face him.

"My name," he repeated in a low, deep tone, "is Curry."

She swallowed nervously and bit at her lower lip. "All right."

"Well, say it!"

"Curry," she said in a hesitant, frightened tone. She didn't recognize him in this strange mood.

"That's better." He let go and leaned back again, flicking ashes into the ashtray he'd set on the other side of him on the sofa.

"Anyway," she persisted, "you know how much her job means, she's worked very hard to make it as far as she has."

His eyes narrowed, glittered, as they met Eleanor's. "I want a son," he said stubbornly. "At least one, maybe two or three. I want a woman who's here when I need her, who puts me first. I don't want a glossy photograph, Jadebud, I want a flesh and blood woman who'll burn like hellfire in my arms when I make love to her, who'll make sons with me!"

She turned every color of red in the spectrum, feeling herself charred with embarrassment.

"I'm sorry," he said curtly. "I forget sometimes how unworldly you really are, for all that you've spent the past three years in an earthy environment. I've spent my whole life here, and I don't find anything embarrassing or shocking about procreation. It's a natural, beautiful part of living. But you wouldn't know about that, would you, not with a mother as icy as yours was."

"Leave my mother out of this! You don't have the right to sit in judgment on her; no one does."

"After what she did to you?" he demanded, meeting her hot gaze levelly. "My God, it was like kissing a rock, Eleanor!"

She turned her face away from him, remembering with clarity those few painful seconds in his arms when she felt his mouth demanding impossible things of hers. "I'd like to forget that ever happened," she whispered unsteadily.

"Do you freeze up on Black like that?" he asked quietly.

"He doesn't kiss me," she said before she thought about it.

"He what?" he asked sharply.

"I told you before, he's my friend, not my lover, and what right have you got to pry into my life?" she demanded.

He shifted, turning so that one long arm rested across the back of the sofa, and his eyes burned where they touched her.

"Not much, I suppose," he admitted. He ran a lean, brown hand through his tousled hair, and watching it, she wondered how that thick, charcoal-colored hair would feel under her fingers.

"I've been rough on you this week," he said without malice. "I don't even know why, but I seem to want to hurt you lately. Maybe it's for the best that you do go. I've never had a complaint about your work, Eleanor, if that's any consolation. I couldn't have asked for a better secretary."

"Thank you," she said demurely, lowering her eyes to her glass as she took another sip of the fiery liquid. It was beginning to relax her a little and she sighed as she rocked the glass so that the ice clinked.

She made a pattern in the condensation on the cool surface of the squatty container. "Is that all that's wrong with you?" she asked after a minute. "That Mandy doesn't want to live on the ranch?"

He took another deep, harsh breath. "She's trying to move up the wedding," he admitted. "We never discussed a definite date, but now she's pushing for next month. I'll be damned if I like being pushed!"

"She loves you," she said, hurting inside even as she defended the redhead. "Naturally, she's..."

"That isn't it. Something's not right about this whole damned thing, and I'm wearing out my mind trying to figure it. She tried to seduce me tonight," he said frankly. "And she damned near succeeded. I'm so hot-blooded, it was all I could do to get out the door."

"Please, you shouldn't be telling me this....," she protested.

"I've got to tell somebody, damn it, who else is there?" He clenched his fingers around the glass and leaned forward, staring blankly ahead. "I don't know what kind of game she's playing, but I don't like it. She's always said 'no' before. Now, all of a sudden, anything goes. It looks very much as if she wants a guarantee. And she knows I'd never turn back if there was the risk of a child."

She got up and moved to the bar, reaching idly for the whiskey bottle.

"What's the matter, little saint, can't you even discuss adult subjects without trying to climb into an alcoholic haze?" he shot at her.

She froze with her hands on the bottle. "It embarrasses me, if you must know," she said in a choked voice.

"You should have entered a convent, then. How old are you now?" he asked gruffly.

"Almost twenty-one."

There was a long pause. "Twenty?" he asked incredulously.

"I'd just turned eighteen when you hired me," she reminded him.

"You always seemed so much older...but that was part of the disguise, too, wasn't it?" he asked bitterly. "You're young with Black, like a filly just feeling her legs. Yet with me, there's something matronly about you, a kind of reserve...even when I took your mouth that night, you turned to stone against me. And I hurt you, didn't I?" he asked with a strange, sweet tenderness in his deep voice. "I bruised you all over because I couldn't make you give in. Not a very satisfactory introduction to passion, was it, Jadebud?"

She felt a shudder run the length of her body as he brought it all back again. "I didn't know...men got like that," she admitted weakly. "I...I thought the first time it was gentle."

"The first time is usually with a boy your own age who'd be afraid to touch you," he replied quietly. "And, yes, it's usually gentle. But a man...kissing is something entirely different for a man, Eleanor. A tightly closed little mouth becomes a challenge; he needs to taste a woman, not just feel the softness of her mouth against his. It's damned hard to explain," he said finally and with soft laughter. "I suppose it all goes back to the basics, to passion. A man my age likes to arouse a woman more than he likes to simply kiss her, because it usually ends up in a bed. That's one reason I never take out a woman who doesn't already know the score. Until Amanda came along," he added gruffly. "And by the time I realized how innocent she was, I was hooked."

"I still think it will work out," she said in a soothing tone, turning to look at him. He wanted the woman, and if he loved her, all Eleanor wanted for him was to see him happy.

He met her soft gaze and his silvery eyes studied her for a long time, from her face to her slender body and back up again. "You're lovely, little girl," he said softly. "As lovely as a dream, and I can't think of anything I'd like better than to draw you down with me on this sofa and teach you how to make love."

She felt her eyes going wide with fear as she set the glass down quickly. He'd had too much to drink, apparently, and she didn't feel like being a stand-in for the woman he really wanted.

"I . . . I'm very tired," she said quickly, moving toward the door. "And sleepy. And I've got a lot to do tomorrow."

"Afraid of me, Eleanor?" he asked patiently.

She turned at the door, her whole look puzzled and uncertain. "I'm terrified of you, Curry, and that's God's own truth," she admitted. "Please don't make it any harder for me. I don't want to be used, like a toy to amuse you when Amanda's not around. I don't want to be flirted with. I'm your secretary and you're my boss, and if it's going to be any other way than that, then please let me go now. I can't bear being played with," she finished on a pained whisper.

"Honey," he said quietly, "what makes you think I'm playing?"

She whirled and left him sitting there, feeling her heart bursting against her ribs as she made her way quickly up the stairs. And when she finally got into her room and ready for bed, that last gentle question kept her awake for another hour despite the fact that her senses were exhausted.

He was at the breakfast table when she went down only hours later, her eyes still bloodshot from lack of sleep, and she wondered idly why he hadn't gone out with the hands.

His pale eyes shivered over her as she sat down across from him, and a hint of a smile curved his mouth.

"It's about time you crawled out of bed," he told her, sipping his coffee as he eyed her. "I want you to come out with me today."

She stared at him uncertainly. "Where?" she asked.

"Roundup starts this morning."

"Oh!" She couldn't hide the surge of excitement that statement created. Every year she'd begged to be taken along when the first of the cattle were brought in from winter pasture to be moved to summer quarters. New calves were branded, and the vet was around to check for disease. It was the most exciting time of the year on a cattle ranch.

"You love it, don't you?" he asked with narrowed eyes. "Every bit of it, from the branding to the culling, even tossing hay to the horses. Yes, Miss Priss," he nodded at her start of surprise, "I hear what goes on around here. You conned Johnny into letting you feed the horses in the stalls. Or didn't you think he'd tell me?"

"I thought ranch managers were supposed to keep their mouths shut," she grumbled.

"They are—but you're forgetting, I don't keep a ranch manager, I keep an assistant manager. Nobody manages this spread except me," he added.

"As if I didn't know." She sighed. "You manage everybody on it, too, when they'll let you."

"You used to let me," he said.

"I grew up," she said smugly.

"Not quite," he said with a meaningful lift of his eyebrow.

She glared at him across the table. "Maybe it depends on the man, did you ever think of that?"

The smile got deeper. "Or maybe the man just didn't try hard enough. Next time, I won't be so impatient."

Her eyes widened and she dropped them to her plate with volcanic eruptions taking place in her blood. "There won't be a next time," she said firmly, although her voice wasn't quite steady.

"Are you coming with me? You'll have to change. That pretty pantsuit will be ruined if you wear it."

She glanced down at the white slacks and matching top. "More likely it'd turn red," she mused. "Jeans and a cotton shirt okay, boss?"

He smiled at her. "And boots. Got yours?"

"Of course. I do ride, you know," she reminded him.

"I haven't seen you on a horse in two months."

"You haven't looked in six months to see what I was on," she teased.

He didn't smile at that. His pale eyes caught hers and held them for a long time with a searching look that made her forget the blistering heat of the cup in her hand.

Bessie came in noisily with the coffee pot and broke the spell. Eleanor held her cup out with a smile while she fought to calm her stampeding pulse.

"Haven't touched your breakfast," the housekeeper scolded. "He ruining your appetite?" she nodded toward Curry.

"Maybe it's the other way around." Curry grinned, winking at Bessie.

"Well, aren't we in a good mood this morning!" Bessie said brightly as she filled his cup again. "What'd you do, foreclose on somebody?"

"You," he told the buxom woman, "are pushing your luck."

"Not likely. Who'd you find with the gumption to put up with you?" she shot back.

Eleanor smiled. "She does have a point," she put in.

"Look who's talking," Bessie scoffed. "You only just got the good sense to leave after three years of it."

The smile faded as Bessie went out again, and she felt an aching emptiness inside her that breakfast couldn't fill.

"Don't think about it," Curry said suddenly, his jaw set, his eyes somber. "Let's take it one day at a time, honey."

"I'm still going, Curry," she told him gently.

He met her eyes. "We'll see."

"*We* won't see anything," she returned, putting the cup down. "I'm not taking any more orders, and you're not going to bulldoze over me...oh!"

He'd moved out of his chair while she was in midsentence to stand by her chair. All at once his head bent, and he pressed a hard, quick kiss against her open mouth.

"Stop talking and get your clothes changed," he told her. His lean hand ruffled her hair. "I can't wait all day."

He was gone out the door before she could come up with a lucid sentence. Her fingers went involuntarily to her parted mouth. She could still feel the warm, hard pressure against them.

He was on the phone downstairs when she got changed into faded jeans, boots, and a blue-patterned cotton blouse. She'd tied her hair back with a blue ribbon to keep it out of her face and left off her makeup. The prospect of spending a whole day with Curry had been too tempting to turn down, but when she heard him call Amanda's name while he spoke into the receiver, all the color went out of the day for her.

"I told you," he was saying gruffly, "I'm not being railroaded, Amanda. Either we wait until I'm ready, or we call the whole damned thing off. You don't want to? Then what the hell are you doing in Houston?" There was a pause and he cursed under his breath. "You couldn't turn it down? Then stay there. Don't 'oh, Curry' me! I want you like hell, but not enough to let you lead me around like a broken stallion. My terms, Amanda. No ifs, buts or maybes. My terms, or nothing. All right." He sighed roughly. "Maybe the breathing space will do us both good. I'll see you in two weeks, and we'll talk about it. Sure. Bye."

He hung up and stood there staring down at the phone, his hard-muscled body as taut as a stretched rope, running a restless hand through his hair. He looked as if he might explode, and Eleanor hesitated uncertainly on the bottom stair.

As if he sensed her presence, he turned, and his pale, troubled eyes looked full into hers.

"Problems?" she asked softly.

He nodded. His eyes traced her slenderness like an artist's brush. "Take your hair down," he said.

"It gets in my eyes," she faltered.

He moved close, and his lean, brown hands reached up to untie the ribbon, letting the soft waves tumble down. His fingers tangled in the softness gently, touching the warm flesh of her throat through it, his breath coming harder and heavy at her forehead.

"Please," she whispered shakily as his fingers contracted bringing her face up to his suddenly blazing eyes. "Please don't use me to keep your mind off her," she whispered.

His jaw clenched, his nostrils flared. "Is that what you think?"

"It's what I know. I...I couldn't help overhearing." She dropped her eyes, licking her dry lips as she fought to keep her emotional upheaval from showing. "I'm sorry you're upset, but hurting me won't help."

"Would it hurt you?" he asked softly.

She didn't know what he meant, but she was afraid to ask. "Shouldn't we go?"

"Norie, don't be afraid of me," he whispered against her temple, using the familiar nickname for the first time. "Little Dresden china doll, I won't hurt you again, physically or emotionally. Don't run from me."

"I...I'm not running, I just don't want..."

"Don't want what?" he murmured, placing his lips against her closed eyelids. "Let me make love to you."

"No!" She pushed away with all her strength and backed against the wall like a stalked fawn, her pale green eyes enormous in her pale face.

His eyes narrowed painfully. "God, don't look like that!" he exploded.

"You...you make me feel like something hunted," she exclaimed. "Please!"

He whirled with a hard sigh and a muffled curse, running his hand around his neck tightly as if there was an ache in it he couldn't ease.

"Come on, if you're not afraid to ride with me," he growled as he reached for his battered work hat and started out the door.

She followed along behind him, the day ruined, afraid of him as she'd never been. She hesitated on the bottom step as he swung into the pickup and threw the passenger door open for her.

"Well?" he shot at her.

She got in, slamming the door firmly. She couldn't look at him.

"Is it Black? I'd just like to know."

She shifted restlessly, staring at the dash unseeingly. "No," she replied.

"My God, it's like trying to pry a clam open," he grumbled as he started the truck. "All right, forget it!" he said, and accelerated out of the yard.

7

In a stoic silence, Curry drove down to the twin barns where his horses were kept. His face was set, and a cigarette burned forgotten between his fingers. He was so unfamiliar like this, she thought. The old days of friendly banter seemed to be gone forever, leaving only cold silence or anger between him and Eleanor.

She stared at the lush green pastures stretching to the horizon. The river was just visible in rare glimpses through the hardwoods that ran along its banks. Both of the truck's windows were rolled down because Curry didn't bother with air conditioning options in work trucks, and it was blazing hot. She missed the ribbon that would have kept her hair out of her face, and blushed when she remembered how she'd lost it.

Curry unknotted the bandana around his throat and handed it to her. "Tie your hair back with that," he said, as if he'd read the thought in her mind. "It's hot as hell out here."

"Thanks," she murmured. She drew the weight of her hair behind her neck and tied it with a double knot, letting the ends stream down. The bandana smelled of Curry's tart after-shave, and she knew she'd never give it back. It would go into her jewelry box with all the other tiny mementos of him that she'd accumulated over the years; things to be taken out only rarely in the future and looked at through tears while she tried to get used to a world that he wasn't in.

"We'll pick up the horses on the way," he said as he lit a cigarette. "Sure you're up to this, baby?" he added with a half smile. "It isn't pretty."

"I'm not a satin doll, Mr. Matherson," she replied, stung by the sarcasm in his deep voice. "It won't be the first time I've seen cattle branded and castrated."

"No, it won't, will it?" He frowned thoughtfully, handling the pickup easily with one hand as he took it over the rocky pasture and Eleanor bumped and bounced in her seat as it absorbed the rough terrain on its shocks.

"Were you hoping I'd pass out from the heat?" she asked, peeking at him from her long eyelashes.

His eyes flashed over her young face. "Flirting with me, Miss Perrie?" he mused.

She shifted pertly in her seat and looked out the window, her heart throbbing. "Me? I wouldn't dream of such a thing, Mr. Matherson," she replied in her best businesslike tone.

He laughed softly. "Brat."

"Male chauvinist," she countered, loving the easy atmosphere that was reminiscent of earlier, more companionable times.

"Me?" Both dark eyebrows went up as he glanced at her. "Honey, I'm one hundred percent in favor of women's liberation."

"You are?" she asked suspiciously.

He took a long draw from the cigarette. "Dead right. I think we ought to liberate women from housework so they'll have more time to wait on us."

"Incorrigible man!"

His eyes glittered over her soft curves with a familiarity that raised her blood pressure two points.

She moved restlessly. "Would you mind not looking at me like that?" she asked uneasily.

"Yes, I would."

"Curry!" she groaned, his name slipping from her tongue as if she'd always used it.

"That's the first time you've ever said that," he remarked with a quick glance into her eyes. "I like the sound of it."

"It slipped out," she replied tightly.

"My God, do we really need the post-mortems?" he growled. "You make me feel sixty when you call me 'Mr. Matherson.' I'm not that much older than you are."

"Fourteen years," she reminded him.

He stopped the truck in the middle of a rise and let it idle, turning toward her with one long, lean arm across the back of the seat while he studied her thoughtfully. "Does it bother you that much?" he asked.

The look in his silvery eyes did, but she couldn't give him the satisfaction of knowing that. She dropped her gaze to the leather seat between them, to the powerful legs covered in blue denim.

"Why should it?" she asked as coolly as she could.

"Because the emotions you arouse in me lately don't have much to do with dictation," he said bluntly.

That brought her face jerking up. She gaped at him, her lips parted as her breath gasped through them.

"And now that I have your attention," he continued casually, "would you mind not trying to build fences between us for the little time I have left to enjoy the pleasure of your company?"

"I didn't realize it was a pleasure," she told him.

"Neither did I," he admitted. "But, then, we don't tend to appreciate things as much until we're faced with the loss of them, do we? I'm going to miss you one hell of a lot, little girl. I've gotten . . . used to you."

"You make me sound like a habit," she murmured.

"One I could acquire without a great deal of effort," he replied with narrowed, considering eyes as he sat there watching her.

"I'd rather we just left it at a business relationship," she said through taut lips.

"Would you?" he asked gently. "How would you know, Eleanor? I've never made love to you. Not in all that time we've been together. You don't know me in a physical sense."

"Don't I?" she whispered, embarrassed, remembering that night. . . .

He drew a deep, harsh breath. "It wouldn't be like that again," he said gruffly. "I wouldn't hurt you."

She studied her folded hands. "I'm not going to stay, Curry," she said tightly, "no matter what you say or do. You don't have to flatter my vanity. No man would be blind enough to want me, remember?" she added bitterly.

"I said that, didn't I? My God, those horrible glasses and shapeless dresses, that staid personality that clung to you like spiderwebs—would any man have wanted you that way?"

"Probably not," she admitted quietly. "Maybe that was what I wanted, I don't know. I thought what a person was inside was the most important thing, not what he or she looked like on the outside."

"That's true, to a certain extent," he admitted. "But, honey, what's on the outside is what attracts a man to look for what's on the inside, didn't you know?" He smiled mockingly. "A man reacts to the look, smell, taste and touch of a woman, little girl. It's the way he's made. The first thing I noticed about Amanda was the silky way her skin felt under my hands."

Amanda. The sound of her name was enough to put the sun behind a cloud for Eleanor. "She's very lovely," she admitted in a subdued tone. "She'll come around, Curry, if you just give her a little time."

"Eleanor," he asked gently, "are you in love with Jim Black?"

She avoided those searching eyes. "I don't have to answer that."

"I'd like to know." He leaned forward to stub out his finished cigarette. "I don't want to see you hurt, in any way."

"Jim isn't the kind of man to ever hurt a woman."

His head lifted arrogantly. "And I am?" he asked narrowly.

She met his eyes bravely. "Yes," she agreed, "you are. You . . . you don't really like women, I don't think, except in a purely physical way. Love isn't in your book of words, is it, Curry?"

He leaned back against the door to study her. "Neither are unicorns and the tooth fairy, honey," he admitted carelessly. His pale eyes glittered with bitter memory. "You know why I feel that way, don't you?"

She nodded.

"You've never asked me about it," he remarked.

"It wasn't any of my business," she said quietly. "I don't like prying into painful subjects."

"No, Jadebud, you don't," he said, reaching out to smooth a strand of hair away from her dusky cheeks. "I could tell you anything, do you know that? Things I could never tell anyone else. It's always been like that between us."

Her eyes avoided his. "I'm flattered that you trust me."

"Is that all it is?" he asked quietly.

She couldn't answer him, was afraid to even think he meant...

He started the truck and pressed down on the accelerator.

Later, riding over the pasture with Curry brought back childhood memories. Rocking gently on the back of the chestnut gelding he'd given her, Eleanor studied the lay of the land she'd spent her life in.

Texas was a land of contrasts, of desert and green pastures, of mountains and flatland, cattle and high-rise apartments, cattle drives and desperadoes and men in handmade Italian silk shirts.

She breathed in the sweet smell of grass and closed her eyes dreamily as the horse moved lazily and the saddle leather creaked in the bright morning sun. In her mind she could picture the old trail riders punching the herd along the Chisholm Trail, the Goodnight-Loving Trail, all the famous cattle trails that ragged, weary cowboys had followed so many years ago. It was impossible to look around and not feel the sense of history here, the ghostly presence of those rugged souls who withstood the ravages of storm and drought and Indian war parties and rustlers. It excited her to think about the proud history of the land that was her own.

"Where are you?"

Curry's deep voice broke her out of her reveries and she darted a sheepish glance toward him, towering over her on his coal black stallion.

"I was riding on the Chisholm Trail," she confessed.

He chuckled, his good humor returning under the wide canopy of sky and cloud. "You baby," he teased. "How many copies of Zane Grey did you cut your teeth on?"

"The first hundred," she replied. "I loved everything he wrote." She studied his shadowed face under the battered ranch hat he wore. "Curry, did you like Western history when you were a boy—you know, about gunslingers and lawmen and cattle drovers?"

He reined in and crossed his forearms over the pommel. After a moment, he pushed his hat back on his head and studied her in a still, waiting silence. "What made you ask that?" he mused.

She shrugged. "I don't know. I was curious." She turned her gaze back to the horizon. "How much farther is it to where you've got the cattle?"

"A mile or so. Think your backside can take it?"

"I'll live," she replied, easing up and down in the saddle. Her legs would probably feel like twin bruises tomorrow, she thought wryly.

"You're nervous today," he observed as they started moving again.

"Am I? I don't feel nervous," she assured him.

"We've never been alone like this before," he said without looking at her. "Bessie was always around, or some of the hands." He turned his head and caught her eyes. "I could drag you off into the trees and no one could hear you if you yelled your head off," he teased gently, but something dark and dangerous began to cloud his eyes as they swept over her face.

She bit her lower lip. "I'm safe, you told me so," she replied with a confidence she didn't feel. "You didn't have the patience, you said . . ."

He drew a sharp, angry breath. "You've got a memory like a steel trap, haven't you, Eleanor? Do you remember every damned word I've ever said to you?"

"I didn't mean to make you angry."

"Then shut up, and you won't," he said bluntly, giving the stallion its head, leaving her to follow or not as she chose.

Several hundred cattle were raising dust and a lot of noise where they were held in pens connected to a network of chutes that were used to sort them according to age, sex and breed. Two men were herding the cattle from one pen into the chute, yelling and slapping the animals on the rump with their hats to move them along. Another man was on top of the railing of the

chute to keep the animals moving along. Other cowboys strad-
dled a two-way gate that separated calves from cows and steers.

"Noisy as hell isn't it?" Curry laughed as they neared the
pens. "The sorting takes a while, and this is only a fraction of
the whole herd."

"Which herd is this?" Eleanor asked, shading her eyes with
her hat.

"The breeding herd—some of it. We'll run them through
before we even start on the grade cattle."

"I don't envy those men their jobs," she said, shaking her
head. She searched the area. "I don't see Terry," she remarked, looking for the local veterinarian's tow head among
those of the cowboys.

Curry glared over at her. "Isn't Black enough for you,
honey? Or are you just collecting scalps as you go along?"

She wondered at the bite in his voice. "I just wondered where
he was, Curry, that didn't mean I want to assault him while he
vaccinates the herd!"

"He likes you," he persisted.

"Horrible glasses and all," she said with a defiant gleam in
her pale eyes.

He got down off his mount with a quick, graceful motion
and strode over to the corrals.

Terry Briant arrived just after the sorting was completed,
while the men were preparing the branding irons. Eleanor took
a place beside the chutes to watch as the calves were herded into
them and chased down to the metal trough at the end of the
chute and the entrance to the branding corral.

Her ears caught the mingled sounds of cows crying for their
calves, calves bawling in fright, cowboys laughing and talking
in a mingled potpourri of English and Spanish as they coped
with the day's work.

The team at the end of that chute, which included the thin,
blond-headed vet, was experienced and fascinating to watch.
The calf's neck would be clamped in the trough and within one
minute he'd be branded, earmarked, castrated, as most male
calves were, vaccinated and tattooed—all in one smooth oper-
ation. The air was thick with smoke and dust and the smell of
burning hair, but Eleanor had seen this many times before, and

she didn't even flinch as she watched—which seemed to amuse Curry to no end when he glanced at her from the branding corral.

One small sick calf was separated from the rest, and Curry brought it out in his arms.

"It's going on dinner time," he told Eleanor, nodding for her to get on her horse. "We'll have a bite to eat and come back."

"All right." She mounted, taking the reins in her hand and steadying the horse as Curry handed the small calf up to her. She swung it over the saddle horn and smoothed its silky coat with a smile.

"Poor little thing," she cooed. "Going to put him in the barn until he heals?"

He didn't answer her. He was looking up into her face, one hand on the saddle horn, the other on the horse's flank, and she doubted if he'd heard a single word. He just looked at her, his eyes steady and unblinking, with an expression in them she couldn't decipher. They sparkled like diamonds, vibrant, piercing.

"Curry?" she asked softly, unaware of the picture she made with her hair just slightly windblown, her cheeks full of color, her eyes lovely in the sunlight.

"You look right at home," he remarked with a half smile. "As natural on that horse with a calf in your arms as a frontier woman might have looked a century ago."

"Frontier women," she reminded him, "were wrinkled and tough as leather and could outshoot, outdrink, and outcuss their menfolk. And besides, they got married when they were barely thirteen and had twelve kids."

"Would you like to have twelve kids?" he asked.

She looked down at him, her eyes involuntarily tracing his angular face and firm, chiseled mouth, the curve of his dark brows, the thick hair that made tiny waves at the nape of his neck. A man like Curry would have sons as tall and tough as he was, as handsome as himself.

"Green and gray," he murmured thoughtfully as he searched her eyes. "What color would their eyes be?"

"Gray," she said softly, as if she knew.

He jerked his eyes away suddenly. "Let's go."

She blushed to her heels as she realized what he'd been saying, what she'd replied... She watched him swing into the saddle, but whirled her mount before she had to look him in the eye.

They went back to the ranch house long enough to eat the thick ham sandwiches Bessie had waiting, but the silence at the table was unusual to say the least. Bessie kept glancing from one of them to the other, trying to puzzle out what was wrong.

It was almost a relief to get back to the turmoil of roundup, Eleanor thought as they made their way once again to the holding pens on fresh mounts.

The strain between Curry and Eleanor was almost tangible. Even the busy ranch hands seemed to sense it. There was an ominous feel about the afternoon as calf after cow after steer was run through the gate into the branding corral. It all went smoothly until one big, enraged Hereford bull managed to escape the men and tear his way into the branding corral without being snared.

Bill Bridges, one of the more experienced cowboys moved quickly to throw a rope on the bull, but he reckoned without the animal's frightening speed. In seconds, the rope was torn from Bridges' hand and the bull was charging at him furiously.

After that, everything seemed to happen at once. Bridges suddenly went down with the bull snorting and hooking its horns at him as he rolled frantically trying to dodge the thrusts.

Curry went over the rail like a track star, a gunny sack held in one lean hand, and started to distract the bull.

"Get him out of here!" he yelled to two of his men, who promptly jumped into the corral and dragged the white-faced cowboy out.

Curry flicked the sack at the bull, and turned to leap back over the ring, but a quick jerk of the snorting animal's head caught him in the side. Eleanor saw him grimace tightly with pain, and he went down like a crumpled bag.

Terrified, without even thinking, Eleanor slipped between the rails and ran to him, picking up the gunny sacks as she did.

"You stupid beast!" she raged at the bull, whapping it across the rump with all her strength with the sack, taking out the terror and fury she felt on it.

Distracted, the bull turned away from Curry, tossing his big head, his red and white coat wiggling with the motion as his big eyes stared at the pale young woman.

Meanwhile, the other hands dived into the corral and got to Curry, ignoring his feverish curses as he ordered them to "get that damned woman out of the corral!"

Jed Docious settled the problem by slinging a hard, wiry arm around Eleanor's slender middle and half carrying, half dragging her to safety while the others danced around to keep the bull from charging. Two other cowboys dragged Curry to safety.

Once outside the ring, Eleanor made a beeline to Curry, who was stretched out on the ground with blood oozing from the wound in his side as one of the men worked to stem the bleeding by applying pressure with a clean handkerchief.

"Are you all right?" she asked him breathlessly. She dropped to her knees pushing at a strand of gritty, damp hair as she looked down into blazing silver eyes in a face gone white under its tan.

"You hotheaded little mule," he began slowly, the whip in his voice was so sharp that it cut. "You empty-headed, idiotic, stupid little fool! You could have been killed in there, you damned lunatic!" He was warming up now, and what followed was louder, rougher, and laced with language like nothing she'd ever heard him use before. Her face had gone red and tears were rolling down her cheeks before he finally stopped to take a breath.

"Boss," Docious interrupted hesitantly, "we need to get you to the sawbones and have him patch you up before you bleed to death."

"What the hell do I need with a doctor?" Curry wanted to know, flashing his blazing glance in the tall cowboy's direction. "Get me the hell in the house and call Jake in off the fence line. He can patch me up."

"Curry, he's good at patching up animals, but . . ."

"Don't tell me what he is, Docious, I know damned well what he is, just get him, will you?" Curry growled. He glared up at Eleanor, whose face was white as paste. "Let Eleanor take over riding fence," he added sarcastically. "Since she's decided she's one of the hands!"

That was the last straw. She turned with a sob and ran for her horse, tears streaming down her cheeks. She rode away without a backward glance.

8

————— *—————*

Eleanor stayed in her room for the rest of the day, refusing Bessie's offer to bring her supper up, doggedly refusing to even ask about Curry even though she was aching to be reassured that he was all right.

Night came, and she turned on the small lamp by her bed, taking up her seat in the armchair by the window to stare blankly out of it with eyes that burned from too many tears.

She heard the door open, and one quick glance showed her that it was Curry. She bit her lip, feeling the tears come again, warm and wet and salty, trickling into the corners of her mouth.

Curry came and knelt in front of her. His shirt was open down the front, and she could see the stark white bandage against the bronzed flesh of his rib cage, his chest with its mat of dark, curling hair. His hands went to her waist and he held her gently, looking straight into her misty eyes, his own gaze dark and quiet with what might have been pain.

"You scared the hell out of me, little girl, do you know that?" he asked softly. "I died twice watching you in the ring with that bull, knowing that any minute the horns could catch you, the way they caught me. You sweet, crazy little fool, what if he'd gored you in the stomach? You might never be able to bear children, did you even think about that?"

She bit her lip, shaking her head softly. "I...I thought he was going...to kill you," she said simply, and her tear-filled eyes met his, shimmering like spring leaves in the rain.

"Honey," he whispered softly, "what the hell good would it do me to live if your life was the price I had to pay?"

A tear worked its way down her flushed cheek. His hands went to her cheeks, drawing her forward, and his lips sipped away the tear, following it back to her closed eyelids, his tongue gently brushing the long, wet lashes in a silent intimacy that throbbed with emotion.

"Curry?" she whispered unsteadily, her hands going involuntarily to his broad shoulders.

His breath came hard and heavy. "What?" he whispered in a voice that wasn't quite steady as his mouth began to explore, to touch and lift and taste the contours of her face.

"Are . . . you hurt bad?" she asked.

"I'll have a scar out of it," he murmured absently.

"You . . . you bled so much," she whispered. Her fingers dug into his hard shoulders as the lazy, brief caresses began to work on her like a narcotic.

"It wasn't any more than a cut and a bad bruise," he murmured. He looked into her misty eyes, searching them in a silence that burned, with an intensity like nothing she'd ever experienced. His gaze dropped to her parted lips and studied them for such a long time that her heart pounded in her chest.

"I'm going to make you want it this time," he whispered huskily. "I'm going to make you ache for it."

Before she could find the words to answer him, his mouth was brushing softly, lazily, against hers, teasing her lips apart, his whiskey-scented breath mingled with hers as his practiced mastery brought a moan from her throat.

His teeth nipped gently at her lower lip, his tongue probed the soft, tight curve of her mouth with a slow, stroking motion that made the trembling start in her untutored body.

She drew back quickly, her eyes wide with surprise as they looked directly into his. She expected to see mockery there, but there was only a vague, patient tenderness.

"It's all right," he said softly. "I'm not going to force you this time."

The tears were drying on her cheeks, the unhappiness being replaced by a wild kind of excitement as his lean hands tightened on her waist.

"I don't know very much," she murmured uneasily as her hands went to his broad shoulders and rested there.

"Forgive me, little one," he said with a slow smile, "but it shows."

She searched his pale, glittering eyes. "Curry, do men really like to kiss like that?" she asked.

"Oh, yes," he murmured, studying the puzzled little face so close to his.

"Why?" she asked.

"If you'll relax and let me do what I want to for the next minute or so, I'll show you."

She sat very still as his dark face came even closer. Her eyes closed, her breath sighed against his firm mouth as it touched and caressed and began to open, pressing her trembling lips apart with a slow, sweet, relentless pressure. She felt the intimacy of it right through her body. It made feelings stir deep inside her that she'd never felt, and as they grew and grew, her sharp nails involuntarily bit into his hard shoulders as she felt his mouth deepen the kiss to an intimacy that brought a choked moan from her throat.

"Oh, Curry!" she whispered brokenly against his mouth.

"Don't talk," he replied, in a voice she didn't recognize.

His lean hands moved under her cotton blouse to caress her bare back, and the touch was like fire. She pressed closer suddenly, her mouth hungry for his, her body blazing under the lean, sure hands that moved with an urgent pressure from her back to the silken curves of her breasts and the length of her slender body.

With a suddenness that left her hanging between paradise and reality, he tore away and stood up. He went to the window without a backward glance and drew in a harsh breath while he pulled a cigarette from his pocket and lit it.

"I didn't mean to go that far," he said finally, in a voice rough with self-contempt.

Her stunned eyes went over his long back, loving him, needing him, still burning from the fever of his ardor.

"Did I do something wrong?" she asked in a subdued tone.

"No, honey, I did." He stared out the window. "Little innocent, don't ever let a man touch you like that again unless you're willing to accept the consequences. It's too arousing."

She blushed. It embarrassed her to talk like this, to feel like this. He made her feel ashamed of her own breathless response and as the bitter words sank in, her cheeks flamed with the memory of what she'd let him do. How could she tell him that she could only have felt that kind of abandon with a man she loved? She dropped her shamed eyes to her lap.

There was a movement as he turned, and she felt the piercing gaze on the back of her neck.

"God, Eleanor, don't look like that!" he growled shortly. "You're out of the nursery!"

She jumped out of the chair and went madly toward the door, feeling like some hunted animal trying to escape the hunter's bullet.

"Baby, don't," he said in a calmer voice as her hand reached for the doorknob. "I didn't mean to snap at you."

She hesitated, hearing the soft thud of his boots on the carpet as he came up behind her and caught her by the waist, drawing her rigid back against the length of his body.

"Men get like this sometimes," he explained patiently, "when they're hungry for a woman they can't have. Call it frustration, Jadebud. I wanted you very much and because of it, I let things get out of hand. I won't let it happen again."

She relaxed a little against him, her mind fighting to cope with the upheaval of her emotions. He had her so confused, she barely knew her own name, and the newness of what she was feeling, added to the embarrassment of the liberties she'd allowed him, brought the tears back to her eyes.

He felt the sob that shook her and turned her into his arms, holding her tight against him while she cried.

"Hush," he whispered at her ear. "God, I'm sorry. I had no right to touch you like that. I'm a man, Eleanor, long past my adolescence. It's damned hard for me to accept limits, if that's any excuse. But what happened . . . happens between men and women," he added, searching for words. "It's a very natural part of lovemaking, and nothing to be ashamed about. You're a normal, warm and responsive woman, and there's not a frigid bone in your body. And for the record, I'm damned glad I was the first."

She buried her hot face against his chest, and he chuckled softly.

"We'll keep it low key from now on, little girl," he said gently. "Come back out with me tomorrow. We'll stop by the store after we get through with the last of the breeding herd and pick up some canned sausages and soft drinks and have lunch on the river.''

"I'd like that," she said softly. Her fingers pressed patterns into his blue-checked shirt, feeling the warmth and hardness of his chest through the soft material.

One of his hands came down to still the movement. "Don't tempt fate," he said quietly.

Her fingers curled into a tight ball. "I'm sorry," she said quickly.

"So am I," he murmured. "If you were a little more sophisticated, I'd strip the damned shirt off and show you how I like to be touched."

She tried to avert her face, but he caught her in time to see the slow burn on her cheeks and he grinned down at her wickedly.

"Little spring bud," he whispered. "You're a far cry from my usual kind of woman."

"So is Amanda," she reminded him quietly, feeling the hurt as she suddenly remembered that flashy diamond Curry had given his new fiancée. Fiancée!

"Is she, Norie?" he asked seriously. His eyes searched hers. "I wonder. It takes experience to try and seduce a man. I don't think you'd know how."

She averted her face. "I think it would come naturally if a woman loved the man."

"Amanda loves my money, all right," he agreed. "But not enough to put up with the ranch twelve months of the year." He drew in a deep breath. "Would you be happy several hundred miles away from a man you loved?" he asked.

She shook her head without thinking, her soft, misty green eyes tracing every hard line of his face, lingering on his square jaw and the firm curve of his mouth.

"When you look at me like that, you're asking for trouble," he said in a husky voice, his hands tightening like steel bands on her slight rib cage.

Her breath came fluttering, the look in his eyes made her hungry and reckless. "What kind of trouble?" she whispered shakily.

He bent, lifting, curving her body into his arms as he trapped her there. "What kind of trouble do you think, you little witch?" he murmured as he caught her mouth roughly under his.

9

She felt her knees turning to water while he crushed her lips under his ruthless, hungry mouth. He lifted her slender body against his, fitting her expertly to its powerful contours. It was like being joined by gigantic magnets, she thought while she could, as if they were glued together so tightly that they could never separate again. She clung to his neck, drowning in the sensations he was causing as he kissed her, yielding completely, loving him until nothing mattered but that he never let go....

A shudder went through his tall body as he drew back, looking down at her through slitted, blazing eyes. His breath came like a runner's, hard and heavy and slightly rasping.

"Lovely little witch," he whispered in a shaken voice. "God, you learn fast!"

"Your ribs!" she remembered suddenly, her eyes dropping to the half-hidden white bandage where his lean hand pressed against the pain.

"It was worth it," he replied. He put her away from him. "I'll see you in the morning. Want some supper now? If you do, I'll have Bessie bring you a tray."

She shook her head.

His teasing eyes dropped to her mouth. "Not hungry any more?" he asked in a voice like a caress.

She shook her head again, with a smile.

He touched a finger to her swollen mouth. "Goodnight, honey," he murmured, and went out the door, leaving her eyes glued to the space where he'd been.

She woke up wondering if the night before had been a dream. There was no sign of bruising on her, no turmoil in the eyes that met hers in the mirror. But she felt a tingle of emotion at just the thought of meeting Curry this morning and she dressed in her jeans and a white cotton top with a feeling of vibrant anticipation.

He was at the breakfast table waiting for her when she came downstairs, and his silver eyes ate her the minute she walked through the doorway.

She flushed at the intensity of the look, surprised by the sudden inexplicable difference in their relationship. It was as if what had happened last night—and it was no dream, she read that in his eyes—had opened the floodgates, and there was no stopping the raging current they'd created.

"Did you sleep well?" he asked in a deep caressing voice when she sat down beside him.

"Yes, thank you." Her eyes darted up for an instant to meet his and dropped quickly. "Did you?"

"I'll tell you later," he murmured. He leaned over and kissed her lightly on the mouth. "You look lovely in white, little one," he added.

She smiled, feeling a warmth like summer sunlight inside her when she met his level gaze. He returned the smile, and a current of electric hunger seemed to link them for several seconds so that neither could look away.

"Well, aren't we affectionate this morning?" Bessie enthused, and broke the magic spell as she walked in with a platter of sausage, scrambled eggs and biscuits.

Curry lifted a dark eyebrow at her, not a bit perturbed. "Remind me to raise your salary in 1996."

"What makes you think I'm going to put up with you that long?" Bessie returned, leaving with a quick wink at Eleanor and a face like the cat that got the cream.

"What if I raised your salary?" Curry teased, and she could feel the laughter in his eyes. "Would you stay?"

She felt the light go out of the world, remembering, and all at once she wondered if these were some more of Curry's ruthless tactics to get his way.

Would he go so far as to court her to keep her on the ranch? She hadn't considered the possibility before, she'd been too caught up in the surge of emotion he'd created between them with those expert kisses. But the mention of her staying brought it all home with a vengeance. Curry was engaged to Amanda, for heaven's sake! That was a fact, and all the teasing kisses in the world wouldn't change it. If he'd wanted to marry Eleanor, or even been in love with her, it wouldn't have taken him three years to find out.

"Never mind," Curry said. His sharp eyes caught the freezing of her features, the stiffening of her body. "We'll take it one day at a time. Eat your breakfast, honey, I've got work to do."

"Should you be pushing so hard with that wound?" she asked, and nodded toward his ribs under the khaki shirt.

"I told you once, I'm as tough as nails," he said with a smile. "It's a little more sore today, but I don't expect to die from it."

"Stubborn man."

"It's my middle name."

She smiled, but her heart wasn't in it. She finished her breakfast quickly, already dreading being alone with him for the rest of the day. When it came to Curry, she had no resistance, and she was afraid of what he might demand of her innocence. He was dynamite at close quarters, she'd learned that already, and the fact that she was in love with him would make it all that much harder to resist him.

How could he do this, how could he use her own emotions against her just to keep her working for him? Secretaries, even private ones, weren't that hard to come by. Not for a man with Curry's looks and charm. Or maybe it was just the principle of it. That he didn't want his old rival Jim Black to get one up on him by stealing his very efficient secretary. Either way, Eleanor thought miserably, she was the one who stood to suffer because of it.

The noise and dust and heat were far worse the second day than the first, and it seemed to take forever to work the herd after they were sorted.

One mean-looking heifer got her foot stuck between the rails and it took a half hour to free her. The men's tempers were running hot, and Curry's was at its finest, when lunch time finally rolled around.

Curry stomped away from the corral, dirty and drenched in sweat, his face flushed with temper, his eyes cruel.

"Let's go," he bit off, joining Eleanor where their mounts were tied.

"Was that the last of the breeding herd?" Eleanor asked.

"Almost. We've got about a hundred or so to go today." He smoked quietly on his cigarette as they rode along toward the small country store down the road. "God, I'm getting too old for this kind of aggravation."

"Jim Baylock's opening a new nursing home," Eleanor suggested. "Maybe we could get your name on the waiting list."

He glared at her through narrowed eyes. "I can't go," he told her. "The damned cattle would cry their eyes out missing me."

She grinned at him. "Only the cows," she laughed.

"Keep it up and I won't feed you."

"If you don't, I'll get weak from hunger and fall off my horse," she threatened.

He smiled at the banter, and she could actually see some of the tautness drain out of his tall body, his set face. He finished the cigarette and threw it down into the dust as they reached the old-fashioned little store with its single gas pump out front.

They bought Vienna sausages and crackers, along with soft drinks, a block of cheese, and moon pies. Loaded with their bounty, they rode down to the cool trees by the river and sprawled on the soft grass to eat.

"We'll get chiggers," Eleanor said lazily. She popped a small sausage into her mouth and savored every bite as she washed it down with an orange drink.

"You can get Bessie to rub you down with alcohol to get rid of them," Curry replied.

"I bet you never get chiggers," she observed. "Your hide's so tough they couldn't get through it."

He grinned. "So I've been told."

She finished her lunch and leaned back against the grassy bank with her arms behind her head. "It's so cool here," she murmured with closed eyes. "So quiet."

"Shangri-la, Eleanor," he agreed. He stripped off his shirt and stopped down at the edge of the river to splash cold water over his sweaty chest and shoulders and neck.

She watched him quietly, her eyes drawn to the powerful muscular body, remembering the feel and touch of it with a hunger that ached. Of all the men to fall in love with, why did it have to be one as unreachable as Curry Matherson? Why couldn't it have been Jim Black? She smiled, remembering Jim's last phone call, his enthusiasm for the little blonde. It sounded very much as if there'd be a wedding before long, and she was glad for the lonely widower. He'd been alone so much over the years, he deserved a little happiness.

Curry straightened up, tossing his shirt to the grass as he dropped lazily beside Eleanor, leaning on one elbow with his long body stretching out on the green grass.

"I love it here," she murmured, closing her eyes to savor the watery voice of the river.

"Is there anything about ranch life you don't like?" he asked with sudden bitterness.

She sighed, drinking in the delicious peace of green shadows and silvery water. "No, there isn't anything about it that I dislike. Oh I'd hate to live in a city, wouldn't you, Curry?" she asked abruptly, enthusiastically, turning to meet his silver eyes and finding a look in them that made her heart turn over. It was a sensuous, totally adult look that appraised every inch of her body, and she was more aware than ever of the masculine appeal of that broad, bronzed chest so close to her with its mat of hair still damp from the water, the bandage slightly dark where the water had just touched it.

"You're trembling, Eleanor," he said quietly. "What are you afraid of?"

"I'm not afraid of anything," she denied shakily.

His fingers slid under the sleeveless white top at her shoulders, lightly stroking the warm young flesh over her collarbone with a teasing pressure that made her tremble.

"Your skin feels like warm silk," he remarked gently. He leaned forward, easing her onto her back and trapping her there with his arms on either side of her.

"Shouldn't we get back?" she asked too quickly.

He caught her frightened eyes and held them with his. "I don't want to go back right now," he said, bending to tease her lips with his. "You don't want to, either, if you'd admit it. I need you, Eleanor...."

He drew her face up to his and kissed her gently, slowly building the pressure until he felt her mouth relax and part, until he heard the soft moan that sighed against his lips. He took her hands and spread them onto his bare, cool chest, teaching her wordlessly how to touch him, how to caress and arouse him.

His body was hard and unyielding where she touched him with slow, nervous fingers, learning the hard contours with a sense of wonder, testing the wiry strength of the dark hair on his chest with a fleeting pressure that brought a groan from the mouth that devoured hers.

She looked up into his face, seeing the passion harden it, darken his eyes as he returned her frank regard.

"God, the way you look when I love you . . ." he whispered huskily, sketching every soft, lovely line of her face.

"You shouldn't be," she whispered unsteadily.

"You want it," he replied flatly, with that inborn arrogance that was as much a part of him as his square, relentless jaw.

She lowered her eyes to the muscular chest under her fingers. So did he, she thought, but only as a means to an end, and he knew it. With a sigh, she rolled away from him and got up, standing under a spreading oak at the river's edge while she caught her breath.

"What's wrong?" he said from a few feet behind her.

"It's not fair, Curry," she said. Her hands fluttered as she clasped them behind her, drinking in the cool breeze that blew off the bubbling water below the bank. "Not to Amanda, not to me. You're engaged."

"I know." There was a harsh sigh, and a long pause, after which she smelled the cigarette smoke that drifted thick and pungent past her face. "Avalanches aren't that easy to stop, little girl. Once they start rolling downhill, it's next to impossible to stop them."

"Riddles?" she asked quietly.

He moved beside her to lean back against the trunk of the mammoth tree. He'd put his shirt back on, although it was hanging open, and she could see marks on his chest where her nails had bitten into the bronzed flesh while he was kissing her. . . .

"I want you," he said bluntly, his eyes catching the way she stiffened at the words. "I want you like hell every time I touch you, and I can't help it any more than I can help breathing. And, damn you, you want me just as much!"

She felt the trembling start in her legs and work its way up. Her eyes closed on the emotion in his deep voice, an emotion so convincing that she almost believed he felt it. But she knew Curry too well. She knew his tactics. It was just another trick, and only a fool would fall for it.

"Physical attraction fades in time," she said. "I don't want an affair with you, Curry, I don't want it with anyone. I want something permanent."

"A ring?" he growled. "Just like every other damned woman, you'll give yourself if the price is right, is that it? I won't be owned, Eleanor. I'm as susceptible to a soft young body as the next man, but there's a limit to the price I'll pay for it."

"Aren't you buying Amanda's?" she asked bitterly, glaring at him.

He paused. "It's different with her. She doesn't want ties, and neither do I."

"You don't consider marriage a tie?" She looked straight into his glittering eyes. "Do you think I'd use the back stairs to your bedroom while she spent the better part of her life in Houston, Curry? Is that what you had in mind for me?"

He had the grace to flush, his eyes stormy and strange. "It wouldn't be like that."

"Oh, wouldn't it?" She laughed without humor. "Do you think I'm so stupefied by a few of your kisses that I'll tell Jim Black sorry and climb into your bed? I'm sorry to disappoint you, but I'm still going. If you thought you could keep me here by blinding me with your potent charm, you lose."

He looked for an instant as if he'd been hit from behind. "You think that?" he asked in an ominously quiet tone.

"Did you think you had me buffaloed?" she replied with a coolness that was smoothly convincing. "That I wouldn't guess what you were up to? I may be naïve, Curry, but I'm not stupid. I've seen you in action, remember, and I know better than most how low you'll stoop to get what you want. You couldn't stand letting Jim Black walk away with anything you considered your property, could you?'' She drew in a sharp breath. ''Did you have to grit your teeth when you kissed me, Curry?'' he asked bitterly. ''After all, you said yourself that no man would be blind enough to want me.''

''What the hell are you talking about?'' he asked in a frankly dangerous voice.

''You know what I'm talking about, you've tried everything short of proposing to keep me here!'' she said furiously. ''You and Jim have been rivals in business for years, and you've never taken a challenge from him that you didn't win. Did it really bother you that much to have him hire me right out from under you? Or was it just that you couldn't stand having a woman around the place who could resist you?''

His eyes caught fire. ''Resist me?'' he growled. ''You little wildcat, I could lay you down in that grass and have you right now if I wanted you, and you'd let me! So don't stand there like some Victorian society matron and tell me how immune you are to me. I just might let you prove it!''

She wrapped her arms around her chest and turned her attention back to the water. She didn't say another word.

''You're still the shriveled up little chicken you were before you shed your disguise, Jadebud,'' he growled cruelly. ''For your information, I wasn't trying to get you into my bed. I thought you might benefit from a little experience if you're going to be tangling with the likes of Jim Black. But from now on, your education can go hang! If you think I'd trade Amanda for a repressed little bundle of piety like you, you're crazy as hell!''

She went white in the face. Absolutely white, her nails bit into her forearms as she fought not to let him see the effect the vicious attack had on her.

''You're free to go whenever you damned well please, Eleanor,'' he added curtly. ''Making love to you every day is too damned high a price to pay to keep you at your desk.''

She heard him walk away and a minute later, there was the creak of saddle leather and the thud of a horse's hooves dying away.

10

*

Roundup went on, but without Eleanor. There were no more trips out to the holding pens, no more quiet rides with Curry. He avoided her like the plague, speaking to her only when it was necessary.

She was grateful for his absence. She felt wounded, and she needed time for the scars to heal.

"Something wrong between you and Curry?" Bessie asked her at supper one night when Curry was still out working on the ranch.

Eleanor stared into her plate. "Just the usual irritation," she said lightly, trying to make a joke out of it.

"Things calmed down for a little while there."

"So they did," Eleanor agreed.

"Don't want to talk about it?" the housekeeper said knowingly.

Eleanor smiled wanly and shook her head. "It's best forgotten."

"Still going over to Jim?"

"Yes, for now."

"And then?"

Eleanor shrugged. "It's a big world," she said with a short laugh. "There's no telling where I'll wind up."

"You'll write?"

She said yes, of course she would, and dug into her meal, knowing full well she wanted no more contact with the ranch, ever, once she left it. It would hurt too much.

Jim Black's phone call the next afternoon came at the best possible time. Curry's continued avoidance, and the lack of work to keep her busy, was driving her to an attack of nerves she'd never experienced before.

"How much longer?" Jim teased. "I'm getting impatient over here, and I just may need your help with a wedding before long."

"Oh, Jim, congratulations!" she enthused. "See, I told you it would work out!"

"Yes, you did, and Elaine and I will never be able to thank you enough for that 'double-double dog dare' that started it all. When, Norie?"

She swallowed. "Three more days. I wish it was tomorrow."

"What about if I talk to Curry?"

"I . . . I wouldn't do that," she murmured.

He drew a hard breath. "I knew I should have kept a check on you!" he grumbled. "If I hadn't been so wrapped up in my own life . . . hon, I'm sorry. It's been bad, hasn't it?"

The sympathy brought tears to her eyes. "Yes," she admitted unsteadily. "It has."

"Are you free the rest of the day?"

She brightened. "Yes. I've got everything out of the way that I need to do."

"Good. How about if I come get you, and you can have supper with all of us tonight? I'd like you to get to know Elaine."

She smiled. "I'd like that very much," she said genuinely.

"I'll pick you up in thirty minutes. That long enough?"

She was ready, dressed in a pale green clinging dress with her hair waving softly around her shoulders, when Curry arrived back at the ranch house just as Jim drove up.

The two men studied each other quietly. Jim was neat in a dark sports coat with matching slacks and a cream-colored shirt. Curry looked as if a whirlwind had hit him, his jeans dusty, his shirt torn and wet with sweat, his hair damp with perspiration.

"I'm taking Norie over for the evening," Jim said as if he expected an argument.

"That's your business," Curry said abruptly. His pale eyes speared the other man.

"I'm glad you finally realized it," Jim replied. "No hard feelings, Curry. I hope you'll come to the wedding."

Eleanor didn't think she'd ever forget the look on Curry's dark face when Jim told him that. Obviously he thought Jim meant Eleanor, and his jaw locked violently, his face seemed to harden to solid rock.

"Wedding?" he asked in a strange tone.

Jim grinned. "It happens to all of us sooner or later, doesn't it? I hope you and Amanda will be as happy as we expect to."

Curry didn't say another word. He turned, sparing Eleanor a glance so hateful she felt as if he'd struck her, and walked straight into the house without a backward glance, slamming the screen door behind him.

"What was that all about?" Jim asked.

She sighed and shook her head. "Beats me," she told him. "If anything, he'll give a party when I leave. He's that glad to see me go."

"Is he, now?" Jim's eyes narrowed thoughtfully.

Eleanor got into the car and sat quietly until he started it.

"Thanks for rescuing me," she told him. "Supper was going to be another ordeal."

"What's eating him?"

"Amanda won't come and live on the ranch after they get married," she explained. "He's furious. He doesn't think she cares enough to stay with him, and he's like a fire-breathing dragon lately."

"So that's it," Jim remarked, as if he'd been thinking something very different. "I knew that wasn't going to work out. Amanda's a lovely girl, but she's not ranch stock."

"It's more than that," Eleanor said, staring out the window as she spoke. "She doesn't love him, Jim. She's more interested in how much she'll be able to spend, and keeping up her career, than she is in taking care of Curry."

"Does he love her?"

"Apparently," she replied, "although he says no. He wants her," she added in a subdued tone. "I suppose that's as close as he can come to feeling anything for a woman."

"He doesn't know what he's missing," Jim grinned.

"You old maverick," she teased. "You look ten years younger. Elaine's influence, I'll bet!"

"You'd be right, too. Oh, what a girl!"

And she was. The petite little blonde, once she got over her initial reserve when she and Eleanor were introduced, turned out to have a live wire personality. There was a loveliness in her that had nothing to do with exterior beauty. She was a caring person, and everything she felt for Jim was in her eyes when she looked at him.

Maude liked her too, and it showed. Eleanor noticed that Jeff, too had been captured by that bright smile and sunny manner.

"Looks like you're not going to have to win anybody over," Eleanor teased the older girl when they were washing up the dishes after supper.

"I know," Elaine replied with a smile. "It was so strange, the way everything seemed to fall into place. I seemed to fit here the first time I walked through the door. I love Maude and Jeff, too, and I'm crazy about the ranch. Jim's teaching me how to ride."

"You'll make a good wife," she told the blonde. "He's needed someone like you for a long time. He got a raw deal with his first wife, I guess you knew that."

Elaine nodded. "I'll try to make it up to him."

Eleanor grinned. "I don't think you'll have to try too hard."

"You're still coming to work for him, aren't you?" Elaine asked suddenly, as if it really mattered to her. "Jim's told me what you had to put up with over there. I hope you'll still feel welcome—I'd like very much to have someone my own age to talk to. We could go shopping together and everything."

"If you and Jim don't mind," Eleanor replied, "I'll come for a few weeks." She looked down at the soapy water. "I...I don't know where I'll wind up eventually. Even ten miles away from Curry may not be enough, I'll just have to play it by ear."

"Do you love him that much?" Elaine asked softly.

Eleanor bit her lip. She nodded, hating the tears that misted in her eyes.

"I'm sorry it didn't work out."

She shrugged. "We don't always get everything we want in life," she said philosophically. "And sometimes there's a good reason. I'll live."

"Couldn't you come sooner?"

"I promised him two full weeks, and that's what he's going to get if it kills me. Anyway," she laughed, "it's just a couple more days. After the time I've already put in, it's going to be a piece of cake."

Curry was waiting for her in his den when she finished breakfast the next morning, dressed in a gray business suit that matched his eyes. He spared her a grudging glance when she walked in the door.

"I've left a couple of letters on the Dictaphone," he said in a voice like ice. "I'm going to be out of town today; you might tidy up in here so that your replacement can find things."

Your replacement. He made it sound so impersonal, as if the three years she'd spent working in this room weren't worth anything at all to him. And that was probably true. Curry wasn't sentimental. He'd tried to keep her, he'd failed, and now he wasn't even making an effort to be courteous. She'd refused his generous offer and he had no more time for her.

"Yes, sir," she said in a subdued tone.

"When's the wedding?" he asked with his back to her.

"I don't know. Soon," she said vaguely.

"You don't sound enthusiastic."

"I think it's wonderful," she corrected. "It's going to be a good marriage. One of the best."

Curry's hands jammed hard into his pockets. He drew in a deep, harsh breath. "I'm going to bring Amanda home," he volunteered into the silence. "It's time she faced up to what marriage means. I'm not going to have my wife living one place while I live in another. She's going to understand that from the beginning."

"You don't give an inch, do you?" she asked sadly, turning away so that she didn't have to meet his eyes. "She's the one who's going to have to make all the sacrifices."

"If she loved me, giving up her career to be a mother wouldn't constitute a sacrifice, and you damned well know it!"

She did, but she wasn't going to puff up his ego by admitting it.

"Does Black want children?" he asked suddenly.

She laughed softly, remembering what Elaine had told her. "Oh, yes," she said with a smile, "a whole huge houseful of them, assorted."

There was a tense silence between them. "Damn him!" Curry breathed violently. "Damn him, and damn you, too!"

She turned, astonished by the emotion in his dark face, his blazing eyes, trying to puzzle out what in the world was wrong with him.

"Don't be here when I get back," he told her in a voice so cold it seemed to choke him. "Get your bags packed today, and get out! I never want to set eyes on you again, do you hear?"

She could only nod, strangled by the demand, her voice buried.

He spared her one last, scathing glance as he opened the door. "Good riddance," he murmured. "I've had enough puritans to last me a lifetime. I wish him joy of you."

And with that last, puzzling statement, he was gone. She stood there white-faced, half relieved that the stress was finally over, that she wouldn't have to stay here and watch him with Amanda while another part of her was already wilting like a flower suddenly thrust from full sunlight into the cool shade.

Tears were pouring down her cheeks when she put the cover on her typewriter for the last time and left the room.

Leaving was harder than Eleanor had ever imagined. It was one thing to know she was going to do it, quite another to make it an accomplished fact.

Three years was a long time to leave behind. There were so many memories in the sprawling ranch house. Nights when she and Curry sat up and watched the late show together while he dictated correspondence during the commercials. Long, lazy afternoons when he'd stop her in the middle of something and they'd go driving, or riding out to see the new calves. Periods of such comradeship that they seemed infinitely closer than boss and secretary. And now, all of it was only a memory.

Jim came to get her, bag and baggage, and Bessie cried.

"Fool man," the housekeeper sobbed, "hasn't got eyes in his head to see with! Amanda'll never satisfy him!"

"It's his life, Bessie, he has to do what he thinks is best," she replied tearfully, defending him unconsciously, as she always had.

"He had such a jewel in you." Bessie tried to smile. "If only he'd realized it."

"Secretaries are easy to come by," Eleanor reminded her. "Remember the first day I came here, and there were four very efficient ones in front of me for an interview? He won't have any trouble replacing me—he may have already done it for all I know."

"He's hired Betty Maris, is what he's done," Bessie scoffed.

"Miss Betty?" Eleanor blinked. "Old Miss Betty who lives just past Smith's store and raises the African violets and hates men?"

"That's right. Oh, she'll make a dandy secretary, and Curry won't cow her," Bessie admitted. "But she's a far cry from you."

"Mandy will love her," Eleanor teased lightly. Her lower lip trembled with tears that wanted to escape. "I'll miss you, Bessie."

"I'll miss you, sugar. Please keep in touch with me. I'll never tell him a thing, I promise," she added knowingly.

Eleanor nodded and, turning to Jim, went quickly out the door without looking back.

The first week was harder than she'd imagined anything could be. Not the work. Jim was patient, and Elaine and Maude and Jeff kept her mind occupied when she wasn't hard at work. But Curry seemed to follow her, always in her mind, on her mind, his face flashing before her eyes, night and day until she thought she'd never again see any peace.

Then, miraculously, after those first days were lived through, she began to lose the paleness and the sparkle came back into her green eyes. It was like living through combat. Taking it one day at a time. She was going to survive it in spite of Curry Matherson.

"Amanda didn't come back with him," Jim remarked over supper one night.

Eleanor concentrated on her mashed potatoes with a vengeance. "Didn't she?"

"Rumor is that he broke the engagement himself."

"Best thing that could have happened," Maude remarked with a nod. "She'd never have made him happy."

"Traveling won't either, but it looks like he's trying it," Jim said as he sipped his coffee. "He'd no sooner got back to the ranch than he took off again. Hasn't come home yet." He frowned. "Maybe the memories are haunting him."

Eleanor knew about haunting, she'd had her share. She could almost feel sorry for Amanda, but the redhead should have known that she couldn't dictate terms to a man like Curry.

"Well, how do you like it here?" Jim asked Eleanor suddenly.

She laughed, gazing around the table to Elaine, Maude and Jeff. "How should I like being surrounded by nice people? None of you turn the air blue, or yell, or threaten to have me drawn and quartered if I don't finish my work exactly on schedule." She glanced at Elaine with a beaming smile. "And I'm having a ball helping Elaine get everything ready for the wedding. I don't even mind addressing invitations.

"Only two more weeks," Jim sighed, his eyes drinking in his pretty fiancée. "How will I live?"

"One day at a time, like the rest of us," Maude laughed.

"I think it's going to be keen, having a mom like the other guys," Jeff volunteered with a wink at Elaine. "I've told everybody."

"I hope I don't disappoint you," Elaine told him with a smile. She was already taken with Jim's son, and it showed. She'd be good for him.

"As long as you don't try to read me any bedtime stories," Jeff cautioned her, "we'll all get along just fine!"

And they all broke up at the plea.

Several days had gone by when Bessie called one night and asked to speak to Eleanor. She'd kept the lines of communication open, but this was the first time Bessie had called at night, and Eleanor had an ominous feeling about it when she picked up the phone.

"Something's wrong, isn't it?" she asked without preamble.

"To my mind, everything is," Bessie admitted with a weary note in her voice. "He's back."

"Jim said he'd been away," came the soft reply, and there was no need to pretend she didn't know who Bessie was talking about.

"Well, he looks like the back end of beyond," the housekeeper said gruffly. "And his temper's so raw I can't even talk to him. Eleanor, I've seen him in all kinds of conditions. Drunk, mad, irritated...but I've never seen him the way he is now. He's pushing himself so hard, I expect any day for one of the boys to bring him in unconscious with a heart attack. I don't know what to do. He won't talk to me, or to anybody else. I'm so worried I can hardly stand it."

Eleanor knew what was coming, and she dreaded the words, but she had to ask, "What do you want me to do?"

"Come over here, and talk to him," she replied, just as Eleanor expected. "He always would talk to you when he wouldn't say a word to anybody else. You can find out what's wrong with him, if anyone can." There was a pause. "Eleanor, we both love that man, despite all his faults. I can almost hate him sometimes, but I can't stand by and let him kill himself. Can you?"

Eleanor stared down at the push buttons on the phone. "No," she admitted weakly. "I can't. When do you think would be a good time?"

"Come to supper. I'll tell him I invited you to come see me. Will you?"

"For you. I'll get one of the boys to drive me over. Bye."

"Thanks, Eleanor. I knew I could count on you."

She hung up the phone with mixed emotions. Could she bear seeing Curry again with all this water under that bridge? Could she bear to hear him pour out the grief that his broken engagement must have caused him? She went upstairs to dress reluctantly. In many ways, this was going to be the hardest thing she'd ever had to do.

* * *

It was almost dark when Decker, one of Jim's ranch hands, let her out at the doorstep. The house looked just as she remembered it, big and warm and welcoming with light pouring out the windows onto the ground. If only things had been different, she'd never have had to leave it, she thought wistfully.

She paused on the bottom step to watch Decker drive away, putting off the confrontation until the last possible minute. Then she went up the steps, remembering belatedly that she had to knock on the door now. She couldn't simply walk in as she'd been used to doing before. Everything was different now.

11

*

She waited breathlessly for someone to answer the door, nervously smoothing the white sleeveless dress down over her hips as she dreaded the sound of booted feet.

But it was Bessie who answered the door, drawing her inside to hug her heartily before she took her into the dining room.

"Curry, I invited company for supper," Bessie called as they went into the dining room, and Eleanor's heart stopped dead as she turned the corner and saw him unexpectedly sitting at the head of the table. She felt as if she'd been shot suddenly, looking straight into those narrow silver eyes without warning.

He looked older, tired, positively haggard, and he'd lost weight. His gaze slid up and down her like an artist's brush, copying every soft line of her body, her face, until his eyes came back up to capture hers and search them.

"If . . . if you'd rather, I can eat in the kitchen . . . with Bessie," Eleanor stammered nervously.

He shook his head. "Sit by me," he said quietly, drawing a chair out for her.

Bessie disappeared, leaving her stranded. She laid her purse down in a chair by the door and sat down next to Curry. Her eyes carefully avoided his.

"How are things going?" she asked casually.

"Fine," he replied carelessly. He lifted his coffee cup to his lips and took a sip of the hot, black liquid. He set it down again. "That's a damned lie," he added quietly. "Nothing's right around here anymore. Is that why Bessie sent for you? Does she really think I need a shoulder to cry on?" he asked in a soft, dangerous tone.

She kept her eyes on the white tablecloth. "She was worried about you; don't be mad at her, Curry."

"Were you worried?"

She kept her face down wordlessly.

He drew in a harsh breath and lit a cigarette. "No," he said for her. "Of course not, why the hell should you be after the way I treated you? Are you happy, Jadebud?" he added in a softer tone.

"No," she said involuntarily, letting the word slip out when she'd rather have bitten her tongue off.

"That makes two of us." He reached out suddenly and caught her cool, nerveless fingers in his. "Honey, if you're not happy now, how can you be happy married to him? Don't jump into anything!"

"Married? Me?" she exclaimed, meeting his eyes with a puzzled look in her own. "I'm not getting married."

"But, Black said...."

"He's marrying Elaine," she replied. "Elaine, whose father owns the Limelight Club," she explained. "They're crazy about each other."

"Oh. I see," he murmured heavily. He took another long draw from his cigarette and meticulously thumped the small ash into the ashtray by his plate. "Rough, isn't it, Eleanor, wanting something you can't have?" he asked.

She gaped at him. He thought... he thought she was in love with Jim!

He glanced at her, mistaking the astonishment in her eyes. "I always could read you like a book," he said quietly. "I've known all along how you felt about him. I'm sorry it didn't work out for you."

She averted her eyes. "I'm sorry things didn't work out for you," she seconded. "I...I heard Amanda didn't come back."

"Hell, I didn't want her back," he said gruffly. "I caught her in her apartment with her photographer. A photographic session, they called it." He grinned like the old Curry. "First time I've ever known it to be done when the photographer and the model had their clothes off."

"Oh," she whispered, reddening.

He glanced at her with a raised eyebrow. "It didn't embarrass me a bit. I took back the ring, wished them luck, and came home."

"Why didn't she tell you the truth?"

"Knowing what I'm worth on the market, you can ask that?" he laughed. "My money has powerful attraction for most women, little one, didn't you know?"

"Only your money?" she asked with a little of her old audacity.

He looked straight into her eyes, and there was something dark and strange and unreadable in his.

"We made sweet fires that afternoon, didn't we?" he asked her quietly, "and the night before it, too. My women have always been secondhand. It was a first for me as well, touching something innocent, cherishing it.... I'll never forget how soft your skin was, how eager you were to learn what I ached to teach you that night."

She licked her lips to take away the dryness, folding her hands before her on the table to stop their trembling.

"It still embarrasses you to talk about it, doesn't it?" he asked gently.

She nodded, unable to find words enough to answer him. How could she tell him it was the closest she'd ever been to paradise?

"There's something I've got to know," he said with sudden urgency, one of his lean hands reaching over to clasp both of hers.

"That night . . . was it me you were kissing, or were you pretending I was Jim Black?"

She framed a reply, but Bessie came in suddenly with the first of the supper, and conversation died away under the smell of fresh greens and perfectly cooked beef.

After supper, Bessie tactfully retired to the kitchen, leaving Curry and Eleanor to sit on the front porch where it was cool and quiet.

She sat down in the porch swing, and he took the place beside her, rocking the swing into a lazy creaking motion.

"I've missed you." He said it quietly, and it sounded genuine. "Miss Maris doesn't live in. I can't drag her out of bed at two in the morning to take a letter." He chuckled.

"I was more accommodating," she agreed.

He put a careless arm around her shoulders and drew her against him. "Jim doesn't work you as hard as I did, does he?"

"No." She let her head rest on his broad chest, relaxing as she heard the slow, heavy beat of his heart under the cotton shirt, felt the warmth of him enveloping her. He smelled of starch and oriental cologne and tobacco, familiar smells that soothed her. This was magic, what was happening now. Magic, to lie against him and feel his breath on her forehead, and know the sweet security of all that lean strength so close to her.

"Bessie says you're overdoing it," she murmured against his shirt.

"She's probably right." His arm tightened. "I hurt, No-rie," he whispered deeply.

She nuzzled closer, one small hand snaking around his neck to hold him comfortingly. "I'm sorry," she whispered. "Curry, I'm so sorry it didn't work out for you."

"Eleanor..." He hesitated, and she felt his other hand come up to tilt her face up to his. "I need you...just for a few minutes..."

She read the hunger in his voice, the ache for what he'd lost, the grief..."

"Take what you need, Curry," she said quietly, her body yielding to his in an unspoken invitation.

"I won't hurt you..." he whispered unsteadily as he bent to her upturned mouth, feeling it open deliciously as his lips touched it so that the restraint went out of him almost immediately. He lifted her across his knees and kissed her like a drowning man who never expected to feel a woman's softness again. There was desperation in the rough mouth invading hers, urgency. His arms contracted and hurt her, bringing a soft moan from her lips.

"I'm sorry," he bit off against her mouth, relaxing his hold just a little. "Oh, God, I want you so, Norie! I want you so!"

"I can't," she whispered brokenly.

"I'm not asking you to," he said in a husky voice. "I'd never ask that of you."

"But, you said..."

He brought her closer, tucking her face into his throat as he
locked the swing back into motion, cradling her soft body
against him in a silence thick with hunger.

"Men are such damned fools," he whispered gruffly. "We
never seem to know what we want until it's too late."

"You...you could take her back, you know," she murmured miserably.

"Hell could freeze over, too," he replied. He moved her body
against his sensuously. "Soft," he whispered, "soft, like down
where you touch me."

She felt the tremors trickling down the length of her body,
new and narcotic. "Don't," she protested weakly.

"Another first, little innocent?" he asked at her ear. His
mouth slid down to her throat, whispering warmly against it.
His hand slid up her rib cage slowly, feeling her tense and surge
up against him as his fingers spread out delicately against her
softness. She moaned and tried to draw away.

"You let me do it once," he reminded her softly, "and not
through two layers of cloth."

"Curry, don't," she pleaded unsteadily.

"Did you ever let him touch you that way?"

"I've never let anybody...!" she protested, falling right into
the trap.

She felt the smile she couldn't see as he gathered her close
again and sat just holding her in the darkness.

"I've got to go," she murmured.

His arms tightened possessively. "In a little while. Not yet.
Not yet, Jadebud."

She swallowed down the emotions he was arousing. "More
games, Curry?" she asked bitterly. "Isn't that where you sug-
gest, casually, that I might like to pack up my broken heart and
come back to work for you?'

He stiffened like steel against her.

She pushed away from him and got to her feet. "That's just
what I thought," she said, reading his reaction. "Sorry, I'm not
the naïve little girl I used to be, thanks to you."

"No, by God, you're not," he replied, rising to tower over
her angrily. "You've turned into a hard, cynical little hellcat
who can't see the forest for the trees. Go back to him and eat

your heart out. God knows there's only one way I want you
and it wouldn't be worth the effort at that!''

He turned on his heel and went into his den, slamming the
door behind him.

The days seemed to go by in a haze after that. Eleanor felt as if
she'd been torn in two, and the half that was left just barely
functioned at all. She didn't think she could ever forget the
whip in Curry's deep voice as he'd told her bluntly that there
was only one way he wanted her, but it wouldn't be worth the
effort. Not that she hadn't known that all along. It was so obvious.

But what had he meant, she couldn't see the forest for the
trees? That had puzzled her. That, and the fact that he really
thought she was in love with Jim. If only it had been true!
Loving Curry was a one-way ticket to heartache. She couldn't
stop. It had become a way of life over the years, and life without him was as flat as a soft drink left out in the sun.

Every afternoon, she had Decker saddle a horse for her, and
she rode. Sometimes it was for a few minutes, others, for an
hour or two. And wherever she went on the property that joined
Curry's, her eyes searched for him. She'd have given blood for
just a glimpse of that tall, commanding figure in the saddle. But
it never seemed to happen that way. At least, not at first.

Then, finally, two weeks after the stormy scene with him, she
was riding along the banks of the river when he came upon her
on his black stallion, an unexpected confrontation that made
her heart race as she drew the chestnut to a halt under a
spreading oak.

His eyes were cold as they drifted over her slender figure in
jeans and a cool blue cotton blouse.

"Lost?" Curry asked gruffly, a smoking cigarette held
loosely between the fingers on his pommel.

She shook her head. "Just riding," she murmured.

"On my land," he told her narrowly.

"I . . . I thought the river was the boundary," she said in a
subdued tone, her eyes drawn involuntarily to the hard masculine lines of his face under the brim of his hat.

"It is, most of the way. But not here." He leaned forward, studying her. "You've lost weight," he remarked quietly. "A lot of it. Doesn't Black feed you?"

"I eat," she replied. She studied his haggard face. "You don't look so terrific yourself."

"I'm pining away for my lost love, didn't you know?" He laughed bitterly. "When's the wedding?"

"Next week. You're invited."

"No thanks," he replied flatly. "I can't stomach the damned ceremonies. What a hell of a way to get a woman into bed."

"He loves her, Curry," she said, meeting his gaze levelly.

"You'd better believe he wants her as well," he returned. "Loving and wanting go together, little girl, for all that you'd like to believe they're completely unrelated."

"I thought you were the one making comparisons between love and the tooth fairy," Eleanor reminded him.

"In the beginning, I did." His pale eyes stared blankly at the river. "I was wrong."

Her heart ached for him. He was hurting in a way she never thought to see him hurt. She hadn't realized how much he'd loved Amanda.

"Oh, Curry, go to her," she said gently, compassion in the look she gave him. "Don't let pride do this to you. Maybe she's just as lonely as you are, did you think about that?"

He stared at her unseeingly. "Pride doesn't have anything to do with it, Jadebud," he said softly. "She doesn't love me."

He said it so simply. *She doesn't love me.* And the pain was in every syllable, in his eyes, his voice, the hardness of his face. She dropped her own eyes. "I'm sorry."

He drew a deep breath. "So am I. Don't you want to try and console me, little girl?" he asked. "We could console each other. A night in my bed might make your path a little easier, too. I'd make damned sure you didn't have any regrets."

She gazed at him quietly. "Do you think that little of me, after all this time?" she asked him. "Is that all I am now, a body to satisfy a passing urge?"

His eyes traced her body carelessly. "What would you like, a declaration of passionate love and a promise of marriage?"

Her eyes flashed. "Not from you, thanks!"

"Don't worry, I'm not that blind yet!" he flashed back a her, his eyes cruel.

She flinched. "Excuse me," she said in a choked tone. " forgot. You've told me so many times how undesirable I am, shouldn't have had any trouble remembering." She whirled th chestnut and started back the way she came, whipping the an imal into a gallop as she reached the pasture.

Her eyes were misty with tears, and she was leaning over th horse's neck, wild to get as far away from Curry as quickly a she could, and she didn't see the gopher hole. Neither did th furiously moving animal, until it caught him and threw him with Eleanor landing underneath.

The last sensation she had was of crushing pain, and the merciful blackness and oblivion.

The first thing she was aware of was the pressure on he chest. Not hard, not crushing, but pressing against her. Ther was a voice, too, with anguish in it, murmuring words sh couldn't understand, whispering things. Hands touched her caressed her, and always and forever came that deep, husk voice.

Through the mists of pain, her hands reached up, and bur ied themselves in thick, cool hair. It was a head pressed agains her breasts, hands gripping her back while a voice pleaded wit her not to leave him. She couldn't understand who would d that, unless it was her friend Jim....

She licked her parched lips and tried to make a sound "Jim?" she whispered hoarsely. "Jim?"

The head stilled against her, the hands stiffened and bit int her, hurting her soft flesh. Then the warm contact was sud denly gone, and she wondered vaguely if she'd dreamed it all a she dropped back off again.

A light burned against her eyes. Little by little she came bac to consciousness to see a man in a white coat bending over he with a tiny light in a steel cylinder. When her eyes opened, h stood erect and smiled down at her reassuringly.

"How do you feel?" he asked.

She searched herself. "My head hurts," she murmured. She ⌐oved in the crisp confines of the white-sheeted bed. "I'm ▸re . . . all over."

"I'm not surprised. A horse fell on you." The man, who was ▸viously a doctor, went out the door and a few seconds later ⌐urry came in. He bent over her, meeting her curious gaze with ▸ormy, dark eyes.

"Are you all right, honey?" he asked softly. "The doctor ▸ys I can take you home now as long as someone stays with ▸u for the rest of the night."

She nodded. "Please, I'd like to go home . . . but, Curry, ▸here is home?" she murmured disorientedly.

"Wherever I am, Eleanor." He brushed the wild, tumbled ⌐ir away from her face. "For now, at least. Come on, baby, ▸'s see if you can sit up."

Bessie was waiting on the porch when Curry carried Eleanor ▸ the steps and into the house.

"Hello, sweet," she said, patting the young girl's shoulder. ▸What can I bring up?"

"Some water and ice," Curry told her. "You'll have to get ▸r into a gown for me."

"I'll get right to it."

Curry climbed the stairs, holding her close against his taut ▸dy, and she leaned back against his broad chest and watched ⌐m every step of the way, her eyes quiet and loving.

He looked down into them once and quickly looked away.

"Jim? Will you call him?" she asked.

His jaw clenched. "I already have. I told him I'd take care of ▸u, and he asked me to keep him posted. He's not coming ▸er, if that's what you hoped," he added gruffly.

"I wouldn't expect him to," Eleanor said gently. "Curry, I'm ▸rry I was so stupid. . . ."

"I drove you to it," he said wearily. "I've done nothing but ▸rt you for weeks."

She traced a pattern on his shirt with a sharp nail. "It doesn't ▸atter."

"Norie, don't touch me like that," he said in a haunted tone, ▸d she noticed that his breath was suddenly ragged. She

looked up in time to see the flash of desire that darkened h
eyes as they glanced into hers.

Her lips parted with the strange hungers she was feeling, th
dazed condition of her mind making her careless, reckless, a
the nearness of him worked on her.

"Like what, Curry?" she whispered, letting her hand slid
inside his shirt against the blazing rough warmth of his ches
tangling her fingers in the mat of hair.

A shudder went through him and he crushed her in his arm
bruising her against his body as he went through the doorwa
to her bedroom and all but threw her onto the bed. He stoo
over her, breathing harshly, looking down at her with eyes tha
made her hungry.

"What are you trying to do?" he asked harshly.

She turned her face away from the accusation in his an
buried it in the cool pillow. Her head hurt, her heart felt as
it had been blown into splinters.

"I don't know," she whispered shakenly. "I . . . I wanted
touch you. . . ."

"You took a pretty hard blow on the head," he said tightl
"You've had a mild concussion, baby, it makes you do thin
you wouldn't normally do."

"That's so," she managed shakily. "I'd never beg you
make love to me if I was myself."

There was a long, static pause. "Is that what you wanted?

She nodded, her fingers gripping the pillow like a lifeline.

"So that you could pretend I was Jim Black?" he asked bi
terly.

"I know who you are, Curry," she told the pillow. Sh
swallowed. "Don't mind me, I'm crazy, isn't that what th
doctor told you? Out of my mind with a concussion, and loon
You'd better go before I get up and try to tear your clothes off.

He chuckled softly. "Baby, I'd let you," he said gently. "An
time, any place. But I think it might be better if you healed
little more first, because you're too weak right now for wh
would happen next."

She barely heard him. Her dizzy mind was whirling rig
away from her, and the last thing she heard was the sound
her name being whispered very close to her ear.

* * *

She woke up the next morning feeling like a new woman, with no sign of headache, no other symptoms of the concussion she'd suffered.

Her eyes swept the room and found an ashtray beside her bed with a number of cigarette butts in it. She frowned. Only Curry could have done it, but why would he have been sitting by her bed?

The door opened while she sat there puzzling, and she turned her head and looked straight into Curry's amused eyes. He had a mug of coffee in his hand, which he set beside the bed, his eyes tracing the soft lines of her body which were visible through the thin nylon gown.

She followed the direction of his eyes and suddenly jerked the sheet up to her throat with red cheeks.

"Isn't it a little late for that?" he murmured. "I sat here and watched you for the better part of the night. You're very restless in your sleep, little one."

The gown was a little large, and the straps had a disconcerting habit of slipping off even when she was awake. Asleep...she met his teasing gaze and realized that he'd seen a lot more than the gown. The blush travelled down to her neck.

He chuckled softly. "You're lovely to look at, Jadebud," he said. "All pink and soft..."

"Curry..." she began irritably.

He laid a long, brown finger across her lips. "Don't start any fights with me this morning. Last night's too fresh in my memory."

"Last night?" she asked curiously.

One dark eyebrow went up. "Don't you remember what happened?"

She thought for a minute and shook her head. "It's all hazy. What did I do?"

"You tried to undress me," he said matter-of-factly. "Then you begged me to make love to you."

She gasped in horror. "I didn't!"

"Oh, but you did." His eyes smiled at her. "I've never been more tempted to let a woman have her way with me," he added.

"I wouldn't have!" she breathed.

He caught a strand of her hair and tugged on it gently as he sat down on the bed beside her. "You really don't remember?" he probed.

"Honestly, I don't." She saw the humor die out of his eyes, to be replaced by something dark and quiet and intriguing. "Curry, did I really do that?" she asked.

"You wanted it, all right," he said solemnly. "God, so did I, but I'm not such a monster that I'd take advantage of a woman with a concussion."

"But then you didn't really want me, did you?" she asked unsteadily, her eyes on the sheet. "You've told me so often enough."

He caught her chin and tilted her face up to his. His eyes were dark and quiet. "Haven't you ever heard of camouflage?"

She shrugged. "I suppose."

"I've wanted you for a long time. You can't know how it's been with me these past few weeks." His finger touched her mouth, traced it. "Do you remember that first night you came down the stairs with your hair down and your glasses off—when we'd had the blowup? I stood there and looked at you, and I felt a kind of hunger I never knew I was capable of feeling. But that was just the beginning. It got worse."

Her eyes dropped to his chest. "You felt that way about Amanda," she reminded him.

"No, Norie," he corrected her. "Not after that. Not at all. The night I came home from Houston, when she'd tried her seduction act—I never told you the real reason I walked away from her. It was because I wanted you, and no other woman," he said, meeting her gaze levelly.

Her face mirrored the astonishment she was feeling.

"Curry, I don't understand," she breathed.

"Don't you? And all the time I thought you were eating your heart out for Jim Black. I wanted to break his neck. He could get close to you, and I couldn't. At least, not until the night the bull gored me," he said with a smile. "The first time I kissed you on the porch, I thought he'd been giving you lessons, and when I found out that you were untouched...I had nightmares about what might happen to you with him. The night after I got hurt, I wanted so much to teach you all the things a woman needs to know with a man...I damned near let it go too far. After that, it was a losing battle to keep my hands to myself. When I lapsed, and I did, I took it out on you because I couldn't let you see how much power you had over me."

"Me?" she asked incredulously.

"Last night," he said quietly, "you did this..." He unbuttoned the top buttons of his shirt, and taking her hand, slid it inside the opening against the moist, bronzed flesh of his body. "It was the first time you ever touched me of your own free will, and you could see the effect it had on me. You wanted me, Eleanor."

She looked deep into his silver eyes, and it all came back. She remembered how she'd felt, what she'd done....

Her fingers moved on his broad chest, touching, loving, exploring.

"I don't want to fight you anymore," she said in a soft, yielding tone.

"What do you want, honey?" he asked gently.

"To love you," she said simply, "for as long as you'll let me."

His eyes searched her flushed face. "Love, in the physical sense or in a deeper sense, Eleanor?"

"Both," she admitted, letting go of her pride as a child might let go of a helium-filled balloon and watch it sail away.

"And if I took you up on that?" he murmured. "If I asked you to come into my bedroom with me, right now, and lock the door?"

She bit her lower lip hard. "I...I'd go," she said, swallowing nervously.

His eyes closed for an instant, as if in relief. "Are you telling me that you love me, Eleanor?"

Tears misted in her eyes. "Didn't you know, Curry?" she asked brokenly. "For three long years!"

He gathered her into his hard arms and crushed her against him, his face buried in the thick, soft hair at her throat. His arms trembled as they contracted around her softness.

"When I got to you yesterday, after the fall," he said huskily, "I held you, listening for a heartbeat that I prayed to hear; begging you not to die. And you reached up to hold my head closer and you said, 'Jim?'" He drew a shaky breath. "And I wanted to ride over a cliff."

"I . . . I remember," she murmured. "I remember thinking that Jim was the only man who'd care whether I lived or died. I really didn't think it would matter to you."

"If you'd died, I wouldn't have survived you by five minutes," he said matter-of-factly, drawing back to look down into her soft, quiet eyes. "Eleanor, I'm in love with you," he said softly.

The sweetness of those words changed her, brightened her, made her suddenly beautiful. "Oh, Curry . . ." she whispered.

"We'll talk later," he breathed, bending to her mouth. "Right now, I'm so hungry I can hardly bear it. Come here, honey. . . ."

He brought her up in his arms and kissed her, long and slow and thoroughly, coaxing her slender young hands to unbutton his shirt, to touch him as he caressed her. Fires burned slowly between them until the room seemed to go around in a burst of flame.

"Oh, God, we've got to stop this," he whispered shakenly, putting her from him. He stood up, looking down at his handiwork with eyes full of love as she fastened buttons and blushed under the possessive gaze. "Why don't you marry me?"

"Isn't it a high price to pay?" she teased.

"I want more than your body, little innocent," he told her, and his eyes darkened lovingly. "I want those sons we talked about once. And picnics by the river. Long nights when we can sit together and talk about the good old days. I want everything with you. A lifetime of memories to store day by day."

"Can we have a church wedding, with all the trimmings?" she asked.

"And a white gown . . . if we hurry," he added wickedly.

She blushed. "I'll get Bessie to start on it tomorrow."

He leaned down and brushed her mouth with his. "Today," he corrected. "If I remember my 'Cinderella's' correctly, the prince didn't waste any time getting her to the altar when the glass slipper fit."

He kissed her once, hard, and pulled her up. "Let's go break the news to your fairy godmother," he said with a loving smile. "Think she'll approve?"

Eleanor tossed her hair and laughed as she hadn't in weeks. "She'll have to. She loves you almost as much as I do."

He threw an arm around her shoulder and led her to the door. "When we break the news we'll go down to the river," he murmured wickedly, "and I'll let you finish what you started last night."

"Only this time," she grinned, "I won't have a concussion."

He drew her closer beside him. "That's what I'm counting on," he teased gently.

She felt the soft pressure of his mouth at her temple as they started down the stairs.

"Going somewhere?" Bessie asked them as they started down.

"On a picnic," Eleanor said dreamily. "We're getting married!"

"Good for you!" Bessie said with a beaming smile. "Now that you've made the announcement, don't you think there's something you'd better do?"

They stared at her, then at each other.

"Well, Norie, you can't go picnicking like that!" The housekeeper frowned. "What would the neighbors say?"

Eleanor looked down at the pale green gown and sighed. "That," she sighed, "is one black mark in my fairy godmother's book."

And she ran back up the stairs to change, her heart moving to a waltz. The fantasy had become real.

* * * * *

Back by popular demand, some of
Diana Palmer's earliest published
books are available again!

Several years ago, Diana
Palmer began her writing
career. Sweet, compelling
and totally unforgettable,
these are the love stories that
enchanted readers
everywhere.

This month, six more of
these wonderful stories will
be available in DIANA
PALMER DUETS—Books 4,
5 and 6. Each DUET
contains two powerful stories
plus an introduction by
Diana Palmer. Don't miss:

Book Four	**AFTER THE MUSIC** **DREAM'S END**
Book Five	**BOUND BY A PROMISE** **PASSION FLOWER**
Book Six	**TO HAVE AND TO HOLD** **THE COWBOY AND THE LADY**

Silhouette Romance®

LONG, TALL TEXANS

**Diana Palmer's fortieth story for Silhouette . . . chosen
as an Award of Excellence title!**

CONNAL
Diana Palmer

This month, Diana Palmer's bestselling LONG, TALL
TEXANS series continues with CONNAL. The skies
get cloudy on C. C. Tremayne's home on the range
when Penelope Mathews decides to protect him—by
marrying him!

One specially selected title receives the Award of
Excellence every month. Look for CONNAL
this month . . . only from Silhouette Romance.

FOUR UNIQUE SERIES
FOR EVERY WOMAN YOU ARE...

Silhouette Romance

Love, at its most tender, provocative,
emotional... in stories that will make you laugh and
cry while bringing you the magic of falling in love.

*6 titles
per month*

Silhouette Special Edition

Sophisticated, substantial and packed with
emotion, these powerful novels of life and love will
capture your imagination and steal your heart.

*6 titles
per month*

SILHOUETTE *Desire*

Open the door to romance and passion. Humorous,
emotional, compelling—yet always a believable
and sensuous story—Silhouette Desire never
fails to deliver on the promise of love.

*6 titles
per month*

Silhouette Intimate Moments

Enter a world of excitement, of romance
heightened by suspense, adventure and the
passions every woman dreams of. Let us
sweep you away.

*4 titles
per month*

SILG-1RR